MERCY RING BOOK TWO

DECLAN

NYSSA KATHRYN

DECLAN
Copyright © 2022 Nyssa Kathryn Sitarenos

An NW Partners Book
Cover by Deranged Doctor Design
Developmentally and Copy Edited by Kelli Collins
Proofread by Amanda Cuff and Jen Katemi

🌟 Created with Vellum

He's everything she's never had. She's everything he didn't know he needed.

Having lost her parents at a young age, raised by her beloved uncle, Michele King is now a successful business owner, providing meals for people by day and getting lost in books each night. A somewhat lonely life...which she attempts to remedy by dating a man she met online. It only takes a few dates before she sees red flags. Breaking things off with a man she barely knows should be easy. But he's not taking no for an answer.

Declan James moved to small-town Lindeman, Idaho, to be near his former Delta Force teammates, men he considers his brothers. His focus should be on their new business, Mercy Ring, a boxing club specializing in giving locals—especially kids—a safe place to exorcise their anger and aggression. But instead, he finds his mind stuck on a certain shy local. Quiet and reserved, Michele is the polar opposite of the women he's dated. And he can't get her out of his head.

He's happy to get to know Michele at her own slow pace...until danger rears its head in the form of an angry ex. Now, Declan has no choice but to stay close, if he doesn't want their fledgling relationship to end before it's barely begun.

ACKNOWLEDGMENTS

Thank you to my team. Kelli, you're my book doctor. Thank you for making everything make sense. Amanda and Jen, thank you for finding all those mistakes that I read over a hundred times and miss. Thank you to my ARC team. You guys are amazing and push me to write the next book. Thank you to my husband for your patience and support, and my daughter Sophia, for giving me reason.

PROLOGUE

*ix Weeks Ago*

FROM BENEATH HER LASHES, Michele cast a nervous glance at Tim. She shouldn't have gotten into the car with him. Stupid. So stupid. How many bourbons had he drunk? Four? Five? She'd lost count.

Jesus.

This was only their third date. Who the heck drank so much on a third date? Was she that unbearable to be around?

She nibbled her bottom lip, just about gnawing the thing off. At least she lived close to the restaurant. The drive shouldn't be too much longer.

When her street came into view, she almost blew out a sigh of relief.

In all honesty, she should have asked him to stop the car the second she'd come to her senses. She hadn't because she was possibly the least assertive person living in Lindeman. Maybe all of Washington.

She placed her hand on the button of her seat belt. "You can just stop out front of the building. No need to come in."

He pulled into a spot in the communal parking lot. "It's a date. Of course I'm going to walk you up to your apartment."

Before she could say any more, he was out of the car and moving around to her side.

Swallowing, she climbed out and walked beside him to the door.

"I'm sorry about tonight," he said quietly.

She wrapped her arms around her waist. "Why are you sorry?"

She knew already, but she was still interested in hearing his take on it. Maybe he'd tell her why he'd felt the need to get wasted and be the worst date she'd ever gone out with.

"I drank too much. I've been stressed, and before this date I had a fight with…" He shook his head. "I'm sorry."

She stopped in front of the complex door. "It's okay."

It wasn't really okay, but she just wanted the night to be over. If she was honest with herself, there had been red flags since their first date. Oh, he'd been nice enough before they met, texting all the right things after they'd found each other on an online dating site. But on their first date, she'd just gotten this *feeling* from him. Like he wasn't quite right for her. And on the second date, there'd been little digs about her appearance. The narrowing of his eyes when she'd talked to their male server.

Yet, here she was, on a *third* date.

Why, Michele? What the heck is wrong with you?

She breathed out a long breath.

Next time she saw red flags, it was a straight no. Especially after tonight. Not only had he drunk nonstop at dinner, but he'd also complained the entire time about the service, the food and other diners. At one point, she'd even noticed a band of sweat across his forehead.

The second she got the complex door unlocked, Tim strode

in, waiting for her in the hall. She gave him a tight smile and walked in around him.

"It's not okay," he finally said. "I'm usually better than this."

She wasn't sure how to respond to that. The people-pleasing side of her wanted to reassure him, but she really couldn't.

When they reached her apartment on the second floor, she unlocked the door and stepped inside. She'd intended to say goodbye there, but he slipped past her, moving into her living room.

Her jaw ticked. Okay, now it really was time for Mr. Slick to leave.

She turned toward him. "Tim, it's late. I'm just going to go straight to bed." *So please leave.*

God, she really needed to get a dog. A big one that would scare unwanted visitors away. She'd been meaning to go down to the shelter for a while but just hadn't gotten around to it. *Tomorrow*, she promised herself.

Tim ran a hand through his hair. "I've screwed up, haven't I? It just all gets to me sometimes. It's so hard. Everything's so *hard*."

What on earth was he talking about?

His eyes turned pained. "Tell me, have I screwed things up between us?"

"Tim—"

"I have."

"I'd like you to go."

Suddenly, he was across the room. When Michele tried to step back, he grabbed her upper arms, keeping her in place. "Tell me this is fixable. Tell me you'll give me another date."

She opened and closed her mouth a couple of times, almost too shocked to speak. "I… No. I think it's best we don't see each other again."

Something crossed his face. Anger mixed with…desperation?

Oh, Michele, for once in your life, why couldn't you lie?

She attempted to tug out of his hold, but his fingers tightened on her arms, digging into her skin.

"Tim. Let me go. Now." Her voice trembled, not just because of his touch but because of the look in his eye. It was wild. Unhinged.

"*No*, Michele. I need you to tell me this is fixable. Give me another chance."

"Tim, you're hurting me!" The man's grip was punishing.

It was like he didn't hear her words; his fingers didn't ease at all. "I need you, Michele. Please! One more date."

"Okay." She swallowed. "I-I'll go on another date with you."

For a moment he watched her, his wild eyes studying her face. Then they narrowed. Dread pooled in her belly.

"You're lying."

"Tim—"

He shook her so hard, her teeth rattled. Fear suffocated her and panic swirled in her gut.

Out of instinct, she kneed him, hitting him right between the legs.

He grunted and doubled over, his fingers loosening enough for her to tug her arms free and run. She raced straight to the bedroom and slammed the door shut. His footsteps were loud on the other side as he stomped down the hall, and her fingers shook as she flicked the lock. Immediately, the handle rattled.

"Michele!"

She took two big steps back. "If you don't leave right now, I'm calling the police."

"Michele! I'm sorry! I'm not myself tonight."

With trembling fingers, she pulled out her phone. Thank God she'd gone with jeans and had shoved her cell into a pocket. "I'm doing it, Tim. I'm calling."

Loud breathing sounded from the other side of the door. Curse words. Then…retreating footsteps.

When the front door closed with a resounding thud, her trembling hand dropped to her side.

What the hell had just happened?

She moved back to the door and pressed her ear to it. Silence. She leaned her back against the door and sank down to the floor. Her heart still beat way too fast in her chest, and her entire body shook. She didn't want to open the door. Not yet.

She was almost tempted to call her best friend, River. Or River's brother, Ryker. But they were going through their own stuff right now. Ryker hadn't been himself since retiring from the military, and River was stressed over her brother's behavior and trying to fix it.

She certainly couldn't call Uncle Ottie. Not with his heart issues. He'd just worry, and that wouldn't be good for him.

Instead, she dropped her head to her knees and stayed like that for hours. Until her eyes started to shutter and her body finally calmed. Then, slowly, she rose, unlocked the door and cautiously poked her head out.

No one. No one she could see, anyway.

Before leaving the room, she grabbed a bottle of antiperspirant spray. She moved out of the bedroom and toward the front door, scanning her small apartment as she went.

When she finally reached the door, she quickly flicked the lock, all the while promising herself she would never again go on another date with a man she met online.

CHAPTER 1

 *resent Day*

"THANK YOU FOR INTERVIEWING, Cheryl. I'll be in contact."

The older woman smiled as she left the shop. The second the door closed, Michele breathed out a sigh of relief. Four interviews, and she didn't want to hire a single one of them. To be fair, she didn't want to hire anyone. What she *did* want to do was expand her business, and to do that, she needed to suck it up and employ help.

Shaking her head, she turned and moved to one of the few small tables in the shop before dropping into a chair.

Running her meal delivery service, Meals Made Easy, was her dream. Her baby. And it was doing so well. Only issue? Success meant expansion. And expansion meant working with other people. She enjoyed working alone. Classic introvert problem.

She glanced around the clean space. The shop was right in the center of Lindeman, Washington. There was a large open kitchen, an industrial fridge and freezer, and a few tables and chairs, mostly used by customers waiting to pick up meals.

She loved it here. And she loved the silence.

When her phone buzzed from the table, she lifted it up, and her heart gave a little kick.

Declan: Morning, sweetheart. You stopping by the club today?

A smile she couldn't stop tugged at her lips. She started responding, only to quickly shake her head and type something else. Then, yep, she deleted that too.

Holy Moses, she was awkward. She never had any idea what to say to him. What *did* you say to the best-looking man you'd ever met, who, for some unknown reason, seemed to enjoy chatting with you?

Michele: River will probably want to. Is that okay?

Yeah, blame it on River. That was the safest thing to do. Definitely don't tell him that you live for those small moments when you run into him.

Declan: Just River?

Crap. The man saw right through her.

She nibbled her bottom lip, debating how to respond, when the door to the shop opened. She looked up to see a boy step inside. He was tall but only looked to be about sixteen, maybe seventeen. He had a piece of paper in his hand and a backpack strung over one shoulder.

She rose from the table. "Hi. Sorry, we're not open today."

He stopped a couple of feet inside the shop. His deep brown eyes bore into her, and between those and his thick dark hair, she knew girls his age would find him attractive.

His hand tightened around the strap of his backpack. "I saw your ad online and wanted to drop off my resume."

Her brows rose. "You're applying to be a kitchen hand and delivery driver?"

Did the kid even have his license? And if he did, how long had he had it?

Something in his eyes shuttered. "Sorry. You're probably looking for someone different."

Guilt slammed into her chest. Crap, had her surprise been written all over her face? *Good one, Chele.*

He started to turn but stopped again at her words.

"I would love to see your resume."

For a moment, she thought he wouldn't give it to her. He glanced down at the paper in his hand. Then, finally, he handed it to her.

"It's not much," he muttered.

One previous job at a pizza shop.

Okay. Well, that was work experience. Her gaze ran over his name—Anthony Garcia—and yep, he was sixteen.

She looked up. "Are you in school, Anthony?"

"No. I, uh, dropped out. I'm new in town. My mom and I just moved into the trailer park, and we kind of need the money from me working."

There was something else that flickered in his eyes at those words. Despair, maybe? Just how badly did they need the money?

His gaze darted down to the resume in her hand, his jaw clenching. Then he shook his head before turning again. "I shouldn't have applied."

"No, wait—"

It was too late. He was already gone.

He'd barely stepped out before River was entering the shop, a huge smile on her face. "Hey, hey! Guess what day it is?"

She shot a final glance out the window as Anthony disappeared down the road before looking at her best friend. A small smile stretched her lips. "Hm, would it be your self-proclaimed Freedom Day?"

A bit dramatic if you asked her, but hey, that was River, and Michele loved her.

"Yeah, baby. Freedom Day! The first day in forever when that overprotective boyfriend of mine is letting me out of prison."

Prison being her home.

Michele's eyes softened. "You were shot, River, and I for one am glad Jackson had you on mandatory bed rest." If he hadn't, there was no way the woman would have gotten the rest she needed to heal so quickly.

"Yeah, I know. The guy's a dreamboat and my savior."

Michele chuckled as she lifted the resumes from the table. She was careful to keep Anthony's on top as she slipped them into a kitchen drawer. "Well, what are we waiting for? Let's get out of here and make the most of Freedom Day, then."

"Yeah, baby."

The second they stepped onto the street, River linked her arm with Michele's. "Is it okay if we make a quick stop into Mercy Ring so I can give Jackson a big embarrassing kiss on his beautiful face?"

Michele almost laughed. Her friend had just been complaining about the man yet couldn't stand to be away from him for long. Not that Michele was complaining. She loved that River had finally reunited with the guy she'd loved for as long as Michele had known her.

They crossed the street. "It's fine. The movie doesn't start for another hour, so we have time."

Besides, stopping inside the new boxing club wouldn't exactly be a hardship. Not if it meant seeing the four tall, dark and handsome former Deltas who ran the place.

River sighed. "Good, because I haven't seen him for hours, and I miss those lips."

"Hours. That sounds like torture."

"The worst kind." River leaned into her shoulder. "I'm so glad we're doing this. I feel like we haven't spent nearly enough time together lately."

"Because you've been recovering from your bullet wound and soaking up time with Ryker."

The entire town, bar River, had thought her brother was dead for a while there. River had fought tooth and nail to find out what had happened to Ryker and to prove he wasn't actually dead. The woman was strong as hell, and she fought for the people she loved. Just one of the reasons she was Michele's best friend.

River's fingers tightened around Michele's arm. "I know. I've threatened him with many forms of physical harm if he ever does that again."

Michele smirked. Ryker was huge and looked every bit the former Delta he was. But she wouldn't discount River for a second. The woman was fierce, and when she set her mind to something, she achieved it.

"How did the interviews go today?" she asked.

It was Michele's turn to sigh. "Okay." She felt River's gaze on her but kept her eyes firmly on the path ahead.

"Just okay?"

"I don't know. Everyone was just so...chatty and full of energy."

"Oh no, that sounds terrible. Imagine the horrible fun they could bring to your workday."

Michele nudged her friend in the shoulder. "You know what I mean. I love the peace and quiet at work. Cooking calms me. It's my 'me' time. I know you don't get it—"

"I do," River said quickly, some of the humor leaving her voice. "You want someone who can enjoy the peace and quiet with you."

No, she wanted *no one*. And she *could* hire no one. She was the boss. But she couldn't keep up with demand on her own, so not hiring would mean turning away customers. The single mom down the street with no time to cook. The professional couple who got home after eight every night. The elderly man whose wife had passed away six months ago.

Nope. She couldn't do that.

"There wasn't *anyone* with potential?" River prodded.

"I kind of narrowed it down to two people. A woman in her late twenties. She's married with kids and seems friendly enough. And an even younger woman who has experience working in the kitchen of a restaurant." She frowned, her mind flicking back to Anthony. "There was also this kid…"

River frowned. "A kid? Wait—that kid I saw walking away from the shop? I was wondering who he was."

"Yeah, him."

"How old is he?"

"Sixteen. He just moved to town. Living in the trailer park with his mom."

A small beat of silence followed. "That's young."

Yeah, it was. And she shouldn't even be considering him, but…

Michele frowned. But what? But she felt sorry for him? But she'd sensed sadness and desperation in him and had a thing for saving people?

They stopped in front of Mercy Ring.

River tilted her head. "Are you considering hiring him?"

Was she? "No." Well, probably not. But then, she wasn't really liking the idea of hiring anyone else, either.

She was about to open the door when River touched her arm. "You can hire whoever you want, Chele, just…be careful. Especially after everything with Tim."

Every muscle in Michele's body tensed at the mention of that name—a name she still tried hard to forget but couldn't.

She hadn't told her friend everything that had transpired. She certainly hadn't told her about the full extent of his harassment since their final date. All the calls. The texts. She couldn't. Not while her friend was recovering from a bullet wound and had only just gotten back the brother she'd almost lost.

"You're obviously not going to date this kid," River continued. "Just make sure he's safe first."

Michele's chest warmed at her friend's concern. "Of course.

Thank you, River." She turned and tugged open the boxing club door. "Now, let's go see that boyfriend of yours so you can kiss his beautiful face."

River looked like she wanted to say more, but she conceded with a sigh, stepping inside.

Michele almost sagged in relief. Good. She loved her best friend, but she didn't want to talk about the continuing mess that was Tim. It was definitely the first and last time she dated some random guy from the internet. Never again. In fact, it wouldn't be terrible if she didn't date anyone for a very long time.

The thought had barely crossed her mind when she glanced up to the boxing ring, which centered the large room. Her stomach dipped and quivered because right there, punching into the pads on Jackson's hands, was a very tall, muscled, and sweaty Declan.

CHAPTER 2

*H*oly Jesus. Declan on any day had her breath running short, but glistening with sweat and his muscles flexing? He had her just...forgetting. How to breathe. How to speak. Basically how to function.

He threw another hard punch into a pad, and his biceps and stomach muscles hardened and flexed.

Only shorts? Really? Could the man not have thrown on a shirt to save Michele's sanity?

Michele was a big reader. She read every kind of romance under the sun, and she read often. She'd always thought no man could hold a bar to the heroes in her books. But Declan had her feeling things that no man, fictional or otherwise, had ever made her feel before, and they'd barely known each other a couple of months. Hell, they were barely friends. He'd only taken to texting her recently.

Jackson's hands dropped. "Okay, my woman's here, I've got to break." He bent between the ropes and climbed out of the ring, eyes only for River.

Declan remained where he was, his chest moving up and down as he sucked in deep breaths. Then, finally, he looked at her

—and his chest stilled, a slow smile creeping across his lips. "Hey."

The deep timbre of his voice had her skin tingling. She opened her mouth to say hi back—you know, like a normal person—but her tongue was suddenly too heavy to speak. So instead, she gave an awkward, I-forgot-how-to-talk smile.

The grin on Declan's face widened.

When a heavy arm dropped over Michele's shoulders, she jumped, swinging her gaze up to find Ryker, River's brother, smiling down at her. She'd known the man since high school. He was like the brother she'd never had.

"Hey, Chele."

She smiled back. "Hey. Settling into the place okay?" Oh good, at least she could actually speak to Ryker.

He lifted one of his huge shoulders. "The boys already had the place cleaned up when I returned from the dead. We've stocked up on a few supplies, gotten the reception desk and office sorted, and now we're ready for our first victims."

She shook her head. "Too soon, Ryker. We're not at the stage of joking about your supposed death just yet." Nor may she ever be. She'd attended his *funeral*.

"But we *are* at the stage of throwing a resurrection party," River called out. She stood with her back to Jackson, his arms curved around her waist.

Ryker rolled his eyes. "I already said no to that."

"And I already said you don't get a say. I had to go to your funeral, you have to go to my party. It will help my heart heal."

Michele's gaze skirted back to Declan as he stepped out of the ring and grabbed a towel to wipe his face. He was looking directly at Ryker's arm over her shoulders. Was it her, or were his eyes slightly more narrowed than they were a moment ago?

No. That was crazy.

When her phone started to ring, she shuffled out of Ryker's

embrace and grabbed her cell from her pocket. A chill immediately skated over her skin at the name on the display.

Tim. *Again.* God, would the man ever just leave her alone?

She should block his number. She knew she should. Crazy as it seemed, keeping the number unblocked was her way of knowing when—or if—he ever decided to forget about her and move on.

She canceled the call and turned back to the group, praying she didn't get another but almost certain she would.

Ryker crossed his arms over his chest, gaze moving between River and Michele. "What are you two doing today?"

"Seeing a movie. It's Chele's turn to pick."

Ryker smirked. "So, some Channing Tatum chick flick where the guy remains shirtless for half the film."

Michele's spine straightened. "Hey. You make it sound like the movies I choose have no substance. There will be love, and there will be a happily ever after. Hence, substance."

Ryker chuckled. "But the guy *will* be shirtless for half the film, won't he?"

"Maybe." So what if he was?

Her phone started ringing again. Her heart sank.

You know what? She was sick of this. Tim had well and truly progressed to stalker mode, and it needed to stop.

Quickly, Michele moved into the small kitchen at the back of the gym, fishing the phone from her pocket again, and this time, answering it.

"Stop."

For a moment, she was greeted by silence. Then a deep, chilling voice said, "You answered."

"Yes, I answered, because you keep. On. Calling. Stop it. This is harassment."

She'd actually gone to the police about him. She'd gone immediately after the man had come to her apartment one afternoon, demanding she let him in. The officer had written some report of the incident and then...that was it. He said nothing else could be done.

"Michele, I said I'm sorry about our last date. Give me another chance."

Another chance? Was he delusional? How many times did she have to say no? "I've told you no countless times. I do *not* want to go out with you again. You need to listen to me and stop calling."

"Come on, you barely gave me a chance!"

Her voice lowered. "Tim, you scared me on that last date. And there is absolutely no chance in hell that I'll be going on another with you. None. So stop calling. Don't show up at my apartment again. Just *stop*."

She hung up quickly, not wanting to hear any more words. Then she turned her phone off completely in case the man called again.

Her eyes shuttered. She hated this. She wasn't strong and fearless like River. She was quiet and calm and craved safety. Men like Tim made her feel sick to her stomach.

"He showed up at your apartment?"

With a loud gasp, she spun around to find Declan standing in front of her, still shirtless, the smile from earlier gone, replaced with a much darker expression. And in the small kitchen, which was more of a narrow walkway than a room, he took up all the space.

"Just once," she said quietly, clenching the phone between her fingers. She almost took a step back. Not because she thought he'd hurt her, but because the look on his face would have *anyone* wanting to step back.

"What did he do?" Declan's voice was quiet, but the quiet was probably worse than if he had yelled. There was a dangerous edge to his tone.

"Nothing." Kind of nothing. "He wanted me to let him in, but I refused."

"So he left?"

"So he left." After twenty minutes of pounding on her door. Something told her Declan wouldn't like the entire answer, though.

He stepped forward, and the air cut off in her throat. He had these honey-brown eyes that she always seemed to get lost in. And when he smiled, the dimples in his cheeks set her heart racing. He wasn't smiling right now.

"I told you to call me if he bothered you again."

He had. Declan had been with her and River when Tim was waiting outside her shop not long ago. He'd scared the man off.

"He showed up at my apartment before that."

The muscles of his bare chest flexed. "Have you gone to the police?"

"Yes. They wrote a report."

"That was it?"

She nodded. He clearly didn't like that.

"Has he shown up again?" Declan asked.

"No." Declan looked like he had a lot more questions, so she pushed her phone into her pocket and stepped around him. "I should get back out there."

She took another step before he reached out, and his fingers closed around her arm. Even though his hold was firm, his fingers so long they overlapped his thumb, they were gentle. And the simple touch had her skin heating all over.

CHAPTER 3

The second Declan grabbed her arm, the touch singed him. And damn, it felt good. He got the same flicker each and every time. It made him want to touch her longer. Hold her tighter.

An array of emotions flicked over her expressive face. Surprise. Caution. Desire…?

Yeah. Definitely a little of that.

He stepped closer, and his voice lowered. "If things aren't okay, I want to help."

Hell, he *needed* to help. He hadn't known the woman for long, but there was something about Michele that sucked him in. That made him want to be her protector. He also wanted to find this asshole ex of hers and beat his ass.

Her mouth opened and closed a couple of times, her biceps tensing beneath his touch. "I'm okay, but thank you."

He didn't believe her. Not for a second. But if the woman didn't ask for his help, there wasn't much he could do. He was nothing to Michele. Not a boyfriend. Barely her friend.

Almost involuntarily, he swiped his thumb against her skin. Then he stepped even closer.

A small puff of air slipped from her lips. Yeah, she felt it too. The inexplicable connection. The pull.

"I want you to call me if that situation changes. Will you do that?"

She gave a short, quick nod. Too quick.

Slowly, he released her and watched as she all but ran from the room. Even though he was pissed about her ex, a small smile stretched his lips. God, she was cute. The little bit of sunshine in his day.

He slipped out of the kitchen and moved back toward the group. Grabbing his water from the floor beside the ring, he smiled again when he heard River arguing with her brother about a terrible movie they'd watched and whose choice it had been.

Listening to his friend and former teammate argue with his sister was fast becoming a favorite pastime of his. The two loved each other, but damn they could fight. It reminded him of him and his sister. By the bemused expressions on Jackson's and Cole's faces, his friends also enjoyed the show.

When Michele's gaze flicked to him, there was a slight widening of her eyes, like she hadn't expected him to be looking back, before she quickly looked away. He almost chuckled.

She was quieter than any of the women he'd ever dated, but it only had him wanting her more.

He walked to the door to flick the sign from closed to open. A kid outside caught his eye. He was standing there looking like he was about to enter, but when he saw Declan on the other side of the glass, he suddenly turned.

Declan stepped out and let the door close behind him. "Hey. Are you here for the introductory session today?"

He turned back to Declan. What was he, sixteen? He was tall, but young. And there was something about his eyes. A wariness. And an anger that lingered below the surface.

The boy straightened. "I'm new in town. I, uh, overheard a

woman at Jodie's Grocery talking about a new boxing club. Said kids were welcome."

Declan gave the boy an assessing look. "That's right. We're a boxing club that specializes in giving locals, especially kids, a safe place to work out whatever they're feeling." He'd put his last dollar on the woman at the grocery store being Mrs. Albuquerque, or more widely known as the town gossip. He'd only been in town for a couple months, and even *he* knew no one's business was safe from the woman.

If he'd expected a response, he didn't get one. The kid just nodded, his hands clenched at his sides.

Declan stepped forward. "What's your name?"

"Anthony."

"I'm Declan. I own this place with my three buddies, Jackson, Cole and Ryker. You're welcome to join the class this morning."

There was a brief eagerness in his eyes. He wanted to.

Then he blinked, and his eyes hooded. "Nah, that's okay." He shoved his hands into his pockets and shuffled his feet, looking like he was going to walk away.

Declan crossed his arms. The fact the kid was here, not to mention his body language, told Declan he wanted their training. "We could kind of use the clients right now, being a new business and all. We've even made the first session free to get some people in."

Not true. Not the first part, anyway. The class had been fully booked within hours of releasing sign-up information. But he already knew the kid needed this place. He either didn't want to admit it or he couldn't afford it. Maybe both.

Anthony opened his mouth to say something when the door opened and River and Michele stepped out.

Michele stopped in her tracks, her gaze falling on the kid. "Anthony?"

"Michele—I mean, Miss King."

She shook her head. "You don't need to call me Miss King. Michele's fine."

He swallowed, looking at the glass doors again. There was something about the kid that was deeply unsettled.

Declan frowned. "You two know each other?"

Michele smiled. "Anthony interviewed for a job at Meals Made Easy this morning."

This kid? Working in a kitchen? Nope. He couldn't picture it. And the idea of a stranger working in close quarters with Michele had him feeling...not great.

"Are you taking a class here?" Michele asked.

Anthony stepped back. "Nah. Just checking it out. I should go."

Before Declan could stop him, the kid took off down the street.

River turned to Michele, nodding. "Okay, now I see the appeal in hiring him. This is Pokey all over again."

Declan frowned. "Who's Pokey?"

River chuckled. "Her massive monster of a dog."

Michele rolled her eyes. "He's not a monster. He's a Great Dane."

Great Dane's were huge...

She turned to Declan. "I got him from an animal shelter. He was just lying there, all sad because no one wanted to give him a home, probably because he's so big. Against River's advice, I adopted him—and I was right. He's a big teddy bear."

So the woman liked saving things. Animals. Teenagers. Another fucking tug at his chest.

"Now she treats him like her child," River said. "She cooks all his meals from scratch, sends him to doggy day care at this big farm twice a week."

Michele smiled fondly. "He loves the farm." She turned to Declan. "They come and pick him up on this bus full of dogs, and he gets home at night covered in dirt and exhausted from a day of running around the huge place."

River nudged her shoulder. "You saved him. Just like you want to save that kid."

"I don't…" She stopped and shook her head. Then she looked up at him, and the guarded expression washed back over her face. "We should get going. I'll see you later, Declan."

River punched him in the arm. "See ya, big guy."

With a wave, Declan moved back inside. Immediately, he felt the eyes of his three friends. The four of them were as close as people could get without actually being blood related. That's what happened after you'd been Delta Force Operators on the same team for as long as they had. When you'd gone through hellish missions and had to save one another's lives more times than you could count.

"Who was that?" Cole asked. Out of the four of them, he spoke the least. The guy was silent but deadly.

"Anthony. He's new in town. Applied for a position at Michele's shop."

Ryker's eyes narrowed. "Hope she's not thinking of hiring a kid she doesn't know. I assumed she'd hire a woman."

Declan's gaze fell on his friend. A friend he'd thought he lost a little more than a month ago. The man hadn't been dead like they'd all thought. He'd been in hiding. Something he was never fucking allowed to do again.

His words had Declan remembering all too well the way his arm had wrapped around Michele's shoulders. The guy was close to her. How close, exactly, and what feelings they had for each other, Declan wasn't sure.

"She didn't say whether she was." Although, from the sounds of it, it was likely.

"How'd the kid hear about Mercy Ring?" Jackson asked as he moved across the room to help Declan organize the boxing gloves.

"Heard some woman talking about the club at the grocery store."

Ryker scoffed. "Probably Mrs. Albuquerque."

"My first thought too."

The others started moving equipment and getting the room ready.

"How's your place going?" Jackson asked.

The three of them—Ryker, Cole and Declan—were renting a large house together in Lindeman. It was spacious, but with three guys living under the same roof, it didn't always feel like that. It sure as hell beat the local inn, though.

"It's like being back in the military," Cole scoffed. "Ryker leaving his shit everywhere. Declan eating every fucking scrap and never replacing a damn thing."

Declan grinned. He did do that. Didn't feel guilty about it either.

Ryker straightened. "What about you? I haven't seen you clean a single dish."

"He's probably too busy cleaning your shit off the floor," Declan replied, getting a roll of sports tape thrown at his head for the jab.

Ryker shot his gaze across to him. "Michele looked a bit pale when she came out of the kitchen."

Declan's jaw ticked. He considered his next words carefully. "Has she told you about the ex who's been harassing her?"

All three men stopped, smiles dropping from their faces. Ryker was the first to speak. "No." There was a lethal edge to his voice.

"I don't think she dated the guy for long, but now he won't leave her alone. Showed up at her apartment. Calls a lot." Based on the conversation he overheard, anyway. "He even showed up at her shop one time when I was there with her and River."

Jackson's eyes narrowed. "Do you have a name?"

"Tim. Don't have a last name, though."

"We can ask River," Cole suggested.

Both Jackson and Ryker scoffed, but it was Jackson who answered. "They have some girl code thing where they don't share information without the other's permission."

Declan turned back to the gloves. "I'll keep an eye on things."

He wasn't surprised by his friends' concern. They were all protectors first. Exactly why they'd joined the military. And the thing they couldn't stand the most? Assholes preying on women. Declan would make damn sure Michele was safe.

CHAPTER 4

*M*ichele shot a quick glance over her shoulder at Anthony. He was dividing the spaghetti carbonara into containers.

It was nearing the end of his first shift, and so far, she'd pegged him correctly. A quick learner. A hard worker. And quiet. So quiet, she could have convinced herself he wasn't there.

So basically, the kid was perfect.

She hadn't told River she'd hired him yet, but she knew she'd get an, "I told you so." Yeah, her friend knew her too well.

She shot a look to the time on her phone. Almost five. She looked back at Anthony again, noticing the frown he'd been wearing all day was still firmly in place.

Why was he so angry all the time? Like he was a stone's throw away from blowing up? Not that it scared her. No, it actually made her want to help him. He was a kid. Was his mother doing anything to help him channel his anger into something else?

"You're doing a great job, Anthony."

His head shot up like her words surprised him. "Uh, thanks. The tasks have been easy enough." There was a beat of silence, then Anthony wet his lips. "I really appreciate you hiring me."

She smiled. When she'd called to tell him he had the job, there had been a full five seconds of stunned silence that followed. She'd almost asked if he was still there.

"Well, so far, you're proving I made the right decision."

He looked like he wanted to say more, but the door to the shop opened and her uncle Ottie stepped in.

A huge smile stretched her lips. "Uncle" wasn't really how she saw him. The man was more like a father. After her parents had died in quick succession of each other when she was only five, her mother from breast cancer and her father from a heart attack, Uncle Ottie had stepped into the role of guardian without hesitation. And there hadn't been a single day when she'd felt unloved.

She moved around the kitchen counter and threw her arms around his shoulders for a tight hug before pulling away.

His hands went to her arms. "Hi, darling. How are you doing today?"

"I'm good. How about you, Uncle Ottie?" Her voice lowered. "How's the heart?"

Her own heart clenched at the question. For the last year, he'd been having chest pains. After a number of medical tests, the doctors had classified him as "at risk" of having a heart attack. It made her feel sick every time she thought about it. Her father had died from a heart attack, and there was no way she could lose her uncle, too.

His eyes softened. "I'm good, darling, and so is my heart."

It wasn't. But she knew he'd be the last person to admit that, especially to her. Because he did anything and everything to keep her happy.

"Well, I've made you some nourishing chicken soup and some Osso Bucco soaked in bone broth. Both are very healing." When she turned, she caught Anthony watching them. His gaze suddenly slid back to the pasta. Michele shook her head. "Sorry, how rude of me. Anthony, this is my uncle Ottie. Uncle Ottie, this is Anthony, my new employee."

Her *first* employee.

Her uncle's eyes widened. She almost laughed. Yep, another person who'd been expecting her to hire a young woman or a retired older lady. To be fair, she'd been expecting herself to do that too.

Uncle Ottie walked around the counter, stretching out his hand. "Nice to meet you, son."

Anthony scrubbed his hands on his jeans before shaking her uncle's. "Nice to meet you too, sir."

A small smile tugged at Michele's lips at Anthony's use of the word "sir."

"I haven't seen you around town," Ottie said.

"My mother and I just moved here from Wenatchee. It's about an hour and a half north of here."

"What had you moving to Lindeman?" Ottie asked.

Good question—one she probably should have asked herself. Whoops.

Anthony paused. "Mom just wanted a fresh start in a new town."

Michele moved to the fridge and grabbed her uncle's containers before setting them on the counter. "Anthony, can you help my uncle carry his meals to his car?"

"Sure."

Uncle Ottie sighed, shaking his head. "This is too much food, Michele."

"Nonsense. You need to eat, and if I don't cook for you, you'll survive on grocery store microwave meals."

"Nothing wrong with those."

"I own a meal delivery service. I am giving you meals. No arguments." She loaded up both her uncle's and Anthony's arms.

At the chiming of the door, she looked up to see Mrs. Albuquerque step into the shop.

She almost groaned out loud. Oh Lord. She did not have the energy for the woman today. She was nice enough, but she was also *a lot*. If she wasn't actively digging for information, she was knee deep in spreading gossip.

"Hello, everyone." Her gaze fell on Anthony. "Why, hello. We haven't met. I'm Jackie Albuquerque. And you are…?"

Anthony shuffled from one foot to the other. "Anthony."

"My new employee," Michele added.

Mrs. Albuquerque's eyes narrowed, assessing. "You're a high school student, I presume?"

His fingers tightened on the containers. It was only slight, but Michele saw it. "I'm not going anymore, ma'am."

"Good heavens. Is that what kids do these days? They just stop going whenever they feel like it?"

Jesus Christ. "Mrs. Albuquerque, I'll grab your meals. The guys were just taking Uncle Ottie's to the car." It was time to move the older woman on. Or move the guys out.

"Thank you, dear." Jackie turned her attention to her uncle. "Ottie, before you go, how's the heart?"

Michele sighed, walking over to the fridge while Uncle Ottie cleared his throat. "As strong as ever, Jackie."

Even if it wasn't, there was no way he'd be telling this woman. It would be all over town by morning.

Her uncle smiled politely. "Excuse us, Jackie. We should be getting this food to the car."

Yes, run.

Michele grabbed the meals from the fridge as she heard the door to the shop close after them.

Mrs. Albuquerque's voice lowered. "How well do you know that boy?"

"Uh, one-interview-and-a-shift well."

Mrs. Albuquerque tsked. "I thought you would hire Cheryl Anderson."

That was a solid no. The woman could talk almost as much as Mrs. Albuquerque. Every shift would drain her.

"I considered her." *Lie.* She set the meals on the counter before going back and grabbing some more.

"You know there's a serial killer on the loose, right?"

Michele banged her head on a shelf of the fridge when she tried to straighten too quickly, half a dozen meals in hand. She turned. "*What?*"

"You haven't seen? It's all over the news. There was a woman killed just last week in Edgemont."

Michele lowered the last of the containers to the counter. "Edgemont? That's just—"

"A fifteen-minute drive. Yes, I know. The woman was stabbed in the chest four times."

A chill swept over Michele's skin. She almost wanted to rub her arms but only just stopped herself. She hadn't heard about the murder, but then, she'd been deep into her latest books for the last week. "You said serial killer. So this woman wasn't the first?"

"She's the fifth, dear. All young women. All stabbed exactly four times while in their own homes, no signs of forced entry."

Michele swallowed as she typed the amount Mrs. Albuquerque owed into the EFTPOS machine and pushed it forward. The older woman had just swiped her card when the door opened, and Anthony and her uncle walked back in.

Mrs. Albuquerque lifted half her meals. "Ottie, do an old woman a favor and help me with my meals."

Anthony stepped forward. "I can help."

She gave Anthony a tight smile. "Very kind, dear, but no thank you."

Michele blew out a long breath. *Jeez.*

Ottie shook his head before walking up to Michele and kissing her cheek. "I'll see you tomorrow, darling."

Then he grabbed half the meals and made his way to the door.

Before Mrs. Albuquerque walked away, she leaned over the counter and whispered, "Be careful." Then they were both gone.

Michele gave an apologetic smile to Anthony. "Sorry. She's a crazy old lady."

God, she hoped there wouldn't be a rumor by morning that she'd just hired a serial killer.

Sighing, she scrubbed her hands over her pants and looked at the time on the wall clock. "It's five o'clock. You officially survived your first shift."

He chuckled, and the sound had a small smile tugging at Michele's lips. That was the first laugh she'd heard from him. Hopefully it wouldn't be the last.

"I did. Want me to stay a bit longer to finish what I was doing and help with the cleanup?"

"Nah, that's okay. Go home, put your feet up, and rest before I see you bright and early tomorrow." It was the first time in weeks she wouldn't be working until ten o'clock at night to fulfill her orders. So it was a good day.

Anthony nodded, moving to the counter to grab his phone and keys before heading to the door. He was about to walk through when he stopped and turned. "Michele, I meant what I said earlier. Thank you. I know you probably could have hired someone quicker and with a lot more experience, but I really appreciate you giving me a chance. With the move, money's short, so…"

Michele's heart softened. There was real gratitude in his eyes. This was why she'd hired him. Well, part of the reason. "You're very welcome, Anthony."

He gave her a small smile before leaving the shop.

What the heck was wrong with Mrs. Albuquerque? Hinting that the kid—a kid she didn't know from a bar of soap—could be a serial killer. That was like saying every random kid she ran into on the street could be a serial killer.

Michele made short work of storing the meals Anthony had

just placed in containers, then quickly cleaned the space. Her gaze flicked to her phone about a dozen times, Mrs. Albuquerque's visit in the forefront of her mind. When the place was clean and ready to go, she finally gave in and lifted her phone, typing in "Edgemont murder".

Half a dozen articles flashed up on the search engine. She clicked on the first one, and a photo of a pretty young brunette came up. In the article below her picture was everything Mrs. Albuquerque had told her. She'd been stabbed in the chest four times, and her murder was comparable to four others in towns close by.

Her gaze paused on the line at the bottom—no forced entry. Also as Mrs. Albuquerque had said. So the victim had known the guy?

She flicked farther down the screen, glancing over the names of the previous victims. Unease swirled in her tummy. They were the same age as her.

When the door opened, Michele started, the phone slipping from her fingers and hitting the floor.

The air rushed from her chest. Declan. He stepped into the shop looking every bit the dangerous former Delta he was. Tall. Well-muscled. Lethal. Cole trailed in behind him, looking much the same.

Declan frowned as he stopped at the counter. "Hey, honey. You okay?"

Usually, his endearments had her warming, but her heart raced too fast for that right now. Was she wearing her unease on her face?

She forced a smile. "Of course. I was just…" She shook her head. "Just about to leave. Can I get you guys some meals?"

Declan leaned over the counter. "Well, we haven't ordered any, but we're hoping you'll take pity on a couple of guys who've been living on eggs."

God, his smile was so disarming. She'd say yes to just about anything the man asked. "Of course. I always have extra meals on hand. Anything in particular you feel like?"

Declan's smile widened, and man did it have her stomach doing somersaults. "Anything you make is perfect."

"And it'll sure beat more eggs," Cole added, just as his phone rang. "Excuse me."

Cole walked out of the shop, and suddenly it was just her and Declan. Nerves skittered up her spine. Swallowing, she turned and headed to the fridge before opening the door. "I'll get you guys a bit of everything."

She didn't have much experience with men. In fact, most of her experience was with fictional guys in books. She could count the amount of men she'd been intimate with on one hand, and not one had made her feel the things Declan made her feel by just being in the same room.

She grabbed as many meals as she could carry. When she turned, yet another gasp slipped from her lips.

Declan was right in front of her. He had a habit of doing that.

He took the meals from her hands, his warm skin grazing hers, causing a shot of awareness to wash through her lower abdomen. Almost immediately, she turned back to the fridge and grabbed more food. She absolutely was *not* hiding or trying to cool her heated cheeks.

Okay, maybe she was a little bit.

She heard his light footsteps and the sound of him setting the meals onto the counter. This time when she rose and turned, she was prepared to see him, even if she didn't think anything would ever prepare her for his touch.

He set the second handful of meals on the counter as she closed the fridge. Then he lifted the phone she'd completely forgotten she'd dropped. He held it out for her, and as she took it, their hands once again slid across each other and, yep, her tummy did little turns again.

He stepped closer. "You seemed scared when we came in."

God, she was so obvious. "Mrs. Albuquerque was just in here talking about some woman who was killed not too far away."

Declan's eyes darkened. "I heard about that."

So it was just her who'd been living under a rock.

"Make sure you're staying safe," he said quietly. "Don't leave the store too late at night and don't let strangers into your place."

Was he closer now? He felt closer, but he couldn't be. She hadn't even seen him move. "I live in an apartment building. People can't get in unless I buzz them up."

Although, that wasn't entirely accurate, was it? Tim had gotten in that night he'd banged on her door. He'd probably slipped in when another tenant entered the building. It wasn't hard.

He nodded. "Don't buzz anyone up."

"Okay."

When he touched her hip, her breath caught.

"Will I see you at the party tomorrow night?"

She bit her lip, trying and failing not to let his touch short-circuit her brain, but it was impossible. Her brain was empty, and she couldn't for the life of her recall what party he was talking about. "Party?"

He grinned. "River's party for Ryker. What's she calling it? The resurrection party?"

Oh, that party. She gave a slow nod. "River would murder me if I missed it." Literally, head on the slaughter.

His head lowered. And when his breath brushed across her cheek, her heart stopped. Then he whispered in her ear, "Save me a dance."

The fine hairs on her arms stood on end.

The door suddenly opened, and she took a step back as a woman walked inside.

"Oh, sorry. Am I interrupting?"

Michele gave a quick shake of her head. "No. Of course not. How can I help?"

The woman smiled and approached the counter. "Hi there! My name's Connie. I live over in Edgemont, and word's getting around about the *amazing* meals you make here."

She shot one more look at Declan to see his wink. Then he dropped some money onto the counter before grabbing his meals and heading toward the door, all while Michele tried to pretend she was a normal functioning woman long enough to serve her customer.

CHAPTER 5

*D*eclan stepped into River's house, only to come to a quick stop. Who the hell *were* all these people? Music blasted, and there had to be at least thirty people in the living room alone.

Cole walked in beside him. "Did you know Ryker was this fucking popular?"

Declan scanned the faces of strangers. "I thought he had three friends. Us."

Suddenly, River appeared in front of them, two small shots of something bright and multicolored in her hands. "You're here!" She foisted the small plastic cups on them.

Declan frowned, turning the cup sideways. The stuff inside didn't move at all. "It's Jell-O."

"Very colorful Jell-O," Cole added.

River's smile was wide. "They're rainbow Jell-O shots. This party is the opposite of a funeral, remember, so lots of color."

Declan lifted the cup and sniffed. Sweet. Too fucking sweet. "Don't think I've had a Jell-O shot since I was fifteen." He lifted it and squeezed the Jell-O out. Yep. It was like candy.

River jammed her hands onto her hips. "Um, what the heck

are you both wearing? I told you the dress code was bright and colorful."

Declan glanced down at his jeans and navy-blue T-shirt. "I made sure I didn't wear a black shirt just for you."

"And I wore a gray one," Cole argued.

Declan just held in a laugh. Cole's shirt was charcoal gray—so almost black.

River looked like she was on the verge of yelling at them. Then she shook her head. "You know what? This is a party. I won't be angry now. I'll just be passive-aggressive later. Now go have fun before I change my mind."

"I'm having fun already," Declan said, handing the woman his empty shot glass.

She rolled her eyes before moving on to her next victim. He didn't miss the muttering under her breath. He was pretty sure he heard the word "death" thrown in there.

Chuckling to himself, Declan moved through the crowd, scanning the faces once again. Was Michele here yet? She had to be. Being River's best friend, she'd probably helped with the setup.

"What's going on with you two?" Cole asked as they stopped at a table. Cole grabbed two beers and handed one to Declan.

"Just messing with her."

Cole shook his head, uncapping his drink. "Not you and River. You and Michele."

Declan paused, beer midway to his mouth.

Cole smirked. "That *is* who you're looking for, isn't it?"

Declan's lips lifted into a half smile. Was he that damn obvious? Or did his friends just see too much? Probably both. "At the moment, nothing, but I hope to change that."

"She's a lot different from the other women you've dated."

True. "I know. There's just something about her. I can't get her out of my head."

"This town's messing with you guys. First Jackson, now you."

"You'll be next."

Declan grinned. It was well known within the group that Cole didn't date. Oh, he liked women. Just nothing that went past one night. In fact, the guy had made an art of ensuring any and all interactions with females were kept short and casual. No commitments.

Cole scoffed. "I don't think so."

Ryker approached, and Declan clamped a hand on the guy's shoulder. "Happy resurrection party, buddy. How's it feel to be back from the dead?"

His friend crossed his arms over his chest. "It feels good. But let's never fucking do it again."

"No, let's not," Cole said quietly, no humor in his voice. "Thinking you were dead was shit for everyone, but we know why you did it."

If he hadn't, assholes would have come after River and their parents.

Declan scanned the room again. "River was all smiles when she greeted us at the door."

Ryker grinned. "The woman takes her parties seriously. Especially, it appears, parties for her long-lost brother. You try the Jell-O shot?"

Cole nodded. "Didn't really have a choice in the matter."

Declan laughed. The sound was cut short when he saw Michele step into the kitchen. River was behind her, lips moving a million miles an hour.

His gaze trailed up Michele's body, taking in the jeans that hugged her ass so tightly his dick twitched. The blue knit top matched her indigo-blue eyes. Her long brown hair was down tonight, something he'd never actually seen before. It cascaded over her shoulders, softening her features.

When she sucked on her bottom lip, Declan's jeans suddenly felt too damn tight.

He moved into the kitchen, catching the last of River's words.

"I can't believe Mrs. Albuquerque would be so judgmental. She doesn't even know Anthony."

"I know. And he's a kid," Michele responded quickly, turning when she reached the island. "He needed a job, and I gave him one. And, can I add, he's been excellent. Hard working. Nonintrusive. He even worked overtime today to deliver a last-minute meal to Mr. Packer."

"You hired Anthony?"

Her head whipped around, mouth slipping open. "Declan, I didn't... When did you get here?"

"A few minutes ago."

River smiled. "Yes, she hired the kid. Didn't I tell you she would? God, I know the woman so well."

"Of course I hired him," Michele said with a laugh. "What was my alternative? Joan, who talks a million miles an hour? Or Cheryl, who's even worse? I wouldn't have gotten a lick of peace and quiet in my day."

Declan frowned. "Do you know much about him?"

She turned back to him, her voice softening. "I know that he needed a job. Come into the shop and talk to him. I think you'll like him."

Oh, he would spend every second in that shop if he could, but that had nothing to do with the kid.

She turned back to River. "Maybe if Mrs. Albuquerque saw that Declan, a big bad former Delta, approves of Anthony, she'd realize the kid's okay."

A scoff sounded from behind him. "Big and bad? The guy's a marshmallow."

Declan shoved Cole in the shoulder as Jackson stepped up behind River and kissed her on the neck.

Michele moved around the kitchen island, clearly making a getaway. "Okay, I'm going to restock the drink bowls."

Over the next half hour, Declan ate and drank with his friends, all the while using every scrap of self-control he possessed to *not* look for Michele every five seconds. And it worked. Until it didn't.

He moved into the crowd, searching her out. Would she give him that dance he'd asked for? No one else was dancing, but hell, he'd use any excuse to hold the woman.

He stopped when he finally spotted her. Immediately, he frowned at seeing the strain lines around her eyes. She entered the kitchen and crossed to the back door before slipping outside.

Why would she be going out there? It was cold as hell tonight.

He was seconds from following when Ryker moved to the door, going outside before Declan could.

He ground his teeth. Had he been watching her, too?

"There's nothing going on between them."

Declan turned to look at Jackson. "How do you know?"

He lifted a shoulder. "Because I grew up with them. They have a sibling bond, not a romantic one. It was hard for Michele when she thought he was dead. We all focused on River, but Michele struggled too. She's good at keeping her emotions to herself."

Yeah, Declan had seen that. He'd *also* seen the way she looked at Declan when she thought he wasn't watching. Like she wanted him but didn't want anyone to know. The way she quickly looked away as soon as their gazes clashed.

Declan glanced around the room. "Who the hell *are* all these people?"

Jackson frowned. "I don't know. I think River just invited every person Ryker's ever had a conversation with. Either that, or she hired a crowd."

MICHELE STEPPED onto River's deck and sucked in her first lungful of fresh air all night. For a moment, her eyes closed, and she just appreciated the peace. No people around. No loud music pumping in her ears.

She loved that they were celebrating Ryker, but God, what she wouldn't do to be tucked up in bed with Pokey and a book.

She moved forward and had just wrapped her fingers around the deck railing when the door opened behind her. She swung her head around to see Ryker walk outside, all million and one feet of him.

She smiled. "Hey. Enjoying your celebration?"

He came to stand next to her, the heat of him warming her side. "Nope. I'd much rather be home with a book and a hot chocolate."

She nudged his shoulder playfully. The man knew her too well. "Don't tease me."

The humor left his eyes. "Seriously though, are you doing okay?"

"Yeah, I just needed some air. Being around people and having to talk a lot kind of exhausts me."

She'd been going for a joke, but the way Ryker looked at her reminded her that it really wasn't. He knew she needed time to recoup. She was an introvert. Whenever she had a choice, she would stick to socializing in small crowds and with people she knew well.

"Thank you for coming," he said quietly.

"Of course." She studied his shadowed face. "I really missed you."

"I missed you too, Chele."

"How are *you* doing?" She wasn't just talking about the whole being dead one second and alive the next thing. Before he'd been declared dead, he hadn't been his usual self. Not for almost a year, since retiring from the military. She'd been told a short version of the story. That his final mission hadn't gone to plan. Cole had broken his back, and Declan had been shot. People had died. People Ryker had met during a mission. People he cared about.

Ryker glanced back toward the yard, but she was almost

certain he wasn't really seeing anything. "Some days, I can almost forget. A lot of other days, it's all I can think about. I have this guilt that pits my stomach."

Her heart ached for the man. She touched his shoulder. "I'm so sorry."

"People died because of me." His voice was almost a pained whisper. "I became a Delta to protect people, to save them. I did the opposite."

"Hey. That's not true." She let go of the railing, turning to face him. "I may not know the finer details of what happened, but I *do* know you would never hurt people you care about. And you would never knowingly allow innocents to die."

His jaw clenched. "Yeah. But my connection to people, good people, got them killed."

She squeezed his arm. "You're *also* a good person, Ryker. If people who were connected to you died, that's on someone else."

He muttered something under his breath. Something that sounded awfully like "someone else who'd pay." Then he nodded before finally looking back at her. "Let's talk about you. What's this I hear about an ex harassing you?"

She sucked in a surprised breath. "Did River—"

"Declan."

"Declan?" She hadn't been expecting that. But maybe she should have. The guy probably told his team everything.

She lowered her hand, turning back to the yard. "He's not bothering me anymore." As of today, anyway. "We went on three dates, and when I ended things, he wasn't happy."

That was the very condensed version.

This time it was Ryker who angled his body toward her. "What do you mean, he wasn't happy?"

"He wanted another date. I said no. He's called me a couple of times since. He showed up at work and at my place."

It made her angry just thinking about. No meant no, and he needed to get that into his head.

She felt Ryker's gaze like a heated beam on her skin. He was the brother she'd never had, always looking out for her like he looked out for River. "Do you feel safe?"

She frowned. Did she? "I feel angry. And frustrated." When Ryker remained silent, she turned to him. "But I'm fine, Ryker. Go back inside and enjoy your party." The man had been through hell. The last thing he needed was her problem to become his.

He watched her for another beat before straightening. "Are you coming?"

"I'll be there in a sec."

He gave her shoulder a gentle squeeze, then he disappeared back inside. Sighing, she looked back over the yard.

She'd made a report against Tim, and the police hadn't cared. In fact, the officer who'd taken her report seemed to think she was overreacting. She wasn't sure if he was jaded, or being lazy, or if he thought she was an attention-seeking woman making a big deal out of nothing. Whatever the case, his lack of concern made her angry as hell.

She straightened and was about to step back into the house when something sounded nearby. A voice. A whisper.

Was that... Had someone said her name?

Frowning, she scanned the yard, but it was too dark to see anything.

"Hello?"

She shot a look over her shoulder at the door. Then, with slow steps, she moved down to the grass. The wind blew hard, causing a chill to sweep up her arms and brush over her face. A voice in her head told her to go back.

Then she heard the soft crunching of grass.

Michele stopped, her heart thudding in her chest.

Suddenly, Mrs. Albuquerque's words came back to her. *Serial killer. Stabbed four times.*

God, what are you doing, Chele? Had she lost her mind?

Quickly, she started to turn. That's when she saw a shadow race from the back of the yard and down the drive.

She sucked in a loud gasp—and when a hand touched her back, she screamed and spun.

At the sight of Declan, she blew out a long breath, grabbing his upper arms to keep herself upright. "Oh God. You scared me!"

He shot a look over her head, then back at her. "Are you okay?"

Michele cast a glance down the drive, where the person had run. She opened her mouth, then quickly shook her head. It was a party. Of course people were around. She shouldn't be acting like an ax murderer had just run away.

"I'm okay. I just scare easily."

Understatement of the century. Damn Mrs. Albuquerque for filling her head with fear.

He scanned her body like he was looking for signs of injury.

Maybe it was the darkness, or maybe she was just feeling on edge and reckless, but she stepped forward and one of her hands grazed up his chest before stopping on his cheek, something she would never normally do. "Declan. I'm okay."

Even in the darkness, she saw his pupils dilate as his hands went to her hips. "I like it when you do that."

She swallowed before responding, his touch causing her brain to short-circuit once again. "Do what?"

"Touch me."

She liked it too. A lot. She should probably move away now. But there was something about the heat of his body that had her remaining completely still. "The darkness makes it easier."

He tugged her closer. It wasn't subtle, and it caused her belly to heat.

"You're telling me, all this time, all I needed to do was flip the light switch?"

She wet her lips. Maybe it wasn't just the darkness. Maybe it was the Jell-O shots River had forced into her hands. Or maybe it was that she finally felt brave enough to explore this intense attraction.

Her thumb grazed his cheek, enjoying the roughness of his day-old shave. "I think I like touching you."

Had those words really just left her mouth? In any case, she didn't think. She knew.

A small smile touched his lips. "I like you touching me, too."

When he started to lower his head, her belly dipped. Her lips separated. Waiting. Anticipating the kiss. She could almost feel his lips...

Until the back door opened, and River's voice sounded.

"Michele? Are you out here? It's speech time!"

Michele dropped her chin to her chest, and Declan swore under his breath. The spell broke. She tried to step back, but Declan's grip tightened on her waist. Then his head lowered, his forehead touching hers. "This isn't over. And you still owe me that dance."

CHAPTER 6

"**W**iden your stance and bend your knees. The power comes from the legs."

Declan stepped back and studied the kid as he adjusted his stance. The next hit had twice the power of the last.

Declan tapped his shoulder. "Good job."

Shooting his gaze away, Declan moved around the room, watching the half dozen people hitting the bags. Most were kids, but they also weren't. Everyone in the room was seventeen or older, but they hit with more force than some men twice their ages.

There were more people in Mercy Ring every day. The growth was steady. Apparently, people from all over Washington State had heard about the new boxing club run by former Deltas who offered a safe space to exorcise anger. Some clients shared their stories. Some didn't.

He looked over at Cole. He was guiding someone else's hit, showing the boy how to throw a punch with precision, rather than blind emotion.

Declan's gaze went to the glass doors when he saw movement.

He straightened when he saw who was outside. That kid again. The one Michele had hired. Anthony.

For a second, the boy looked like he was going to come in. His hand even went to the handle. Then at the last second, he turned away, took two steps, and stopped again.

A slow smile spread across Declan's mouth. What was it with this kid? He wanted to come in, but he didn't. He crossed the room and pushed through the door.

The second Anthony saw Declan, his eyes widened. "I was just passing by."

Declan held the door open for him. "Come in."

Anthony glanced through the door then back at Declan. He shook his head. "I don't have any money."

"I'm not asking for any."

Something flashed in Anthony's eyes. Anger, perhaps? Pride? "I don't need charity."

"Didn't say you did."

Anthony stood there for another beat. The anger slowly eased from his face. Then he strolled inside, and Declan trailed behind him.

"Drop your bag, take off your shoes and come into the ring with me." Declan moved around the kid. He lifted wraps and two focus mitts before climbing between the ropes.

When he looked up, it was to see Anthony frowning. "Are you serious?"

"Do I look serious?"

Another beat passed, then Anthony did as ordered, setting his bag on the floor and toeing off his shoes before climbing into the ring. Dropping the pads, Declan stepped forward and grabbed Anthony's left hand before wrapping it. "You ever hit before?"

"I've thrown a few punches."

Not a surprise. "They land?"

"Every one of them. I'm a good fighter."

Declan grabbed his other hand and wrapped it the same way he had the first. Then he lifted the pads. "Show me."

Anthony only hesitated for a second. Then he swung, throwing the first hit and quickly following it up with a second. The kid had force behind his hits, no doubt, but they were unrefined. Sloppy and emotionally driven.

He continued to hit the pads, and Declan didn't stop him. Not yet. This was anger he was releasing. A lot of it.

When Anthony's breaths grew heavy and his hits slowed, he finally dropped his hands.

Declan dropped the pads to his sides. "How'd that feel?"

"Good." Anthony's chest moved up and down in quick succession.

"For someone without training, you're not bad. But you're exerting unnecessary energy. You need to use more core and legs, and less upper body." Declan dropped the pads to the floor and turned sideways, demonstrating a hit.

Anthony nodded, copying the action.

Declan spent the next ten minutes guiding and refining Anthony's movements. The kid picked up everything quickly, and he was eager to learn.

When Declan lifted the pads again, Anthony started hitting. This time, he didn't grow tired so quickly. But that anger was still there. Simmering behind every hit. Darkening the kid's eyes.

"Wanna talk about it?" Declan asked.

Anthony didn't stop or slow. "Talk about what?"

"Whatever has you hitting like a demon."

Two more punches. "No."

Fair enough. Not everyone wanted to share, and that was their choice.

Three more punches, then Declan asked, "Where's your mom working?"

A small hesitation. Then another punch. "She hasn't found work yet."

"Is that why you dropped out of school? To support her?"

"I dropped out of school because I wasn't learning shit and it was a waste of time."

Three more punches. Anthony's form started to wane.

Declan pushed back with his pads. "Michele's safe with you, isn't she?"

Suddenly, Anthony stopped. His hands dropped and a new wave of anger washed over his face. "You think I'd hurt her?"

Did he? He studied the kid. There was anger, but there wasn't that *other* thing. The thing he'd seen in the eyes of many assholes. "No."

The kid swallowed, his jaw clenching then unclenching. "Good. Because I wouldn't."

"Good." He lifted the pads. "Again."

MICHELE TOOK SLOW, *careful steps into the grand ballroom. Her gaze skittered over the men in their fitted dress coats and matching pants. The women in their beautiful, long ball gowns made from the most exquisite tulle and silk. The dresses were tight at the chest and puffed out from the waist to the floor.*

Beautiful. All of them.

She glanced down at her own dress, a puff of air slipping from her lips at the generous cleavage that pushed against the corset. Holy Christ. She was dressed just as beautifully as the others.

The dress felt heavy on her heated skin. Or maybe it was the dense crowd of people surrounding her that made her hot. They were every-where. Drinking. Talking. Taking small pieces of fancy food from men holding trays.

Laughter and classy English accents fluttered throughout the room, rivaling the soft music.

More slow steps. Each one felt lighter. Like she was walking on a cloud. She stopped at the edge of the dance floor and watched the couples swaying. The way they moved... It was like they were floating around the room. There was so much grace and ease, like each of them had done this very dance a million times before.

Her body itched to move forward and join them, but she didn't know the steps and she had no one to dance with.

A smile was just tugging at her lips, when a man on the dance floor turned his head and looked at her. Her stomach dropped, and she took a quick step back, the smile melting from her face.

Tim.

He turned as he spun his partner. When she saw his face again, she blinked. It wasn't him.

A small frown tugged at her brows. Then she felt it. The prickle on the back of her neck. Like someone was watching her. Like he was watching.

Slowly, she turned her head, searching, frustration welling in her stomach.

Nothing. Nothing but beautiful people laughing with their beautiful friends.

She turned back to the dancers, wanting to lose herself in the hypnotic grace of their movements again, but her heart was still beating too fast. The skin on her forehead now beaded with sweat.

The prickling intensified, only this time it was accompanied by a tightening in her chest. Her breaths whooshed in and out as she scanned the outer edge of the dance floor. That's when she saw him again. Tim.

Her heart crashed to a halt in her chest. She blinked, hoping he'd disappear. He didn't.

He took a step forward, right onto the dance floor. Then another. And like the Red Sea, the people parted, continuing to dance around him like they'd choreographed their movements.

What the...

Michele took a hurried step back. No. This wasn't happening.

Tim never stopped moving. His footsteps, while not quick, were constant. The distance between them diminished. And he only had eyes for her.

The sweat on her forehead grew, and it had nothing to do with the dress or the crowd. It was him. All him.

Run!

The voice was a shout in her head.

Quickly, she turned and moved into the crowd. But where the people on the dance floor had parted for Tim, the crowd did the opposite for her. They blocked her at every step. The people in their beautiful clothing and painted faces suddenly felt like a million barriers keeping her from getting out. Away.

Her breaths quickened, her heart beating so fast, she swore it would burst from her chest.

She tried not to look. She really did. But as if her head had a will of its own, it turned. A scream suddenly tore from her chest when he was there. Right there. Right behind her, his silvery eyes boring into her.

He grabbed her upper arm and squeezed, just like he had that night.

With strength she didn't know she possessed, she yanked her arm from his hold and ran. There was no skirting around people this time. She pushed and shoved, forcing anyone in front of her out of her way.

God, where was the exit? No matter how far or fast she moved, she never seemed to get any closer.

She cast another glance over her shoulder. But she didn't feel safe.

She was just turning around again when she ran into a big chest. She scrunched her eyes shut and would have fallen back if warm hands didn't keep her steady.

She was on the verge of screaming again. Shoving the man. Only the hands on her arms were holding her differently now. Instead of punishing, they seemed gentle. Protective, even.

Slowly, her eyes fluttered open, and there in front of her was Declan. She sucked in a sharp breath.

He towered over her, and just like the other men, he wore the most perfectly fitted dress coat and pants.

Her words came out in a throaty gasp. "Declan, he's here!"

It was almost like he didn't hear her. He bent down, his lips brushing across her cheek, then her ear. "Dance with me."

Her mouth opened and closed a couple of times. "No. Y-you don't understand! Tim, h-he's here."

Those lips brushed her ear again, repeating the words. "Dance with me, Chele."

Her heart started to slow. Suddenly, even though she knew she should get out, she wanted to say yes. She wanted this man to hold her, even if it was just for a moment. "I...I don't know the dance."

But God, she wished she did.

There was another swiping of lips against her cheek. Then those strong hands slid down her arms and took her hands. "You do."

The words had barely left his mouth when his arms were slipping around her waist, and suddenly they weren't in the crowd anymore. They were on the dance floor.

"How—"

She didn't have time to finish what she was saying because they were moving, and it took her a full lap of the dance floor to realize she was doing it. Somehow, she was doing every twirl and dip and turn like she'd done it a thousand times before.

She looked up into Declan's caramel-brown eyes. They were watching her, as if she was all he saw. As if he didn't need to see where he was going or what he was doing. All he needed to watch was her.

"This isn't real," she whispered. "You're not real."

That hint of a smile widened. "Then what am I?"

"A dream." He had to be. "A beautiful figment of my imagination." But hell, she'd take it all, real or not, because dancing with him, being held by him, was everything she'd known it would be.

His hand left her back to spin her around. She moved in perfect unison with the other women on the dance floor. Then she returned to him, his hand once again pressing to her back. The thick material of her dress didn't feel so thick anymore. The warmth of his touch seeped right into her skin.

"Do you want it to be real?" he asked, those fingers around her hand strong as they led her forward.

"It doesn't matter what I want."

"It always matters."

When Declan stopped, Michele looked around, frowning. The other dancers moved around her like she and Declan weren't even there.

"What do you want, Michele?"

She looked back up at him. You. *The word whispered in her head. Or maybe it didn't. Maybe it had slipped from her lips, because his eyes were closing. His hands slipped onto her hips, tugging her closer.*

Their lips almost touched when a deep growl cut through the moment.

CHAPTER 7

*M*ichele's eyes snapped open at the sound of Pokey growling. And maybe something else... Footsteps on the other side of the door?

She closed her eyes and listened, but all she heard was Pokey.

Asleep. She'd been asleep. Declan hadn't really been about to kiss her—as much as she wished he had. Argh.

Slowly, she pushed up into a seated position. The open book on her chest fell to her lap. She'd fallen asleep reading on the couch. Again.

No wonder she'd dreamed about some Regency ball. Her book was historical romance, and she'd been smack bang in the middle of a chapter about a ball.

She lifted the book and folded the corner of the page before setting it onto the coffee table. Then she grabbed her phone. Seven thirty. Her gaze shot to the window. Yep, already dark outside.

How on earth she had fallen asleep when she'd been at a good part in the book, she had no idea. The hero had been crawling back to the heroine, begging for forgiveness after majorly screwing up, always a favorite part of hers.

When Pokey growled again, she frowned, glancing over at him. He sat by the front door. "Hey, boy. What are you growling at?"

Was there someone out there?

The idea had unease prickling at her skin. Then she shook her head.

Stop being silly, Michele. She was probably just remembering Tim in the nightmare. Since when did a nightmare morph into a dream, anyway? Wasn't it usually the other way around? Not that she was complaining.

Her muscles creaked as she rose and moved to the door. She looked through the peephole. Nope. No one outside. Maybe the guy across the hall had come out and gone back in? Maybe he'd been carrying food. She'd fed Pokey, but the Great Dane was always hungry.

"There's no one out there, Pokes." She bent down and scratched his head. "Mommy feels like being naughty and having ice cream for dinner. Want to come to the shop with me?"

Pokey dug his head into her palm but still seemed to be keeping an eye on the door.

She rested her forehead on his neck. "Then Mommy's going to stay up way too late reading her book." She'd regret it tomorrow, but that was future Michele's problem.

She grabbed Pokey's lead and attached it to his collar before unlocking the door and stepping into the hall. The second the door closed, Pokey growled again, staring at the stairs at the back of the building.

"What is it?" She glanced down the hall to the stairs that led to the back parking lot. For a moment, she was tempted to walk down there, just to check that it was clear. The second the idea popped into her head, though, she shook it off. She lived in an apartment building. It was probably a neighbor coming or going.

"Come on, let's go get Mommy some ice cream. I'm thinking rum raisin tonight."

She pulled Pokey in the opposite direction, toward the stairwell that led to the front of the building.

For a lot of her life, she'd been a health nut. With her mother dying of cancer and her father of a heart attack, she'd wanted to do everything she could to prevent either. And she was still healthy. But after her uncle, a man who had been pretty damn healthy his whole life, started having heart issues too, she'd thought, you know what? Life's short and she needed to live it. Embrace her curves and just...be. Now her diet was a bit more balanced.

Quickly, she moved down the stairs, Pokey following closely beside her. She hadn't had him for long, but God, she loved him.

The day after the Tim incident when he'd grabbed her and she'd hidden in the bedroom, she'd gone to the animal shelter. He'd been sitting there in his kennel, looking miserable. And when he'd looked up at her, his eyes had been so sad, like he'd already given up on anyone choosing him. As if he knew he was too big and too old to be anyone's choice.

She'd knelt beside the kennel, and for a moment, he'd seemed confused. Her heart had broken. Then, finally, he'd moved over to her and pushed his face against her hand through the gate. She'd known then that there was no leaving that place without him.

Blowing out a long breath, she pushed outside into the cold night air and moved toward her car.

"You can have a treat too, Pokey." She was pretty sure she had some peanut butter bacon doggie donuts left. She'd only made them a couple of days ago. Yes, she made Pokey fresh dog treats at her shop. She also cooked all his meals fresh, because, well, cooking was what she did. It would be criminal of her to make meals for all these people but not her own dog.

She'd just arrived at her car when she stopped abruptly. "What the..."

A flat tire. Like, all the way flat. How the heck had that

happened? She hadn't noticed running over anything when she'd driven home from work today.

A sudden tingling on the back of her neck had her gaze shooting around the area. Someone wouldn't have done this... Would they?

Quickly, she turned and walked back to the building. Her gaze continued to shift around the area until she stepped inside. She was being silly. She must have run over a nail or something without realizing. Pokey wasn't barking, so she assumed there wasn't anyone else around.

She took the stairs two at a time. Thank God she was only on the second floor.

She'd just unlocked her apartment door when Pokey started growling again. This time it was a low, deep growl she'd never heard before. Almost threatening. And it wasn't aimed toward the hall anymore. He was looking at her apartment door like there was someone in there.

The skin on her arms crawled. Pokey's growl grew louder. He stepped in front of her body, almost like he was refusing to let her pass.

Instead of going inside, she moved back.

On instinct, she turned around. She left her floor, apartment door unlocked and everything, and ran back down the stairs and outside. She didn't stop until both her and Pokey were locked inside her car.

She lifted her phone, and for a moment, she debated who to call. The police? River and Jackson?

Then someone else came to mind. And like her finger had a mind of its own, she clicked on his name.

He answered on the first ring. "Hey. This is a nice surprise."

She swallowed, watching the building entrance from a distance. "I'm sorry to call so late..."

It wasn't that late. But hell, her mind was as muddled as the rest of her.

The humor left his voice. "You sound scared. What's wrong? Is it your ex?"

Had her voice trembled? Or were her breaths loud enough for him to hear? Maybe both. "I left my apartment to go to the shop, but my car had a flat tire. Then when I went back upstairs, Pokey was growling like someone was inside my place."

Rustling sounded over the line. "Where are you now? Are you safe?"

"I'm in my car. I've locked the doors. Pokey's with me."

"Don't move. I'll be there in five minutes."

CHAPTER 8

*D*eclan placed one hand to the door and pushed. It wasn't closed, but that wasn't a surprise. Michele had told him she'd left it unlocked and ajar. She stood close behind him, with Pokey behind her.

He stepped in slowly, gun in hand and pointed in front of him. Before they could move any further than a few feet, he reached over Michele's head, closing the door behind her and flicking the lock. "Wait here."

She nodded quickly, her knuckles white as she held Pokey's lead. She was scared. With good reason. Someone might have flattened her fucking tire, then Pokey had growled at a possible intruder in her apartment. It made Declan pissed as hell.

While Michele waited by the locked front door, Declan moved through the apartment, first checking the kitchen and dining area, then the living room, followed by the bathroom. He left her bedroom until last. If there was anywhere to hide, that was the most likely place. He checked the closet. Under the bed. He even checked the windows, making sure they weren't just closed but locked.

There was no one here.

He stepped out of the bedroom. Michele hadn't moved an inch. "We're clear."

She all but sagged against the door.

"Are you sure you locked the door when you first went down to your car?" He moved around her and unlocked and opened the door before checking the knob and lock. No sign of tampering.

She moved over to the couch. She'd just lowered when she dropped her head into her hands and sighed loudly. "Yes. I'm sure." When she looked up, her eyes were pained. "I'm sorry. The tire thing scared me, and Pokey's been growling since I woke from a nap, but if there's no one here and no signs of forced entry, I must be overreacting."

Declan crossed the room and crouched in front of her. He pressed his hands on her knees. "Don't ever apologize for calling. I *want* you to call. Even if it's for the smallest thing." He lifted a hand to her cheek, and she released a quick breath. "I'm going to have a better look at the tire tomorrow."

Her gaze skirted to his. "Okay. Thank you."

He swiped his thumb across her cheek. "If it looks like someone did it on purpose, you should make a report to the police."

She swallowed, something flickering in her gaze. "I can do that."

"We can also look into new locks and an alarm."

Her mouth opened and closed, but she didn't say anything.

His voice quieted. "If it's okay with you, I'd like to stay the night."

Her eyes widened a fraction. He wasn't sure if it was in surprise or relief. Maybe a bit of both.

She shook her head. "You don't have to do that. I don't have a spare bed."

"I don't have to, but I'd like to. It would ease my mind because I'd know you're safe. And I'll sleep on the couch."

"No. It's too small."

He almost laughed. "Trust me, I've slept in places worse than this."

She blinked. "Um. Okay."

Something in his chest lightened. The woman trusted him. She'd called him when she was scared. She'd agreed to let him sleep on her couch. He was becoming that person for her—and he fucking loved it.

"Where were you going?" he asked.

Her cheeks reddened. "To get ice cream."

"What flavor?"

A small grin stretched her lips. "Rum raisin."

"My favorite."

That seemed to surprise her. "Really?"

"Yeah, honey." Deeper reddening of her cheeks. God, he loved how easy it was to read this woman. "You eaten?"

"No, I got distracted by a book. It's a bad habit of mine." He watched the way her eyes warmed at the mention of her book. He knew she liked reading. Her uncle owned a bookstore here in town, and Declan had seen her in action, grabbing as many romance novels as she could carry at one time.

Quickly, she stood, forcing him to lean back. "Want a drink? Something to eat?"

He rose too, already missing the feel of her cheek in his palm. Her head tilted back as she looked up at him. The woman just barely reached his shoulders. "Water would be great."

"Sure."

As she moved into the kitchen, all but running from him, he took his cell from his pocket and sent a quick text to Cole.

She returned a second later with a glass of water but whisked her hand away the second their fingers grazed. "I should feed Pokey."

It was about twenty minutes later—twenty minutes of Michele finding every little thing to do to keep herself busy—when the knock sounded on the door. Michele finally stopped.

She frowned as she moved over to it. When she tugged it open, Declan moved behind her to see Cole on the other side, two bags in hand.

"Cole?" Michele asked.

Cole passed the bags over. "Enjoy, guys."

Michele looked up at Declan, and he lifted a shoulder. "I asked him to pick up some food."

Her eyes did that softening thing again.

He looked back over her head to Cole. "How'd you get into the building?"

"Some woman was down there and let me in."

Christ, he didn't like that. What was the point of a lock on the outside door if just anyone could get in?

Cole lifted a shoulder. "Guess I look charming enough to be allowed entry." He smiled. "I'll see you both later."

"Thanks, buddy."

When the door closed, he moved over to the couch and set the Chinese food down before walking over to the kitchen with the second bag.

"You asked Cole to bring us dinner?" she finally asked, barely having moved away from the door.

"I did." He opened the other bag and took out the rum raisin ice cream to put into the freezer. It was a good choice by Michele.

When he looked at her, it was to see she'd made a little bit of progress toward the kitchen, but not much. "And you got the ice cream."

He grinned at her. "I did. Am I winning some brownie points?"

For a moment, she was silent. Then she surprised the hell out of him by closing the last of the distance and wrapping her arms around his waist. "Thank you."

He didn't hesitate. He wrapped his arms around her and

tugged her close. And damn, did it feel good. "You're welcome, honey."

~

MICHELE LEANED back on the couch. She was well and truly full. Declan was still eating, the smile on his lips something she could look at all day, every day. The man could eat. He'd easily had twice as much as her and looked like he wasn't close to being done.

She was in shock. Not because of how much he ate, though that *was* impressive. He'd come to her aid at a moment's notice. He'd offered to stay the night. Organized food. Even had her favorite ice cream brought over. He wasn't like the guys she was used to dating. Not even close. He was something else entirely. Something closer to those book heroes she fantasized about.

When he caught her staring, his grin widened, and her cheeks heated.

She cleared her throat. "So, how have you found everything since leaving the military? Has it been a hard adjustment?" The guys had all been in the military for around sixteen years, their entire adult lives.

Finally, he lowered his bowl to the table before angling his body toward her. He'd removed his jacket, and his thick biceps and chest stretched the material of his shirt. Oh Lord. Why did he have to be so sexy?

"Some people struggle with change," he said. "I don't. I follow my instincts. We had a hellish last mission, and after that, my instincts told me I was done, and it was time to explore something else. I don't regret it. How could I? Look where I am."

With her? Was he talking about with her?

She swallowed. "I, um, heard you got shot."

He straightened and lifted his shirt. Her mouth went dry at the sight of his six-pack. Holy Christ, the man was insanely muscled. She'd seen it all before from across the room while he was in the ring, but up close...it was so much better. Then her gaze moved to the scar on the left side of his chest. Her lips separated. She'd never seen a gunshot scar before.

"My war wound," he said quietly.

There were other scars, too. Something that looked like it could be the slice of a knife across his lower belly. A small circular scar barely revealed beneath his shirt, near his shoulder.

As if her hand had a mind of its own, she reached over and grazed the bullet wound with her finger. Then, slowly, her finger trailed to his other scars. His muscles tensed and rippled beneath her touch. When she looked up, it was to see the relaxed look on his face gone, something harder taking its place. Something more...intense.

She snapped her hand away like she'd been burned, her eyes lowering to her lap.

For the love of God, Michele, act normal. Act like you don't *want to jump the guy or for the guy to jump you.*

"That must have been scary," she finally said.

Good. That sounded normal, didn't it?

When she looked up again, his eyes were still a shade darker. Finally, his shirt lowered. "Less scary because I had my team around me. They got me out of each situation and to medical attention."

She gave a slow nod. She hated that he'd gotten hurt, possibly come close to death more than once. She'd experienced loss. After losing both her parents, some days—most days—she feared it would touch her life again. And that fear was crippling. Especially after thinking she'd lost Ryker, then River being shot.

"Bet your family's glad you're out and safe."

Declan chuckled. The sound had her insides turning molten. He just had to have a sexy laugh too, didn't he?

"My parents and sister are as easygoing as me. We love one

another, but we also respect one another's need to live our lives. They're happy as long as I'm happy."

"They sound wonderful," she said quietly. Suddenly, she wanted to meet them. She wanted to see if his sister looked like him. If his father had the same protective nature and his mother the same easygoing smile.

Maybe one day, a voice whispered in her head.

"So, what are you reading?" he asked, pulling her out of her thoughts.

Her brows rose at the change in subject, her gaze flicking to the book on the edge of the coffee table. The cover had a woman in a turquoise-green ball gown. Her head was thrown to the side, her eyes closed, while a shirtless man stood behind her and kissed her neck.

Crap. She'd never moved it.

"It's a historical romance," she said, biting her bottom lip. "It's about two people who are born into different classes and have to go through hell to work out how they can be together."

"Will they?"

She frowned. "Will they what?"

"Be together?"

"Always. That's the number one rule for any good romance book. There always has to be a happy ending."

A ghost of a smile touched his lips. "And that's what makes a happy ending? Two people ending up together?"

"In a romance novel, yes." Most definitely yes.

"What happens if they don't?"

"Then it's a tragedy." Plain and simple.

The way he looked at her... It was like he saw the words behind the words. Like he saw every little part of her.

"And that's what you love about romance books?" he asked. "That there's a guaranteed happy ending?"

"Yes. But that's not all. I love that, for a period of time, you're taken away from your world and thrust into another. One with a promise of love. I like that everything that happens in the book is necessary for them to end up together. Even when bad things happen, it all leads to love."

"Is that what you want in your life? Love?"

She sucked in a quick breath. No one had ever asked her that before. "Love would be nice, but…" She stopped, not entirely sure she wanted to expose her deepest wants and desires to this man.

He stretched his arm over the back of the couch, and his thumb grazed her shoulder. Her skin tingled. The man's touch was like electricity.

"Tell me."

She waited for the zing of his touch to dim. It didn't. "I've never had any big plans for my life. You know, some people dream really big, but then when they get what they want, they just want more. Like nothing's ever enough." She paused. "After my parents died, all I really wanted was a perfectly ordinary life with minimal loss. An ordinary home. A dog to greet me at the door. And all of my favorite authors living on my bookshelf."

Yeah, ordinary had been something she'd craved since experiencing the pain of losing the two people who were the center of her world.

For a moment, Declan was quiet. His throat bobbed as he swallowed, and his eyes were just as intense as they had been before. "Do you have that?" he finally asked.

"Most days. These last couple months haven't been great. I thought we'd lost Ryker. My uncle has heart issues. And then River was shot…" And Tim. But she didn't want to think about him right now.

"So…ordinary is what you want?"

Her gaze flicked to her book, and a smile stretched her lips. "Well, an above-ordinary kiss like the ones the heroines get in my books would be nice."

The second the words left her lips, she flushed. Why the heck had she gone and said that?

The corners of Declan's mouth lifted. "You haven't had any above-average kisses?"

She swallowed, but she couldn't blink. "Not one." Another truth she probably should have kept locked away. No man had ever made her feel much of anything. Not with a kiss. Not in bed. Maybe that was why she read so much. She wanted to feel *something*.

The smile slipped from his lips, and the thumb on her shoulder shifted until his hand grasped her upper arm. Then he moved closer. And slowly—so slowly she could almost convince herself he wasn't moving—his head lowered. The hand on her arm trailed back up, sliding along her neck and onto her cheek. She remained so still that no part of her moved. It was entirely possible her heart stopped with the rest of her.

Then his breath brushed her lips. "You deserve more than an ordinary kiss."

He closed that final distance, and the second his lips touched hers, her belly gave a little flip and her heart took off in a gallop.

His mouth swiped across hers, his hand sweeping into her hair.

Her mind fogged and her insides turned molten. Oh, Lord. It was like she was floating.

She pressed her hands to his solid chest and leaned into him. His lips were soft, but everything else about him was hard. He touched her waist with his other hand, and it was as gentle as the hand in her hair.

It was amazing. But she wanted more. She wanted to taste the man.

She opened her mouth, and as if he heard her thoughts, he slipped his tongue between her lips. She hummed, her fingers digging into his chest. He felt so strong beneath her touch. His arms surrounded her, protecting her from the outside world.

For a moment, she lost herself, and she wasn't sure she ever wanted to be found again. Because the kiss... It was intoxicating and stimulating and everything else she'd dreamed but never experienced.

The hand on her waist slipped beneath the material of her shirt, touching her bare back. The heat from his hand penetrated her skin, zinging straight to her core.

His fingers tightened, pressing into her skin. At the same time, his hand fisted in her hair while his tongue continued to taste and massage her own.

She felt paralyzed. Unable to move or think.

Endless minutes passed. And when his head finally rose, she wanted to tug him back. Pull them both back into the abyss of that deep kiss.

His lips returned, but this time to her cheek, trailing across to her ear. He tugged at her earlobe with his teeth. She whimpered as he whispered into her ear.

"How was that?"

There were so many words she could use, but her mind felt simple right now, so she went with simple words. "Not ordinary."

CHAPTER 9

"*A*re you freaking kidding me? You *kissed?*"

Michele grinned as she added some more salt to the Bolognese sauce. She'd known her best friend would be as excited as she was. "Yep. And it was every bit as amazing as I dreamed it would be."

At River's squeal, Michele tugged the phone from her ear. God, her best friend was going to burst her eardrum.

"This happened last night and you're only just telling me now?" River finally asked. "You should have called the second you woke up, woman. Hell, you should have texted me last night!"

Well, last night she'd been way too busy trying to fall asleep while ignoring the tall, dark and handsome man on her couch.

"I wanted to tell you, not text you, but I couldn't very well call while he was in the next room. And I knew you had work this morning—"

"Screw the photoshoot. I would have taken a break and screamed over the phone for a bit like I'm doing right now!" River sounded like she was trying to catch her breath. "Next time a tower of hunk kisses you, or heaven forbid you have sex, call me the second you're alone!"

Oh Lord, Michele couldn't even think about having sex with the man. The kiss alone had been, well, a lot, in the best possible way.

"What happened this morning?" River asked.

Michele grabbed a spoon and gave the sauce a mix. "We had breakfast together, and he was perfect and charming and kept making these jokes that had me laughing like a crazy person. Then he changed my tire and left for work."

Some of the humor left River's voice. "You sure there was no foul play there?"

The smile slipped from Michele's lips. "I don't have any evidence that someone did it, and nothing else happened." Thank God.

"But you went to the police?"

Pfft. What a waste of time that was. "They didn't even write up a report this time. He said something about flat tires being common."

It had been the same officer as last time. Some old guy who looked at her like she was a delicate princess making a big deal out of nothing. Luckily, Declan hadn't been with her. She was sure he wouldn't have taken well to the guy's condescension. Asshole.

"Is there a chance someone *was* in your apartment?"

She shook her head. "No. Nothing was touched or tampered with. The door was locked when I left and still locked when I returned. There's no chance."

Zero. Zilch.

She moved away from the sauce and grabbed some containers from the cupboard before setting them on the counter.

"But Pokey—"

"Is probably losing his mind in his old age." Heck, the shelter hadn't even known the true age of the poor dog.

The door to the shop opened, and Anthony stepped in. His

hair was windswept, and a frown was firmly etched on his face. Not that the frown was anything new.

"I've got to go. Anthony just got back from making some deliveries."

River sighed. "Okay. Just...be careful."

"I'm always careful. It's you who's not."

River spluttered. "I should be offended but..."

But it was true.

She leaned her hip against the counter. "Love you."

"Love you too, Chele."

The second she hung up, she looked at Anthony. The kid never looked happy, but he was kind and sweet and a hard worker. That was all she needed.

"How'd it go?"

He lifted a shoulder as he moved to the sink and started on the dishes. "Everyone was really happy to receive their meals."

"Yeah, people love delivery day. Especially the oldies." She studied him, seeing the muscles in his arms tensing as he worked. For a young kid, he was pretty toned. "Is everything okay?"

He gave a quick nod. "Yeah, I'm just a bit over today." He paused, then scrubbed a hand over his face. "Sorry. Probably shouldn't be telling you that."

"That's okay. Is it something to do with your mom?"

"No." His response was quick.

When he didn't expand on his answer, she nodded, spooning the pasta she'd prepared earlier into the containers. "You don't have any siblings?"

The glass he'd been moving from the sink to the dishwasher slipped from his hand and dropped. Glass shattered all over the floor.

Michele quickly dropped the spoon and moved over to the sink. Anthony cursed under his breath before bending down and lifting a large piece of glass. Almost immediately, he cursed again as bright red liquid dripped from his hand.

At the sight of the blood, nausea swelled in her belly. She *hated* blood. Like, bordering-on-phobia kind of hate. "Oh my gosh, you're bleeding!" She took a few deep breaths.

In and out, Michele. No being sick when the kid's bleeding.

She moved around the glass and grabbed a towel from the counter, then ran back to him and pressed it to his hand.

"I'm sorry," he said quietly, his brows tugged together.

"I'm not worried about a broken glass. I'm worried about the cut." And the blood. But that was her problem. She took the towel off and inspected the wound. Nausea churned in her gut.

"Are you okay?" he asked. "You've gone really pale."

She looked up to see him frowning at her. "I'm fine. I'm just worried about you." It was only part lie. She *was* worried about him, but that wasn't why her stomach was rebelling.

He shook his head. "It's shallow. I'll be fine."

It was shallow. She was just a big baby.

Blowing out a breath, she moved away and grabbed the first-aid kit from a cupboard before returning to him.

He attempted to pull away. "You don't need to do that. I'll just go home and wrap it up."

Oh, no he would not. "Don't even think about it." She tugged his hand back and, using an antiseptic wipe, cleaned the wound. "You hurt yourself in my shop, so I'll fix you in my shop." That was non-negotiable, no matter what the injury did to her insides.

He didn't fight her after that, allowing her to grab a bandage and apply it to the wound.

"If it continues to bleed tonight, I want you to go to a doctor to see if you need stitches. Okay?"

He gave a quick nod.

"Is it feeling all right?" she asked quietly as she stepped back.

"Yeah, it's fine."

Thank God the wound was covered. She tilted her head to the side. "Did my question about having a sibling startle you?"

All the muscles in his body seemed to tense and contract.

Strange. Why would a question about having a sibling cause such a strong reaction?

He tugged his arm from her hold. "No. I'm just a klutzy idiot sometimes."

"No, you're not." She tilted her head toward the door. "You go home and rest. It's just about finishing time anyway."

"I'm so—"

"Don't you dare say sorry again. Now go rest."

A ghost of a smile tugged at his lips. That was the first hint of a grin she'd seen from the guy today. It was enough to have Michele's own lips tugging up.

He swallowed. "I should clean this up before I go."

"Nope. I've got it. Go home. I'll see you tomorrow."

Another hint of a smile. Good. She liked a smiling Anthony.

"Okay. Um, thanks." With a nod, he headed out of the shop.

Well, how about that. Maybe the kid was actually starting to like her. And maybe, eventually, he'd like and trust her enough to open up to her. She knew he had secrets. Heck, anyone looking at the kid would see it. And for some reason, she wanted to help him. Maybe it was the flicker of vulnerability she saw when he thought no one was watching.

She was just about to clean up the glass when her phone rang. The second she saw the name on the screen, a full smile stretched her lips.

"Hi, Declan."

"Hey, honey. How's your day been?"

Were they at the stage in their relationship where they called throughout the day to check in? Did kissing put them there? If it did, she was all for it.

She bit her lip, trying to stop another smile as she grabbed a trash bag and set it beside the glass. "It's been okay. Not very eventful." Unless you call almost being sick at the sight of a tiny speck of blood eventful. Declan didn't need to know she was that much of a wuss. "Yours?"

"Mine's been awful."

She paused. "What happened?"

"I didn't see you."

Oh, this man. The smile returned and she bent down, carefully lifting a shard of glass and putting it into the bag. "You saw me this morning."

"I need more of you."

Her stomach did a little somersault. Holy Jesus. He had all the right words.

"What are you doing tonight?" he asked.

A sliver of excitement skittered up her spine. "Taking Pokey for a walk, then dinner and reading."

"Want some company?"

The grin on her face grew so wide that her cheeks started to ache. "Company would be nice."

More than nice. Company from Declan would be pretty damn fantastic.

She stretched to grab a piece of glass near the cabinet but lost her balance. When she reached for the cabinet door to stop from falling on the glass, the phone slipped from her hand and clattered to the floor. *Crap.*

As she reached to pick it up, the door to the shop opened. Her head turned—and her mouth slid open when she saw who entered.

Slowly, she rose to her feet. "Tim... What are you doing here?"

Tim stepped into the shop, and the door thudded closed behind him. To the untrained eye, he was handsome but unassuming. He stood a little over six feet tall, with thick dirty-blond hair and silver eyes. But the look in those eyes... It was exactly the same as the last time she'd seen them. Dangerous.

"Michele. How have you been?"

She straightened. "I told you I didn't want to see you again." *Multiple times.*

He ran a hand through his hair. "I know. I just... I can't get you out of my head. I'm begging you, please give me another shot. Just one more date."

Did the man have rocks in his head? "No."

He clenched his jaw, and a vein popped in his forehead. It had the fine hairs on her arms standing on end.

"I know I messed up on our last date together—"

"Messed up? You scared me, Tim. You grabbed me so hard you *bruised* me. And since then, you've done nothing but harass me. I'm not going on another date with you. Ever. You need to stop calling. Stop texting. Stop showing up. And leave me alone."

He continued to walk toward her, his eyes pinched at the corners. She took two large steps back and hit the counter. Her heart pounded hard in her chest, her breaths moving in and out of her faster than they should.

"I've tried that, Michele."

"Try harder," she breathed.

When he moved closer again, she beelined for the other side of the kitchen but only made it two steps before strong fingers wrapped around her upper arm.

She sucked in a breath. "Let me go."

"Please, Michele."

"Tim, take your hand off me right now! This is the last time I'll ask."

What exactly she would do next, she had no idea, but she wasn't just going to let the man intimidate her.

His head lowered, his breath brushing her face. "I need you."

That was the last straw. She was a second away from kneeing the guy between the legs when the door chimed. A second later, he was ripped away from her and thrown into the opposite counter.

Michele's mouth slid open as Declan grabbed Tim by the collar. "What the fuck are you doing here?"

Anger contorted Tim's face. "Get your hands off me!"

"No. She's told you more than once she wants nothing to do

with your ass. So again, what the hell are you doing here, and why the fuck are you touching her?"

When Tim's jaw clenched shut, Declan tugged him away from the counter and slammed him back into it, hard. "Answer the fucking questions, asshole."

"Get your hands off me before I cut you to fucking shreds!"

Cut him? Did Tim have a knife?

Declan lowered his head, his voice quieting, turning lethal. "Try it, and see what I do. Now answer my question before I break you."

Michele's heart contracted in her chest when Tim's hand suddenly moved.

Oh God, he *did* have a knife.

She lurched forward, and immediately her foot slid on the broken glass. She was midfall when Declan swung around and reached for her. But he was too late. The second her right hand hit the floor, a shard of glass sliced into her palm.

A cry of pain slipped from her lips. Declan shouted her name, then he was by her side. She faintly heard the sound of the shop door opening and closing before Declan spoke.

"Are you okay?"

She raised her trembling hand to see the large shard of glass still penetrating her hand. And the blood. God, there was so much! Michele took deep breaths to quell the sudden nausea.

Declan cursed under his breath. "We need to get you to a hospital."

She nodded, because if she spoke she was sure she'd be sick. All she could focus on was keeping her lunch inside her stomach, and the darkness from hedging her vision.

CHAPTER 10

*D*eclan ran his hands through his hair. He'd done so
many laps of the hospital waiting room that people
were openly staring. He didn't give a damn. He was too angry to
stay still. The emotion practically vibrated off him. Tim had
fucking *touched* her. Then she'd been hurt while Declan was in
the same goddamn room, while that asshole ex of hers had run
the hell out of there like a coward.

When the doors opened, Ryker, River and Jackson rushed in.

"Where is she?" River asked.

"With Ottie in room ten."

She took off.

Ryker stepped forward. "What happened?"

"That damn ex showed up again. I was on the phone with her,
and I heard him when he entered her store. I took off and got
there just in time to see his hands squeezing her arms as he
towered over her."

The memory made him want to go out, hunt the man down,
and scare the asshole so badly he didn't even *think* of going
anywhere near her again.

Both of his friends looked as murderous as Declan felt.

"I pulled him off and was ready to throw a punch when she fell, and glass cut into her hand."

Jackson frowned. "Where did the glass come from?"

"She said something about Anthony dropping a glass before he left, but to be honest, she was pretty out of it. She went completely pale after falling."

"She can't stand the sight of blood," Ryker said, glancing down the hall like he was itching to go check on her.

Declan stored that piece of information away, hating that he hadn't known. "When she's up to it, I'm going to take her to the station." And they were going to damn well listen this time.

"Why aren't you with her?" Jackson asked.

"I wanted to give her some time with her uncle." The second Ottie had gotten there, Declan left the room. Honestly, he'd still been so damn furious. She didn't need his heightened emotions darkening her space. But there was no way he was leaving the hospital.

"I don't like this," Declan said quietly. "We need to find out who this guy is and make sure that asshole stays the hell away from her."

Ryker ran a hand through his hair. "We know anything about him?"

"We can call in that favor from Blake Cross," Jackson said, eyes on Declan. "Ask his team to do a background check on the guy."

That wasn't a bad idea. When Ryker looked confused, Declan explained. "We helped the guy get his wife back a few months ago. She was kidnapped and put into a pretty bad situation."

"We also kept their daughter safe while the father, a former SEAL, flew out to Seattle to get his wife back," Jackson added.

Even if they hadn't helped him, Blake and his friends seemed to be good guys and would likely lend a hand anyway. "They own and run a security business in Cradle Mountain, Idaho, called Blue Halo."

Ryker nodded. "Let's call him."

Just then, Ottie stepped into the waiting area. The man looked tired.

"How is she?" Ryker asked before Declan could.

"Good enough. They just finished stitching her hand. It'll scar but no tendon damage or anything like that." He turned to look at Declan. "She told me what happened. Thank you for running down there."

"I wish I'd gotten there faster." Mercy Ring was just down the road from Meals Made Easy, but damn, the distance had felt too long today.

"I'm sure you got there as quickly as you could, son." He nodded his head down the hall. "She's asking for you."

The words had barely left Ottie's mouth when Declan was moving, but he'd only taken a couple of steps before the older man touched his arm, and for the first time, a small smile graced Ottie's mouth. "She was a bit anxious about the blood, kept nearly passing out, so they gave her some morphine for the pain and anxiety."

Declan frowned. Why was the guy telling him—

"She's very…relaxed."

It clicked. "Relaxed as in high on pain medication. Got it." He gave a quick nod before walking down the hall. When he pushed inside the room, he saw Michele sitting up in bed and River standing beside her. Both women were smiling, and when Michele looked up, her smile broadened.

"Hey there, big protector of mine!"

Declan crossed the room, and for a second the rage eased and a smile tugged at his mouth. Then his gaze caught on her hand, and the anger returned, blasting through his system. He lifted her arm gently, softly grazing the bandaging. "How are you feeling?"

She curled her fingers over his hand. "I feel really good, actually."

River laughed. "She's loopy as hell on pain meds."

Michele's smile softened. "Nurse Peach was very kind."

"Her name is Nurse *Leach*. And I'm wondering if she gave you too much."

Michele was just opening her mouth when the door opened and Ryker, Jackson and Ottie entered the room.

Declan moved back as Ryker headed straight to the bed. When he touched her shoulder, Declan had to clench his fists to stop from pulling the guy away. God, he hated watching other men touch her—even Ryker, a man he trusted with his life.

"How you doing, Chele?"

She lifted a shoulder. "I've been better. The morphine helped, even if River tried to make me feel bad for it."

River rolled her eyes. "I never made you feel bad, just voicing my suspicions."

"I'm taking you home," Ryker said.

Declan stepped forward. "No, you're not. I am."

Ryker turned, but before he could respond, Michele spoke.

"Ah, shouldn't it be *my* choice who takes me home?"

"Yes, it should," River said, sounding far too amused.

Ryker smiled. "Who would you like to take you home, Chele?"

"I love you, Ryker. But I'd like Declan to take me home." Then her gaze found his, and she gave him a half-drunk smile.

Before anyone could respond, a nurse walked into the room but came to a quick stop when she saw how many people were in the small space. "Oh my, someone's popular." She moved forward, handing Michele some papers. "Here's your discharge paperwork, dear, you're free to go."

Once the nurse left, Michele swung her legs over the side of the bed. "Okay. Time for you all to go."

The way she said "go" was almost in song form. Declan chuckled under his breath.

It took far too long for everyone to say their goodbyes and leave. When it was just the two of them, she tilted her head to the side, a smile playing at her lips. "It's just us now."

"It is." He stepped forward and shifted a strand of hair from her face. "You sure you're okay?"

Because he just needed the word from her, and he'd be out there, tearing down the world to find this guy.

"I am now." She pressed her cheek into his hand. It was exactly what his anxious chest needed. "Just don't leave me."

Oh, he wasn't going anywhere.

MICHELE SHOT Declan a look from below her lashes. Whereas she was sure she looked as relaxed as she felt, the morphine the nice nurse had given her still causing a languid calm in her limbs, Declan looked the opposite. The muscles in his arms were bunched and corded, and his jaw was so hard it looked like it was carved from granite. And worse, he hadn't said a word the entire drive from the hospital.

He pulled into a parking spot outside her building and climbed out. She'd only gotten as far as opening her door when he was there, lifting her from the car like she weighed nothing.

She shook her head, patting his chest. "I can walk. Put me down."

"No."

No? Who was this surly man, and what had he done with the smiling, friendly Declan she'd gotten used to?

"Declan…" She shook her hips and straightened her legs, trying to get out of his hold.

"Michele, stop it."

"No. I can walk." God, the man's arms didn't budge. What, were they made from steel? Maybe if she twisted around like a pretzel…

She pushed at his chest with her good hand and giggled as she tried to roll.

"What the hell, Michele?"

Almost...there...

He huffed, carefully setting her on her feet. Good. This was good. No, she didn't have the warmth of his chest, but she didn't need him to carry her. She could walk just fine.

She moved forward—and almost immediately started veering off path.

Declan growled, grabbing her shoulders and resetting her course.

She grinned at the ferocious-looking man. "You're a bit grouchy tonight. I kind of like it."

He reminded her of a big angry bear. One with cute dimples and caramel eyes. For a moment, she *did* get lost in those eyes. When she stumbled, Declan shook his head, sliding an arm around her waist and tugging her close.

Okay. This was better. She snuggled into his side.

"You're going to be the death of me, woman."

She giggled again as they stopped in front of the door. She pulled out her key, and immediately, Declan slid it from her hand.

Man, he was take-charge tonight.

He opened the door and tugged her toward the stairs. She almost tripped on the first step, and when Declan tried to lift her again, she shook him off.

"I'm okay."

Two more steps and another trip.

"Nope."

The word had barely left Declan's mouth when her world tipped upside down.

No. Not her world. Her body. Declan had thrown her over his shoulder.

She tapped his back. "Hey!"

"You can't walk for shit right now, Chele."

"Chele? You never call me that." She struggled for about two point four seconds, then exhaustion got the better of her. And the

82

sight of Declan's ass. It was an inch from her face. It was a nice ass.

"Yeah, well, I'm angry, so I'm not myself," he muttered. When he reached her door, he set her gently onto her feet. "Key?"

"Are you angry at me?"

"Key, Michele."

"I didn't mean to drop onto glass. In fact, I would have preferred not to." She would have thought that was obvious, but maybe he needed reminding.

"Do you want me to grab it from your pocket?"

"It will probably scar, you know, and I'll have an eternal reminder of—"

Declan moved closer, one hand going to her back pocket—aka her ass—and the other to her waist. Holy hotness. The man was holding her *ass*. Even slightly high on morphine, she couldn't deny that his hands on her felt good.

He pulled the small chain of keys from her pocket. When he turned toward the door, he kept one hand on her back, like he thought she'd fall or run if he wasn't touching her. Run? Ha. No. Not from this guy. Fall? Very likely.

He pushed the door open and tugged her in behind him.

Immediately, Pokey was there, rubbing against her. "Oh, I'm sorry, boy! You've been home by yourself all day and didn't get your walk or your dinner tonight."

Pokey almost pushed her back into the hall. In fact, she was sure she'd have fallen again if Declan wasn't still touching her back, holding her in place.

"I'll feed him," Declan said from behind. "Let's get you into bed first."

At the word bed, her eyes closed. Yes, please. Sleep sounded heavenly.

That warm arm slid around her waist. Declan's voice gentled. "Come on, honey."

The second they were in her room, Michele kicked off her

shoes. As she stepped forward, she undid her jeans and shoved them down her legs.

A curse sounded behind her, and she was vaguely aware of the fact that she should be at least semi-embarrassed right now, but she just...wasn't.

Maybe River was right. Maybe the nurse had given her too much. Not that she cared.

When she reached the bed, she tugged her shirt over her head. "Fuck, Michele..."

She turned, but he wasn't looking at her. He was standing near the door, a hand over his face like he couldn't bear to look at her.

She frowned, crossing the room and touching his arm. "Declan?"

He looked down at her, and something akin to pain crossed his features. "Dammit, Michele, I can't..."

He didn't finish, instead lifting her against his chest like he had by the car and carrying her to bed. It wasn't until the sheet was tugged over her chest that his gaze finally met hers again. "I'll get you some dinner and a drink."

She grabbed his arm before he could take a step. "I'm not hungry. Just feed Pokey. And can you take him for a walk?"

"Of course. But are you sure you don't want anything, honey?"

She smiled. "I like it when you call me that."

Finally, one side of his mouth lifted, and there it was. One half of that beautiful set of dimples. "Good. Because I plan on calling you that a lot."

He tugged a small bottle of pills from his pocket, her pain medication, and set them on the bedside table.

When he stood, she touched his arm again. "Are you coming back?"

"Yeah, I'm getting you some water."

"Good." Otherwise, she might have begged. "Then will you sleep with me?" More words she probably wouldn't have spoken if she was feeling herself. "I don't think…" She paused, her brain really wasn't working. "I don't think I'll be able to get much sleep on my own."

In fact, she was sure of it. Tim would fill her head.

There was a beat of silence, and even in her drug-induced haze, she felt a trickle of nerves. That he'd say no. That she'd feel the weight of rejection press on her chest.

Then his gaze softened. "I'll sleep with you, honey. Give me ten minutes to feed and walk Pokey."

The tightness in her chest eased. "Eat something too. You must be hungry. There are plenty of meals in the fridge and freezer."

This time she was rewarded with two dimples.

He left the room, dimming the light as he went. Her eyes shuttered and she did that in-between thing, where she'd start to drift to sleep, but then memories of the day came back to her, stabbing into her conscious mind.

God, she was angry. Angry and frustrated and all the things in between. The man needed to learn that no meant *no*. How dare he barge into her place of work and scare her?

She scrunched her eyes again. Where was that morphine when she needed it?

Before long, the sound of footsteps in the room pattered through the silence. Her eyes remained closed as Declan moved to the opposite side of the bed. There was the rustle of clothing, then the bed dipped behind her.

Michele swallowed. Should she turn around and touch him? Lean on him? The idea of sleeping in his arms… It was everything she craved right now.

She was moments from doing just that, when his arm suddenly wrapped around her waist and tugged her body into his. His chest was bare, and so were his legs, and holy ham on a cracker, he felt good.

She snuggled closer, feeling the whisper of his breath on the back of her neck.

"It wasn't just the blood that made me want morphine." Why the heck had she admitted that?

For a beat, he was silent. Then his rumbly voice vibrated against her back. "He scared you."

"Yes." For a moment, she wondered if he was going to ask her about him. So far, he'd asked very little.

"Tomorrow, we're going to the police." It wasn't a question.

"What if they don't care again?"

"Why wouldn't they care?"

She lifted a shoulder. "Because they didn't care the first time. Or the second." She sighed. "But we can try again." She wet her lips before asking her next question. "Earlier today, with Ryker, you weren't...jealous, were you? When he said he was taking me home?"

"With you, I'll always be jealous if another man wants to take you home."

She rolled over. She couldn't see him very well in the darkness, so she reached up and touched his face. "You're the only man who's ever made me feel anything. You never need to worry about me and anyone else."

That hand on her hip pulled her a touch closer. "It's the same for me."

She closed her eyes and felt his forehead touch hers. They lay there like that for a while. Sleep still refused to come.

Then he whispered, "You're safe with me, honey."

His words were like a switch, giving her permission to shut down. To relax. "I know."

"Sleep." He swiped his thumb across the skin of her hip.

She closed her eyes, and the warmth of Declan's body seeped into her. The strength of his arms around her created a cocoon of safety. Finally, she slept.

CHAPTER 11

*M*ichele's breath stopped in her chest. Like, completely stopped. Not a scrap of air got through. Because Declan surrounded her. His hard front pressed to her back while his chest moved against her in even succession. And those arms…one lay over her waist, his hand curving around her belly, sitting dangerously close to the top of her panties. The other arm was between her side and the mattress, wrapped around her chest with his hand over her breast.

Yes, her *breast*. In his palm!

She scrunched her eyes closed. How the heck long had he been holding her like this? An hour? Two? All freaking night?

The thin lace of her bra may as well not even be there. All she felt was him.

Slowly, she peeled her eyes open and shot a quick look at the small thread of light poking through the curtains. It was morning. Good. So she could get up and not look like she was running from him even though she most definitely would be.

She should be focusing on the dull ache in her injured hand, but nope, all her focus remained on Declan and the way he held her now-aching breast. The way his fingers warmed her lower abdomen.

No man had ever made her breast ache, and he wasn't even doing anything! In fact, before Declan, it had gotten to the point where she'd started to wonder if something was wrong with *her*. That maybe *her* body just didn't work the way it was supposed to when she was intimate with boyfriends.

Okay. Time to get out of bed...somehow. Sooner rather than later, because her body was getting entirely too heated and achy.

Maybe she'd try her legs first. Yeah, her legs. That sounded safe.

Slowly, she shifted her right leg. Immediately, her hips shifted, and holy mother of pearl, she felt him behind her. Right on her ass. He was hard, and he was large.

Her breath shuddered from her lips. *Note to self, do not, under any circumstances, move hips.*

Was it even possible to get out of bed without moving her hips? Argh. What the heck was she supposed to do? Maybe she could lift the hand on her waist and then roll off the bed. That sounded easy enough...kind of.

Carefully, she reached down to the hand on her belly and wrapped her fingers around Declan's thick wrist before lifting. Or at least, trying to lift. Instead of going where she tried to move it, the damn thing tightened around her and tugged her closer. His groin ground into her backside. And that hand on her breast... Yep, that tightened too. The man was palming her.

A sharp breath escaped her throat. Actually, it was more of a groan than a breath.

Then a low growl sounded from behind her.

"You shouldn't move like that." His deep, gravelly voice had her eyes widening. He was awake? And it didn't sound like a just-woke-up voice. "Mmm. You feel so good."

His hips rocked, his hardness moving against her ass a second time, pressing into her.

"Declan…" Her voice was so quiet, it was barely a whisper.

"Yeah, sugar?"

When his lips touched her neck, her back arched, ass grinding against him and her breast pushing into his hand. Her nipple tingled, crying out for attention.

As if Declan heard her thoughts, he squeezed his hand. Another moan slipped from her lips.

He nuzzled her neck again. "Mm, I like that sound."

The hand on her breast continued to tease and massage, and her butt rocked and ground harder. When the hand on her breast shifted, there was a panicked moment when she thought he was going to let her go. She opened her mouth to object, but then his fingers slipped inside her bra.

Her stomach did a little flip at the feel of skin against skin. When he found her hard nipple, she whimpered. Then his thumb and forefinger began to thrum and tease.

The dull ache turned into a steady throbbing throughout her core, burning her lower abdomen and tingling across her skin.

"How's your hand?" he whispered.

It took her foggy mind a full five seconds to remember the injury. "It's fine."

Not just fine. Nonexistent in this moment. In her mind, at least. All she could think about were those fingers on her hard peak, and that hand that was so close to her panties.

The very hand that began to move, slowly lowering.

He'd barely slipped his fingers between her lower belly and the material when she caught his hand with her uninjured one.

"Declan, I…" She stopped, not entirely sure how to explain.

The hand on her breast paused, the mouth against her neck lifting. "Do you want me to stop?"

Stop? Never. But there were words she needed to say. "I haven't… I mean, I'm not sure if I can…"

Heat burned her cheeks. She tried to tug away from him, but his hand on her waist didn't budge, keeping her right where she was. The mouth on her neck nibbled on her skin for a moment. "Tell me, honey."

"A man's never made me…" God, why couldn't she just say it?

Because she was thirty-freaking-one. And because every time a man touched her, it started off kind of hot and heavy, but she could never quite get where she needed to go. And because she had been called frigid and just about every other word under the sun on the matter.

She could almost feel Declan frowning behind her. "Never?"

Thank God. He knew what she was trying to say. She didn't need to speak the words. That might just kill her. "No. And I just… I don't want you to be disappointed when you can't."

There was a long moment of pause. *"When?"*

Okay, she was officially too embarrassed to stay here.

She tried to move away again, but his arms tightened, not giving her an inch. Not a single. Freaking. Inch. And that hand on her bare breast began to move again. Small swipes against her nipple. They tormented her.

She sucked in a sharp breath, even as she said, "There might even be something—"

"Don't finish that sentence."

Wrong with me. Yeah. She'd definitely wondered.

His entire body was tense around her, and there was a hard edge to his voice when he asked, "Who said that to you?"

"No one."

"Michele."

Okay. Someone *had* said it. More than one someone, though not in so many words. "Some exes."

Another kiss pressed to her neck as those fingers on her breast moved again. "Do you want me to touch you?"

Her mouth opened and closed, his thumb now drawing slow circles around her nipple. "Yes," she breathed.

His mouth latched onto her neck while his hand slipped further beneath the material of her panties. Her breath caught.

Then his finger grazed her slit, swiping across her clit. Her entire body jolted.

He did it again—another jolt.

Her breaths became choppy, and heat pooled between her thighs as his finger continued to swipe and graze. As her nipple continued to be thrummed between his fingers.

Suddenly, she was impatient for more. She ground against him, reveling in the deep growl from his chest. The hand between her thighs shifted, his thumb replacing the fingers on her clit, and his finger pressing against her entrance.

Oh God. She parted her thighs, giving him better access, and the second his finger pushed inside, a whimper slipped from her lips. He stretched her. Tormented her.

She threw her head back and he took advantage, kissing her neck once again, alternating between sucking and licking.

She'd never felt this before. *Any* of it. Like her entire body was on fire. Like if Declan stopped, she'd die or shatter or something equally annihilating.

It was as if her hips had a mind of their own, grinding against him faster, pressing down every time he pushed back inside.

She moaned and hummed with his thrusts, each breath shorter than the last. When a second finger slipped inside, her cry shattered the quiet. The stretching of her muscles around him had her gripping the strong arm at her waist, anchoring herself.

His thumb continued to circle her clit, his fingers still working her nipple.

She was close. So damn close she was only just hanging on. She dug her fingers into the skin of his forearms, and her teeth penetrated her lower lip.

Declan's lips moved to her ear, his breath brushing her skin. "You need to let go, baby."

She opened her mouth to respond, but the words never made it to air. All she could do was breathe. Hold him and breathe.

He nipped a spot behind her ear, and she shuddered violently. When he crooked his finger inside her, he whispered again. "Let go."

Just like when she struggled to sleep last night, his words gave her permission.

Her body erupted, convulsing around his fingers. Those fingers didn't stop, though. They continued to penetrate her, to slip in and out of her wetness. She cried and shuddered, her body barely moving because he held her so tightly.

He remained still behind her as the shudders dulled and her breaths eased, becoming less deep and loud. Then his mouth pressed another of those gentle kisses to her neck.

Holy Christ. She didn't even know what had just happened. Whatever it was, she wouldn't be forgetting it anytime soon, if ever.

She sucked in a final deep breath as he slid his fingers out of her and removed his other hand from inside her bra. She bit back a groan at the movement. Then she was on her back, Declan hovering over her as he supported himself with his forearms, looking devastatingly beautiful with his day-old beard.

His hardness pressed against her thigh, but instead of doing anything about it, he gently brushed the hair from her face, looking at her so closely she wanted to squirm.

"There's nothing wrong with you, beautiful," he said softly. "You're perfect."

Perfect. The man had given her the best orgasm of her life and now he was calling her perfect. Her lips slipped open, but before she could say anything, her phone rang from the side table. Still, she couldn't take her gaze from Declan. He commanded all of her attention.

She reached down, but he quickly grabbed her forearm, lifting it and pressing a kiss to the inside of her wrist. "If you touch me, I'll lose my mind and it'll be too damn hard for me to stop."

"A Declan who loses his mind in bed doesn't sound so bad."

He laughed, and it bounced against her chest. Then he lowered his head and kissed her on the lips for the first time that morning. It wasn't a passionate kiss but a gentle, slow caress. One that pierced her chest and squeezed her heart.

"I want you at *your* pace," he said quietly, as if sensing she needed to go slow. "And I *do* want you. All of you."

More beautiful words that sent her heart racing.

She swallowed. "You're almost too good to be real." Maybe she'd read so many books that she'd conjured up a perfect model of all the heroes combined.

A slow smile stretched his lips. Her phone rang a second time. When she didn't move, Declan's smile widened and he reached across her, his chest pressing her into the mattress before he lifted the phone and handed it to her.

She glanced at the screen. Anthony…

Oh crap, Anthony! It was nine o'clock. Crap, crap, crap!

She quickly answered it. "I'm so sorry. I'm still at home. I'll be five minutes. Or maybe ten." How had she forgotten about work?

When she hung up, Declan didn't budge.

His eyes were harder than they'd been a moment before. "Take the day off."

"I can't. I have too many orders."

He leaned down, kissing her cheek. "You're injured."

"It's all stitched up, and I have p-pain medication." She stumbled on her words because of his mouth…and the rest of him.

"Maybe I can convince you." He ground his hips against hers —until a banging sounded on the door.

"Michele?"

She sighed at the sound of River's voice and shoved at Declan's big chest with her good hand. He groaned, then rolled to the side as she scrambled to get out from under him.

CHAPTER 12

"I really don't think this is necessary."

Declan took his eyes away from the men who were installing a system on her shop door. "I disagree."

Especially when the police were doing shit-all about Tim. He ground his teeth just thinking about their visit earlier today. The officer had written another report, taken down all the information Michele had on Tim, and said he'd try to speak to the guy. When Declan had pushed for when they would speak to him, the cop's response had been "soon."

Asshole.

His jaw clenched at the memory.

Michele gave a quick nod. But when his gaze darted down, he saw she was digging her fingers into her arms. She was nervous.

His chest tightened as he walked over to her, taking her hands in his and tugging her close. "Any extra security is a good thing."

He'd already installed new locks and an alarm at her apartment. No one would be getting in or out without her permission. They hadn't told her super yet, and they didn't intend to. Not until the guy asked. The longer she was the only one with a key, the better.

When she frowned, he slipped his arms around her waist. "Why don't you want added security?"

She touched his chest, and damn but he loved it. "It's not that I don't want it. I just... I'm so frustrated. At him. At the damn police. I have a right to feel safe without all this stuff, and I don't."

Fuck, that tore at him. "You *do* have a right to feel safe," he said quietly. "And I'm going to make sure you are."

It wasn't even just Tim he was worried about. There was still that serial killer on the loose—and he'd murdered another woman just yesterday. A woman Michele's age, who lived close to Lindeman. It was a serious fucking concern.

She exhaled through parted lips, then sank into him. "I don't know what I'd do without you."

He smiled, lowering his head and pressing his lips to hers. "Have dinner with me tonight." He wanted as much of this woman as he could get. His lips trailed down to her neck.

Her hands subtly pressed against his chest. "Declan, Anthony and the installation guys are here..."

Why the hell should he care about people seeing him kiss his woman? And yes, he was referring to Michele as his woman. In fact, he wanted *everyone* to know she was his. He wanted his claim staked loud and clear. "I don't care. Have dinner with me."

She sighed. "I can't. It's Wednesday night."

"What's Wednesday?"

"Dinner with Uncle Ottie. It's kind of our tradition."

Hm. Maybe one day he'd weasel an invite to this Wednesday night tradition. Until then... "Okay. I guess I'll allow it."

Another laugh. "You'll allow it?"

"Mm-hmm." He kissed her lips again, and she hummed. "But I expect texts. And calls."

"Should I just keep you on speakerphone?"

"Now you're getting it."

He kissed her smile just as the door to the shop opened and Jackson and River stepped inside. Jeez, River had already shown up at Michele's apartment this morning. How many visits did friends need?

River's smile stretched across her face. "So, you guys are at the PDA stage of this relationship? Sleepovers, PDAs..."

Michele scowled. "Shh, River!"

Declan laughed. He sure as hell didn't mind people hearing he'd slept over.

She tugged out of his arms, and damn if he didn't want to tug her straight back.

River followed Michele into the kitchen, her mouth moving a hundred miles a minute as per usual, while Jackson stopped beside him, a ghost of a smile on his face. "Looks like things are going well."

"They are." He could barely think about what happened this morning without getting hard.

Jackson's voice lowered. "I called Blake last night."

The smile dropped from Declan's mouth. "And?"

"He got back to me this morning. His team was able to hack into the dating site portal where she's registered. They found the few guys she responded to, including the only one named Tim. Problem is, the guy deleted his profile."

"Deleted?"

Jackson nodded. "It was only active for a couple of weeks."

So just enough time to meet Michele? That sure as hell didn't sit well with him.

"He didn't leave a trail," Jackson continued. "No picture on his profile. The only information he put in the address section was Seattle. No bank details because he signed up for a free trial. Even his last name makes it impossible to find him. Johnson is the second most common surname in the US. There are hundreds of Tim Johnsons in Washington alone."

"If that's his real name."

"Yep."

Declan blew out a frustrated breath, his gaze rising to

Michele, still talking quietly to River. Anthony stood behind them, stirring a pot. "The police are being lazy as fuck. They don't want to deal with it."

Jackson scowled. "We'll deal with it, then."

"Exactly." His gaze shot to the security system. "I've told her to make sure the buzzer system is always on, once it's installed."

When customers pressed a button outside, Michele or Anthony would have to press one inside to disengage the lock and let them in. No more surprise visits from Tim.

"Good plan. Let me and the guys know what we can do."

Declan lifted his chin. "Will do."

He looked over at the women again. River was taking a spoon from Michele's hand and appeared to be giving her grief for being at work.

Good. The woman needed someone else telling her.

At the sound of footsteps, he looked over to see a woman walk into the shop, smiling.

Michele moved away from River. "Connie, hi! I got your message. I'm so glad you loved your last meals and want more."

"Oh my gosh. They were *divine*! I just wish you delivered that far, but I'm happy to come back and get more. I'd drive across the country for them." She glanced over her shoulder at the work-men. "What's going on here?"

The smile on Michele's face became strained. "Just adding some security."

River slung an arm over her shoulder. "Hi, I'm River. The best friend."

Declan turned back to Jackson as the women started chatting. "How's River doing? Bullet wound almost healed?" They were a bitch to recover from. He knew that all too well.

Jackson scoffed. "I'm lucky if I can get her to rest for one-hour increments." He shook his head. "By the way, we have some new kids coming in this morning."

Declan nodded. "I'm going to wait here until the alarm and locks are done, make sure everything's in place before I go."

STABBED TO DEATH. No forced entry. Young woman in her late twenties.

Michele read and reread the article. Her steps were slow as she walked to her uncle's shop around the corner. The only reason Declan had approved of her walking by herself was because the sun was still bright, and there were plenty of people around.

Twice, she'd walked into said people because her eyes were glued to her phone. But honestly, she couldn't stop reading. There had been *another* murder. This one in Ellensburg. God, that was only a five-minute drive from Lindeman. In fact, the last three had been almost as close.

The fine hairs on her arms stood on end. Who was this guy? And why hadn't they caught him? How many more women had to die?

She was just nearing a corner when, for a third time, she crashed into someone. Her phone fell from her fingers and clattered to the ground.

Mrs. Albuquerque bent down to lift the phone before she could, but she didn't return it straight away. Instead, she studied the screen and shook her head.

"That poor woman." She looked up. "You know they're calling him the Washington Walk-In Killer because he just seems to walk right into these homes and murder his victims. The neighbors aren't even woken with screams or anything."

A shiver raced up Michele's back. She slid her phone from the older woman's fingers. "I didn't know that." And it probably wouldn't have bothered her if she'd never learned that fact, either.

Mrs. Albuquerque leaned forward, her voice lowering. "I'm certain it's either a really good-looking man or a kid."

Michele frowned. "What makes you say that?"

She lifted a shoulder. "Everyone knows it's easier to trust good-looking people. And if a teenager came up to your door asking for help?"

Hang on... "You're not still insinuating Anthony might be the killer?"

Mrs. Albuquerque raised a brow. "I'm saying, you should be careful."

Oh, Lord. "He's a good kid." No, she hadn't known him for long, but she just knew. It was hard to explain. It was in the little things he did. The hard work he put in at the shop. The extra tasks he did without her asking. The moments when he'd slide something out of her hands because it was heavy.

"Hmm." The older woman straightened the strap of her bag. "I heard the kid dropped a glass, and you fell and hurt your hand. Are you okay?"

She glanced down to her bandaged hand, not sure who the woman would hear that from or what exactly she'd been told. Where this woman got *any* of her gossip, Michele had no idea.

"Yes, he accidentally dropped a glass, and after he left, I slipped and fell on it." Mrs. Albuquerque hadn't mentioned Tim, thank God. Maybe that part hadn't circulated to her. "It's fine. Just a couple of stitches."

Mrs. Albuquerque's lips thinned, almost like she didn't believe her. Maybe she thought Anthony had stabbed her while she wasn't looking or something equally ridiculous.

"Well, you have a good evening, dear. Say hello to your uncle for me."

Then the woman just walked away. After basically accusing her, again, of hiring a serial killer.

Shaking her head, she slid her phone back into her pocket and continued to her uncle's store.

The second she stepped inside, a wave of nostalgia and peace washed over her. Not just because she was surrounded by old books—the musky smell never failed to calm her—but because the place hadn't changed since she was a kid. There were the same big bookshelves covering every wall of the shop. The same old ladders. Even the counter in the middle of the room was the same exact one, just with a few more scratches.

She walked over to the desk as her uncle moved around it and wrapped her arms around his middle. She leaned into him. God, she loved the man. He became her entire world after her parents had passed away. And he was the kindest, gentlest man she'd ever known. How she'd gotten so lucky, she had no idea.

Michele pulled away and studied his face. "How are you doing today?"

He shook his head. "I should be asking you that. *You're* the one who sliced your hand open yesterday."

"I'm fine." She waved her hand in front of him to prove it. "It's all stitched up, and anything I couldn't do at work, Anthony did for me."

He'd been a godsend. The second he'd found out that she'd sliced her hand on a piece of glass, guilt had swamped his face. Then he'd bent over backward the entire day to make her job easier. "What about you? How's your heart?"

"It's fine, darling." They were the same words that always came out of his mouth when she asked that question. He moved back behind the desk. "I went for my walk, ate my healthy meals, and avoided stress. You, on the other hand, look anxious."

"Well, that's because I ran into Mrs. Albuquerque on the way here, and…" She shook her head, not even sure she wanted to repeat the woman's rambling about the serial killer and the possibility he could be a kid. And not just any kid. Anthony.

Ottie chuckled. "Yeah, that woman has a gift for rubbing people the wrong way."

"She even knew about my hand. How is that possible?"

"I swear she has cameras up everywhere, and she just spends her days watching them."

"Either that or she has a bunch of minions crawling around town, reporting back to her." Neither would surprise Michele. She set her shoulder bag onto the counter. "I brought a lentil lasagna for us to have for dinner. It's chock-full with hidden vegetables. Is that okay?"

A lot of people would probably groan at the suggestion of a lentil lasagna for dinner. Not Ottie. "You know I love everything you make."

Her eyes skittered over to the shelf of new books. Wednesday was the day new shipments came in, and she could already see a couple of her favorite authors sitting up there.

Ottie laughed again. "Go. I know you've been waiting for the delivery."

A small squeak left her throat as she moved to the shelf. Holy heck. They were beautiful. She ran her fingers over the line of covers. Very little could match the excitement of touching a new book that you just knew would be amazing. A whole fictional world sat inside. Hours of being immersed in another reality. Really, how could a person *not* love reading?

She was just lifting one from the shelf when a text came through on her phone.

Declan: Hey, honey. How's your hand doing?

A smile tugged at her lips as she replied.

Michele: It's fine. How's work?

Declan: Busy. Is your dinner almost finished?

She chuckled. The man knew full well it wasn't.

Michele: It's five o'clock, so no.

Declan: Damn. Guess I'll have to be patient and wait.

The wait would probably kill her more than him. She was just about to respond when a small groan sounded from her uncle. Her gaze shot up to see him holding a hand to his chest.

Her heart constricted, and she ran across the room and touched his back. "Are you okay? Is it your heart?"

His brows tugged together, then he straightened, his hand dropping. "I'm okay. It was just a little tightness."

Just a little tightness? "Maybe we should go to the hospital, just to be sure."

He shook his head. "No. I'm okay."

"Uncle Ottie—"

"Michele, I'm *okay*. I had an appointment just a couple of days ago, and my blood pressure and cholesterol were down."

Down. But not necessarily where they were meant to be. "What about your stress levels?"

He smiled, but it looked a bit forced. "Like I mentioned before, my stress levels are fine."

She wanted to push the matter, but she knew that when her uncle decided on something, there was no turning him around.

"You've been taking your medication?" she asked quietly. "Eating the right foods?"

She needed the reassurance that he was doing everything he was supposed to be doing. Because if she lost him to the same health condition that took her father…

No. She couldn't think about that.

His eyes softened as he looked at her. "I am. All is fine. Now, go grab your books and let's get home so we can eat this wonderful lasagna you've made."

Again, she wanted to say more. Ask more. But she kept her lips sealed and moved back over to the bookshelf, her excitement from moments ago now gone. Before grabbing any more books, she lifted her phone again and sent a quick message to Declan.

Michele: Sorry to ruin our plans but I think I'm going to stay at my uncle's house tonight.

Not that the plans they'd had were concrete. Still…

Declan: Everything okay?

Michele: Yeah. I just need to spend some time with him. See you tomorrow?

She didn't stay at her uncle's often, but her room had remained untouched since she'd moved out, so she knew it was always ready for her.

Declan: You're not running from me after what happened this morning, are you?

She sucked in a small puff of air, momentarily distracted from her worry about her uncle.

Michele: Why would I run?

Declan: Because you feel what I feel.

She almost didn't want to ask. But she had to.

Michele: What do you feel?

Declan: That I want you. All of you. All the time.

Her mouth slipped open, and goose bumps pebbled her skin. That *is* what she felt. An insatiable yearning. The man had started to seep his way into her world and her thoughts.

She tried to type out a response three times but deleted every message, not sure what to say. Every message felt...wrong. Like she couldn't match his intensity.

Before she could decide on her words, another message came in.

Declan: I'll see you tomorrow, honey. Stay safe xx

CHAPTER 13

*D*eclan looked down at his phone. No message from Michele. Not a surprise. It was early, but damn he was addicted to her. After texting him that she was going to stay with her uncle last night, he'd texted her before bed and just gotten a "good night" in response. He was tempted to walk over to her shop and bring her a coffee or something as an excuse to see her. Would that make him look desperate?

Better question, did he care if it did?

The sound of fists hitting bags had his gaze moving around the gym. Even though it was early, a few people were here. A couple of kids before school. Several grown men.

His gaze zeroed in on Anthony. The kid had shown up this morning, barely said a word, and started pounding the shit out of a bag.

Slowly, Declan walked over to him, crossing his arms when he stopped. "Wanna talk about it?"

He was sure he knew the answer he'd get. But maybe—

"Nope." Two more punches. The hits looked good. His form had improved by a landslide in just the one session they'd had. It made him wonder how good the kid could be after a couple more.

Declan studied the kid's eyes. Fire. Angry, hot fire.

He shot a look to the ring that centered the room. "Want a round with me?"

Anthony stopped, his gaze finally meeting Declan's for the first time. Without a word, he nodded.

Turning, Declan headed to the equipment wall. Once they'd both put on gloves, they stepped into the ring.

Declan raised his fists and waited, instinctively knowing Anthony was keen to throw the first punch. He didn't need to wait long. The first two jabs came hard and fast. Declan dodged them easily.

Next, Anthony tried for a hook, quickly followed by another jab. Declan blocked them both.

He waited until the fifth attempt before finally hitting back. He didn't punch hard, just tapped the side of Anthony's head.

Anthony's eyes narrowed.

Interesting. He was angry that Declan had gotten a punch in. Because Anthony *hadn't*?

Anthony lunged forward, throwing a sloppy cross punch.

Declan dodged out of the way. "Soften your knees. You're standing too tall. It's making you unstable and slowing you down."

Anthony lowered, dancing around on his feet and trying for another cross punch. Declan dodged the hit before throwing one of his own, yet again catching Anthony on the side of the head. "Your hands are too low. You're exposing your head."

Anthony breathed hard and raised his fists.

Declan nodded. "That's it."

Anthony jabbed, and again, Declan dodged it and quickly threw an uppercut to his gut. The punch landed, but Anthony lurched away just before contact, making the hit worse.

"Don't do that," Declan said quickly. "Moving away only gives the punch more momentum. If you can't block it, absorb it. Tighten your stomach muscles, shift slightly so the blow hits your side, and absorb it with your obliques."

Anthony frowned, but he didn't argue. He swallowed and nodded. He was still angry, but he was hungry to learn.

Declan spent the next twenty minutes in the ring with the kid. Refining his form. Letting him work out his anger. He even let the boy get a couple hits in.

Finally, Declan stepped back, lowering his hands and nodding. "That was good. Feel better?"

There was a flash of something in Anthony's eyes. Like for a moment, he'd been pulled away from whatever was tormenting him, but Declan's question tugged him back into it.

"Yeah."

Why didn't Declan believe him? "Your mom end up finding a job?"

Anthony pulled off his gloves. "Yeah. I should get going. I have a shift with Michele in an hour."

Declan gave a slow nod. "You're welcome to shower here if you want."

Anthony's gaze flew across the club toward the locker room, then back to Declan. "Is that okay?"

"Of course."

As Anthony moved out of the ring, Declan walked over to the office and grabbed his phone from the desk. Finally, the message he'd been waiting for.

Michele: Hey. My morning's been good. Just making sure Uncle Ottie consumes more than coffee for breakfast. I'm stopping at my place to drop off Pokey then going to work.

Declan: Coffee sounds like a well-rounded breakfast to me. In fact, I could bring you some this morning.

There was a pause between texts, then…

Michele: I would love that.

Thank fuck, because he needed to see the woman.

Declan: It's a date then. I'll be there around ten.

He wasn't even joking. Every time he got to see her, he considered it a date.

"Is it Michele who's put that crazy-ass grin on your face?"

Declan looked up as Cole came to stand beside him. "Sure is. Maybe you should find a woman to date. It might untwist those panties of yours."

Cole didn't react to the dig. But then, Declan hadn't expected him to. The guy had perfected the art of keeping his emotions in check.

"I don't need to date."

Declan pushed his phone into his pocket. "Oh yeah, I forgot about that whole nothing-is-forever, can't-be-happy-until-the-day-you-die, warped view of yours."

This time, a hint of a smile curved the big guy's mouth. He grabbed a mint from the desk and unwrapped it. "I prefer to see it as valuing independence over co-dependence."

Yeah, yeah, whatever. "Get your anti-love sentiment away from me."

Cole popped the mint into his mouth. "You asked."

"Actually, I didn't."

Ten minutes later, Anthony came out of the bathroom just as Declan frowned at the newspaper he'd opened on the front counter. He never read the newspaper. Hell, he wasn't sure many did anymore. But the gym had ordered a subscription, and on the front page was a big photo of the last woman killed by that deranged murderer.

Fuck, he hated that this asshole was still out there and his victims were piling up.

Anthony stopped beside him, and Declan almost felt the kid's muscles tense. "Any new information?"

Declan scanned the page. "Based on a neighbor's description, they think he was driving a light blue Honda. They also suspect he's about six-one with light brown hair."

The cops or FBI or whoever was running the case might know more than they were sharing. Declan knew how it worked. They rarely shared everything they had because they wanted the perpetrator to feel safe in their ambiguity. They wanted to use the information to find him, without the killer changing tactics.

MICHELE SHOT a glance at her phone. Almost ten—and almost an hour past Anthony's start time.

Blowing out a breath, she lifted her phone and called him for what had to be the fourth time that morning.

Straight to voice mail. Again.

She chewed her bottom lip, tightening her fingers around the phone. She'd done all she could with one hand, but there was a ton she couldn't do at the moment, and a heap of orders that needed filling.

Maybe he'd just slept in. He was a teenager, after all. That happened.

But then, what if he hadn't? What if something was wrong? With him or his mom? And neither of them knew many people in the area…

Maybe she should check on him. She knew he lived at the trailer park. There was no harm in paying a little visit, was there?

Yeah. One quick look.

With a small nod, she headed out of the shop, locked the door behind her and climbed into her car. She made it all the way to the trailer park before remembering Declan saying he'd be stopping at the shop.

Crap! He'd said ten. That was in five minutes.

She pulled out her phone and sent a quick text.

Michele: Anthony didn't show up for work today. I'm just at the trailer park checking on him. Be back in a sec x

Almost immediately, her phone started to ring.

"Hey."

"Hey." Declan sounded worried. "Anthony didn't show up? He was at Mercy Ring this morning."

Michele frowned. "He was? No, he didn't make it to work. I'm going to check his trailer."

"You should have sent me out there. That trailer park isn't safe."

She shot a glance around the deserted area. "It doesn't even look like anyone's here."

"Do you know which trailer is his?"

She tugged her key from the ignition and slipped from the car. "He wrote Lot Thirteen on his resume."

Declan cursed. "Michele—"

"Hang on, I think I see him. I'll call you back."

She closed the door and locked the car before jogging toward him. "Anthony!"

When he didn't stop or pause, she sped up. He was just opening a trailer door when she touched his back. "Anthony, you didn't show up at Meals Made Easy and I was wo—"

She stopped when he turned. Not Anthony. It was a middle-aged man with a scar across his brow and an angry look on his face.

"What the fuck are you touching me for, woman?"

She snatched her hand back and hurriedly moved away. "I'm sorry, I thought you were—"

"Who? Some guy you're here to fuck?" His gaze slid down her body.

She frowned at his crude words.

He stepped toward her. "Actually, maybe I don't mind you touching me." Two more steps forward.

She rushed to move back, but then his hand shot out and snatched her arm. Her heart stopped at the way his calloused fingers bit into her skin.

He smiled. "Where're you going?"

"Let go."

He was just tugging her closer when Anthony was suddenly there, squeezing between them and shoving the guy in the chest. The hand dropped from her arm.

"What the hell are you doing?" Anthony growled.

Michele's eyes widened at Anthony's hard tone. He didn't sound like a kid in that moment. Not even a little bit. His voice held a dangerous edge.

The guy scowled. "She touched me first, kid."

For the first time, she noticed his words were slurred. Had the guy been drinking this early?

He shoved Anthony. Anthony stumbled back a step but almost immediately righted himself and shoved the guy again. Her heart thumped when the guy threw a punch.

A punch that Anthony dodged, then quickly countered with his own.

Michele gaped when Anthony lunged, his arms wrapping around the guy's waist and sending them both to the ground. For a second, she was completely frozen. Until the guy got Anthony onto his back and started throwing punches.

Michele lunged forward.

She was just reaching for the guy's arm when strong hands wrapped around her waist and lifted her away. She looked up to see Declan behind her, looking big and so damn furious she almost didn't recognize him.

"Stay here." His voice was so low and hard, a shudder rocked her spine. Then he moved forward and grabbed the guy off Anthony before throwing him into the closest trailer.

"What the—"

"You like beating the shit out of kids?" Declan interrupted him, moving forward and grabbing the guy by his shirt. "How about you fight someone a bit closer to your age?"

The guy threw a punch, but Declan dodged it easily, grabbing the guy's arm and flipping him around. He pulled the arm up so high, the man howled.

Anthony rose to his feet, spitting blood from his mouth.

"Get the fuck off me!" the stranger yelled. "You're breaking my damn arm! They came to *my* trailer. I'll do what I damn well want—including touch that bitch!"

If the tensing in Declan's muscles was anything to go by, it was the wrong answer. He pulled the arm higher, and the guy screamed again. Oh God. He *was* breaking something. Maybe not the guy's arm, but his shoulder. Or at least dislocating it.

Declan's voice lowered. The quiet was worse than any loud shout he could have used. "I ever catch you touching either of them again, even an accidental pat on the shoulder, I'm gonna pull your insides out through your fucking throat. Got it?"

Michele was pretty sure her heart was beating out of her chest.

The guy breathed hard but didn't respond.

Declan slammed him against the trailer before finally letting him go. When he turned, he looked double the height and breadth he normally did. He almost had *her* shrinking away.

His gaze zeroed in on Anthony. "Where's your trailer?"

When Anthony remained silent, Declan stepped forward. "I'm not in the mood, kid. Where's your damn trailer?"

Anthony turned and started walking. Declan walked up to her, and with a surprisingly gentle grasp, he took her hand in his and followed behind.

She spared a quick glance at the guy over her shoulder, seeing him clutching his arm and shooting death stares at them. His arm hung at an odd angle. Dislocated. Definitely dislocated.

Swallowing, she turned back to see Anthony stopping at the oldest, dirtiest trailer in the park. He walked up the steps and unlocked the door.

The second Michele stepped inside, her stomach heaved and she almost gagged. The place smelled disgusting. Like something had died in here. And it didn't look much better. There was mold and condensation everywhere. And God, it was freezing cold.

"You're living here?" she asked quietly, wrapping her arms around her waist.

He clenched his jaw as he dropped to the single chair in the room. "It was available and it was cheap. So yeah."

"Tell me what's going on with you, and tell me *now*," Declan demanded.

"No."

Declan growled. "Anthony—"

"If I tell you, you'll send me back, and I don't want to go back!"

Michele frowned. "Send you back where?" When he didn't answer, Michele stepped forward. "Anthony. Where is your mother?"

"I don't know. She skipped out on me and my sister a few years ago. My sister basically raised me even before that anyway. She was eighteen when Mom left."

So he'd lied to her. "Is your sister here?"

Another clenching of his jaw. "No. My grandmother got custody of me a month ago."

Something flashed in his eyes. Dread pooled in her stomach. "Why? Where's your sister?"

This time it wasn't just a flash in his eyes. They flooded with a dark, all-consuming anger. "She's dead."

CHAPTER 14

*D*eclan felt Michele tense beside him. No wonder the kid never fucking smiled.

"How?" she asked quietly.

"Her boyfriend killed her. Beat her to death." He didn't look at them when he said it. Instead, he stared at a strand of material that had pulled free from a ragged hole in his jeans. "Then the asshole skipped town."

She stepped forward and touched his shoulder. "I'm so sorry, Anthony."

Another click of his jaw. "Thanks. Anyway, my grandmother didn't want me, and I can't stand the woman, so I left."

"Is your grandmother from Lindeman, or did you skip town and come here?"

He swallowed. "She lives in Wenatchee." Anthony briefly met Michele's gaze. "Like I told Ottie."

"Why come here, then?" Declan asked.

"Rang around to find something cheap. This was available. It was lucky Michele had the job available and hired me."

Declan's eyes narrowed. "That doesn't tell us anything, Anthony. You might have called around to find a place to live when you moved here, but that doesn't explain why you settled here in Lindeman to begin with."

Anger darkened his eyes as he stood. "I just drove, okay? I was angry at the world, so I got in my car and I drove. I stopped at the shitty motel here in town, and the next day I looked for a job and a place to live. Lindeman had both."

There was more to the story. He was moments from demanding answers when Michele touched his arm. "We need to get ice on his face."

When she looked at Declan, she was almost pleading with her eyes. Pleading with him to table this conversation for the moment and move it somewhere else.

"Fine." But he was returning to the topic, and he was returning soon. "Before we leave, though, where were you this morning? Why didn't you go to work?"

Anthony wet his lips and looked at Michele. "I'm sorry. I went to Mercy Ring this morning, then lost track of the time."

Bullshit. Declan exhaled before glancing around the trailer. "Grab your shit."

Both Michele and Anthony's gazes shot his way.

Anthony was the first to speak. "What?"

"Grab your shit. You're coming back to my place."

The kid looked somewhere between hopeful and nervous. Like he needed the help but didn't want to believe he was getting it, in case he was reading Declan wrong. "I can take care of myself."

"You're a kid, and there's no way you're staying in this place another night. It's a damn health hazard. Get your stuff, Anthony." He reached for Michele's hand. "We'll wait outside." He didn't want Michele standing in this mess of a trailer another second.

He tugged her outside, not waiting for a response from Anthony. The second they were out, he pulled her body into his before wrapping an arm around her waist. "Are you okay?"

She gave a short nod, her gaze darting to where the guy had been. He was gone now. "I'm okay."

His voice hardened, but there was a thread of pain to his words. "Don't do that again."

She frowned. "What?"

"Don't walk toward a fistfight. It's dangerous."

She pushed at his chest, but he didn't give her an inch.

"He's a kid," she said firmly. "And he only got into the fight to protect me."

"I don't care. Not only would you *not* have stopped them, you would have gotten hurt." She'd been a step away from a fist or elbow colliding with her face, and it made him see red. He was damn grateful he'd gotten to her when he had. "Next time, call for help. Hell, grab a rock and throw it at the asshole's head. But don't get closer and don't touch them."

Because that's what she'd been about to do. She'd wanted to pull the guy off Anthony. He'd never run so fast to get to anyone in his life.

She nibbled her bottom lip. Then finally, she sagged into him. "You're right." She smoothed her hands down his chest. "So, you're really taking him back to your place?"

He gave a quick nod, his fingers skirting beneath the material of her top and touching warm skin.

"Will you get into trouble?" she asked. "Because he's supposed to be with his grandmother?"

"I'll make contact with the woman." Whether Anthony wanted him to or not. He was also going to make sure he learned the rest of the kid's secrets.

When Anthony stepped out of the trailer, Declan walked Michele to her car. "I'll show Anthony his room at the house, then send him to the shop."

He kissed her before watching her drive off, then he turned back to Anthony. "Follow me to my place."

He didn't wait for the kid's response, instead heading back to his car and slipping behind the wheel. There was a spare room in the house he rented with Cole and Ryker. All it had in it was a bed, but for now, it would do. And it was a far cry from the trailer. He'd have to run it past the guys, but once he explained the situation, he was sure they'd be fine with his decision.

When he reached the house, he led Anthony inside. Cole and Ryker were at the club, so the place was empty.

Anthony's eyes widened as he stepped in. "This place is huge."

"Living with two other fully grown men makes it feel small." And now there was another guy in the mix. "This is the living area. Kitchen's to the left. There's a bedroom down the hall to the right that Ryker stays in, and we've converted the room opposite his into a gym."

He headed up the stairs, and Anthony followed.

"The spare room only has a bed in it, but it's comfortable." He stepped into the room.

Anthony followed closely behind but didn't immediately go inside. "Why are you doing this?"

"Because you need help." Simple as that.

"You don't even know me."

"That's something we should change, isn't it." It wasn't a question. He moved in front of Anthony. "It sounds like you've had a hard few months."

Pain flashed in Anthony's eyes.

"I know there's more you're not telling me," Declan continued. "And I intend to find out the whole story." Not today. Today had been a lot. But soon.

Anthony remained silent.

Declan squeezed his shoulder. "Put your shit down and get to the shop. Michele needs your help."

Then he left the kid to it.

$\sim$

Michele was just lifting her bag to leave for the day when the buzzer rang. She looked up and her brows rose before she smiled, pressing the button to let Ryker in.

"Hey! Wasn't expecting to see you here. I was just walking over to Mercy Ring to see Declan."

He shoved his hands into his pockets, and his arm muscles rippled. "I know. I'll walk you."

She tilted her head to the side. "Did Declan send you?"

Because since this morning, the man had been messaging her all day, probably checking that she hadn't gone and walked herself into another fight.

"No. But we did decide it might be best for one of us to walk you in and out of your shop from now on. Should have started doing it after Tim's visit the other day."

"We?"

"Me and Dec. The other guys agree as well."

Okay. It was sounding like they'd all met up and had a conversation specifically about her. "Did you think about, I don't know, including *me* in this conversation?"

"We thought about it." A smile grew on his lips. "But we knew you'd agree with us anyway. You'd have no other choice."

She shook her head, but a smile played at her lips. "Funny."

She walked around the counter, grabbing her bag on the way, and stopping in front of him. "Fine. You can walk me to Mercy Ring. But no scolding me for almost getting in the middle of a fistfight this morning, and no talk of Tim or the serial killer. You can talk about how pretty I am and how good my cooking is. Deal?"

Another twitch of his lips. "Deal."

"Good."

She moved over to the new alarm and set the code. Once she was outside, she pulled her key out, but Ryker slipped it from her hand and locked the door.

"Still as take-charge as ever, I see," she mumbled.

He handed the key back and walked beside her. "Is that so bad?"

"No." Declan was like that too. Maybe it was a military thing. Or just a Delta thing.

Ha. Yeah, right. Ryker had been like that way before joining the military.

She linked an arm through his. "So. How are you doing?"

There was a slight flicker of his eyebrows tugging together. It was so quick she almost missed it. Probably *would* have missed it if she hadn't known every inch of his face for so long. "I'm good. Mercy Ring is doing well. I have my team back together. I'm home."

But... He didn't say the word, though he may as well have. "You know, it's okay to *not* be okay. You lost people you cared about in that last mission."

He shook his head. "I wasn't okay for over a year, and look where that got me."

"That wasn't your fault, either." Homeland Security had pulled him into a sting because he'd been in the right place to help. It had been what ultimately led to Ryker faking his death. She snuck a peek at him. "Have you talked to the aid worker? Blakely?"

His muscles jumped beneath her touch. Wow, maybe the woman meant more to him than he let on.

"No."

She looked back at the path in front of them. From what Michele had heard from River, Blakely had worked with the same Middle Eastern family Ryker had befriended, one of the families killed during his last mission.

When they stopped in front of Mercy Ring, he was reaching for the door when she tightened her hold on his arm. "Ryker, reaching out to her might help."

If she knew the families who'd lost their lives, she might be the only person able to grant Ryker the forgiveness he wouldn't grant himself.

He blew out a breath, looking down the street but staying silent.

"Has she reached out to *you*?"

Ryker hesitated. Michele was sure she'd gotten her answer. The woman had. She swallowed, dropping her hand. "Will you just think about it? Please?"

"Thanks for looking out for me, Chele."

Not an answer to her question.

He held the door open, and she only just kept in the sigh as she stepped inside. Then she spotted Declan. He stood in the ring, shirtless, arms crossed over his large chest as he watched men dancing around each other. Every so often he'd say something, and the guys would nod.

Ryker squeezed her shoulder before moving toward the office.

She went back to watching Declan. She had to admit, his focus was sexy. So was the crease between his brows. The way his biceps bulged when he crossed his arms.

Declan called the men to stop. It wasn't until after they'd pulled off their gloves that he finally looked her way. Then a slow smile curved his lips.

Man, the guy was swoon-worthy. A guy she'd always believed was fictitious, that she'd never meet in real life.

But he's real, the voice whispered. Real and taking up way too much space in her head.

He climbed out of the ring, and every step toward him had her heart kicking faster. When his arms slipped around her waist and his chest pressed against hers, a low hum escaped her throat.

"How's your day been, gorgeous?"

She chuckled as he kissed her neck. "You mean since ten thirty this morning when I said goodbye to you at the trailer park? It's been good."

When he lifted his head, his eyes hardened. "Anthony get there okay?"

She gave a small nod. "He arrived before eleven and got straight to work, completing all the jobs I gave him."

He lifted her wrapped hand and kissed the bandage over her palm. Her lower abdomen did a little dip. "Good."

The guys who'd been in the ring shouted out a goodbye from the door, then Ryker tapped Declan on the shoulder. "I'll see you tomorrow." He smiled and winked at her before walking out. She heard the lock click behind them.

"So he moved his stuff into your house?" Michele asked when it was just them.

"Yep. Into the spare room."

Her skin crawled at the memory of the trailer. The place had been the definition of a dump. The more she thought about it, the more she was certain the trailer wasn't even safe to inhabit. If Declan hadn't offered to let the kid to move in with him, she probably would have offered her place, just because there was no way she could have left him there.

Her hands smoothed down his chest. "You look good, bare chested and giving directions."

"Do I now?" He lowered his head and nuzzled her neck again. "I can do it more often if you like."

Michele giggled, but the sound quickly turned into a heated sigh as his lips trailed up her neck and onto her cheek. The second he reached her mouth, she groaned, leaning into his kiss.

Her lips parted and Declan's tongue slipped in, rolling across hers. It wasn't just his mouth and tongue that were wreaking havoc on her, though. It was the way every inch of his body sealed against hers. The way his fingers slid down her spine before closing over her ass.

Suddenly, he lifted her into his arms. Her fingers funneled into his surprisingly soft hair. One of his hands trailed up her side, sliding over her cheek before grasping her neck.

When he tilted his head, he deepened the kiss. He stepped forward. Then there was a wall behind her.

Her core throbbed at the feel of being pressed against his hard stomach. She wanted to grind against him. To push her aching breasts into his chest.

When he tore his mouth from her lips, it slid down her throat, leaving a trail of fire.

Another groan flew from her throat.

Then, suddenly, the lights flicked off, sending the room into near darkness.

Instantly, Declan's body stilled and hardened. The hand on her hip tightened. In the dark, the silence felt eerie. Declan slid her body to the floor. Something that moments ago would have made her feel achy, now just left her chilled.

He slipped her hand into his larger one. When something sounded from the side of the building—a car engine, maybe—he quickly navigated through the dim room and into the office before pulling a handgun from the drawer. Her lips parted, but she remained silent as he pulled her into the small galley kitchen. At the back was a door. He silently flicked the lock before slipping through it.

Michele stuck close behind him as they walked into the back parking lot. The breath rushed out of her when she saw it was empty. Not a soul in sight.

"Maybe it was just a faulty light switch," she said quietly. *Please let it be a faulty light switch.*

The clenching of Declan's jaw told her he didn't agree.

He tugged her toward the power box several feet from the door. Before he reached it, he veered away and knelt, inspecting a small amount of liquid on the edge of the asphalt. Oil? He reached down, touching it. It was wet.

"A car was here."

Her eyes widened as music abruptly started playing from inside the gym.

Declan grabbed her hand again and tugged her back inside. Michele frowned. It was some kind of classical, orchestral song. They stopped beside the wireless speaker that sat on the front desk.

He lifted the small speaker. "Someone must've hooked their music to the speaker using our Bluetooth."

The fine hairs on Michele's arms stood on end. It was a common portable speaker system, easy enough for someone to hook into if they connected to the club's Wi-Fi. Declan's gaze shot out to the street. He didn't move to go out there, instead lifting his phone and opening Shazam, a music app that helped identify songs.

When the song title came up, Michele's skin iced.

Come, Sweet Death by Bach.

The music stopped. The connection was gone.

CHAPTER 15

*D*eclan dropped his bag onto the floor of Michele's bedroom before heading back into the living area. She was placing pizza and salad onto the dining table, throwing tentative looks his way from beneath her lashes. With good reason. He was pissed.

They'd gone to the police station. Another wasted fucking trip. Apparently, nothing could be done without evidence. And when he asked if they'd located and spoken to Tim, the asshole had said, "We're working on it." Yeah, right.

The guy was trying to scare Michele without stepping over any lines that would get the police involved.

It made him see red.

He collected some cutlery as Michele grabbed drinks, then they both sat at the table. He'd been silent the entire drive home. They both had. Did it eat at her as much as it ate at him? She didn't look nearly worried enough.

They ate together, still without a word being spoken.

Declan had eaten half an entire pizza when her words finally cut through the silence.

"Are you okay?"

The slice paused halfway to his mouth. "I should be asking you that."

She gave him a look as if to say *no, you shouldn't.* Then she reached out and squeezed his forearm. "I'm sorry."

He frowned. "Why are you sorry?"

"Because you didn't get the result you wanted with the police."

He hated that she was apologizing. He lowered the slice to the plate. "Why exactly did you break up with him?"

Her head lowered, and she ran her index finger along the edge of her plate. A sick feeling churned in his gut. He wasn't going to like this.

"I was dumb. There were red flags from the first date, but I went on three with him."

"What kind of red flags?"

"The first date was more of a feeling that nothing was quite right. Everything felt too...rehearsed." Her roaming finger moved to the edge of the table. "On the second date, there were less subtle things. At the end of the night, he went in for a kiss, but I pulled away. He looked angry but recovered quickly."

Declan's hands fisted.

She drew in a long breath. "It was the third date where he *really* scared me, though."

Yep. He hated this. "How did he scare you?"

She wet her lips. "He had a few drinks that night at dinner. He was...I don't know, on edge about something. He was sweating too, and his hands were shaking. It was subtle, but I saw it. I shouldn't have even let him drive me home, but...I don't know. I'm not strong and assertive. I'm not good at saying no."

He grabbed her hand. "Don't say that. You *are* strong, Michele." And the fact she thought she wasn't had more fury racing through his veins.

"When he dropped me off, he didn't ask to come up. He just followed me," she continued.

His voice lowered. "What did he do?"

"I tried to close the door, but he slipped in before I could. He was talking, almost muttering, about how he shouldn't have drunk so much, but everything had been getting to him lately." At her next pause, his gut gave another kick. "I stayed by the door, hoping he'd leave. Then he grabbed my arms and asked if he'd screwed things up. Asked if I'd still go on a fourth date with him. I said no, and this angry look came over his face. When his fingers tightened on my arms, they were like manacles."

It took everything in Declan to remain as he was. To not walk out of the door and hunt this asshole down. "What happened next?"

"He wasn't letting go of me, so I lied. I told him I'd go on another date." She shook her head. "That was worse. He knew I wasn't being honest. And there was something in his eyes that almost looked wild. It scared me. I tried to pull away, but he didn't let me. I still remember the feeling of his fingers digging into my skin." She slipped her hand from his and ran both of her hands over her arms, as if to brush off Tim's hold.

The asshole had *touched* her. Bruised her. He wanted to kill the fucker.

He reached over, grazing the skin of her arm, replacing her touch with his.

"When he wouldn't let go," she continued, "I kneed him between the legs, ran to the bedroom, and locked myself in."

"And he left?"

"Eventually."

More gentle grazing of her arm. "You told the police this?"

"I didn't go to the station until he started harassing me with phone calls and texts, and by showing up at my apartment building. By that stage, the bruises on my arms had faded. The officer looked at me like I was making a big deal out of nothing. He even said that when Tim showed up at my apartment, it could have been to apologize."

Declan cursed under his breath. Asshole.

"I know. It made me angry as hell, but I didn't know what to do. There was no way I was telling Uncle Ottie. He's got his heart issues and can't be stressed. And River had just been shot…"

Declan stood, no longer able to sit still. He moved in front of her, took her hands, and tugged her to her feet before slipping his arms around her waist. "You have *me*."

She lay her head on his chest. "Thank you. I don't know what I did to deserve you, but I'm not questioning it."

He kissed the top of her head. "I'm the one who should be saying that."

She looked up, and the second their gazes clashed, her blue eyes darkened to the shade of the dark sky at night.

His arms tightened around her waist, and the second her fingers wrapped around his neck, he lowered his head and took her mouth.

Fuck, her lips were soft. And that damn scent of hers surrounded and pressed into him.

With a low growl, he lifted her up, molding her body to his. He pushed his tongue between her lips and slid against hers.

He could drown in the woman, and he'd die a happy man.

"Where are we taking this?" he asked between desperate kisses. He knew where *he* wanted to take this, but he needed her words. He needed to know she was exactly where he was.

"The bedroom."

Blood roared between his ears, his body hardening to an almost painful degree.

Turning, he carried her to the bedroom. Using one hand, he tugged her shirt over her head. The second it was off, her hands were on his, doing the same.

Then he felt her skin, hot and smooth, pressed to his. It was agony.

He eased her to the center of the bed, lowering with her and caging her with arms on either side of her body. This woman—

everything about her called to him. She was his obsession. And tonight, she was all his.

~

WARMTH COILED in Michele's belly as Declan kissed down her cheek. Her neck. When he stopped at her chest, he took one pebbled nipple between his lips and sucked her through the material of her bra.

Her back arched, and a fiery cry fell from her lips, splintering throughout the room. Declan's hands immediately slipped behind her, unclasping the bra and tugging it away. Then he was sucking her bare nipple, his hand grazing the other.

Oh God. He was everywhere. It felt like every part of him was touching, *burning*, every part of her.

Desperately, she tugged at his hair. Her hips lifted of their own volition, pushing against him and crying out for attention.

Declan chuckled, and it was a vibration against her chest. Her hard peak slipped from between his lips, and his mouth started to trail down.

Suddenly, she couldn't breathe. As well as her sanity, the man was stealing her breath.

She caught her bottom lip between her teeth and dug in, almost penetrating skin. He tugged her jeans and panties down her legs. Then his long fingers wrapped around her ankles, tugging her so that her ass was right on the edge of the mattress, her knees bent and feet on the bed.

Before she could comprehend what he was doing, he was on his knees between her thighs, his mouth so close to her apex that his breath brushed against her flesh. She shuddered. Then he lowered his head, his lips wrapping around her clit, and suddenly, her vision grayed and blurred.

Her cry was louder this time, her hips jolting at the sudden sensation. But even though she bucked, she didn't move an inch. Not with Declan holding her so firmly.

Holy Jesus, she wouldn't survive this. The man was killing her.

His tongue swirled and swiped, toying with her. Her breaths sawed from her chest, her clit pounding against the onslaught.

When it all became too much, she sat up, her feet hitting the floor as she tugged him up. Her heart beat too quickly, to the point where she was almost certain it would beat right out of her chest.

He straightened, and even with him kneeling and her sitting on the bed, he was taller than her.

Her turn. She needed to touch him. Feel him beneath her fingers. The need almost suffocated her.

Her hands went to his jeans, undoing the button then the zipper. Each sound was loud in the quiet room, like a knife hitting glass. She reached inside his briefs and wrapped her fingers around him.

A low growl ripped from his chest, and when she looked up, it was to see his eyes closed, his brows tugged together like he was in pain.

It wasn't enough. She wanted more.

She began to move her hand over his length, feeling him. He was long and thick, and he just seemed to get bigger in her hold. She stroked her hand from the base right up to the tip, enjoying every little scrunch of Declan's brows. Every tensing of his muscles.

He dipped his head, his temple touching hers. Then his hand was covering the apex of her thighs, touching her entrance. And slowly, he slid inside her. Her other hand went to his arm, her nails digging into his flesh.

Her exploration of him became stilted and slow as he began to move his finger in and out of her. Her breaths grew choppy, her eyes scrunching shut. And when he slipped a second finger in and his thumb went to her clit, she stopped moving altogether as her head flew back with a groan.

"Declan..."

Suddenly, his mouth latched onto her breast again, and it was like the man was claiming her. As if every little part of her belonged to him now. She couldn't move. She couldn't think. All she could do was breathe through the slow thrusts of his fingers and the suction of her nipple.

She was seconds from breaking when his fingers slipped out of her. Her eyes popped open to see his grin was wide as he rose, sliding off his jeans and grabbing his wallet from his pocket. Then he was back with her, donning a condom.

His hands wrapped around her thighs, lifting them to his waist. She threaded her ankles behind his back, and he leaned over her.

God! She felt him there, right at her entrance. And he felt just as big as he'd felt in her hand. One of his hands remained on her thigh, while the other skirted behind her neck.

His face lowered, hovering over her lips. "You torment me, Chele. Drive me absolutely insane."

She didn't have a chance to respond, because he was kissing her again and sliding inside her.

She gasped into his mouth and his tongue plunged, dancing with her own. He eased in slowly, stretching her, only stopping when he was seated deep.

It was taking everything in her to *breathe*.

He paused, his mouth continuing to work hers. The hand on her thigh held her tightly, thumb grazing her sensitive skin.

When his hips rolled back, her breath caught. Then he thrust forward. This time it was a whimper from her throat. She arched her back as he thrust again and again.

There was strength and power in every movement. There was also restraint, like he was barely holding himself together. Like it was taking everything inside him to gentle his movements.

She slid both her hands through his hair, shifting her hips forward to meet him on every thrust. His hand on her neck lowered, taking hold of her breast while he rubbed the tight bud with his thumb.

Her entire body felt on fire. She wanted more, but she was also on the brink of shattering.

When he rose and pushed her back onto the mattress, he hovered over her, and the thrusts hit at a new angle. She groaned and writhed, her ankles remaining tightly around his waist.

His thrusts grew faster. Harder. His face pushed into her neck, teeth latching on. When he rolled her nipple between his thumb and forefinger, she lost the last bit of herself.

She cried out as a shudder coursed through her limbs, and her core clenched around his length. He kept thrusting through her orgasm, prolonging everything. Then he growled, his body tensing and hardening around her. He thickened inside her, his fingers digging into her flesh.

Finally, the world stopped moving and her breaths evened out. But neither of them moved. She wasn't sure if she wanted them to ever move again.

God, but he owned her. All of her.

CHAPTER 16

*D*eclan leaned back in his chair. The football game was on, and everyone was here at his, Cole's and Ryker's place, including Anthony, Michele, and River. Even Erik had come over. The guy was a new friend of the team, and he came to Mercy Ring for a few rounds every so often. He was both former military and a former boxer.

Michele's voice from the kitchen hit him in the chest. She and River were baking. It took everything in him not to look. Hell, he'd watched her more than he'd watched the game.

Pokey rested his head on Declan's legs. Yeah, Pokey was here, too. He gave the mutt a pat.

"You still doing that government contract work, Erik?" Jackson asked.

The guy kept his cards close to his chest and gave away very little about himself. Not that Declan cared. He'd proven to be a good man, which was all they needed to know.

"Sure am. Flexible hours. Little commitment. It's a good gig." He took a swig of his beer. "I hear Mercy Ring's been busy."

Didn't surprise Declan that he changed the subject quickly. He usually did when they asked personal questions.

Declan nodded. "Yeah, it's been great."

Better than they'd envisioned. Businesses frequently started slow and took a few years to build up. Hadn't been the case for them so far.

He shot a look to Anthony. The kid sat in an armchair and had barely said two words all day. Not that he was the most talkative person in the room usually.

Cole was talking about their clients, but Declan tuned him out. He switched his attention back to Michele in the kitchen, where she hovered over River's shoulder as the other woman stirred something in a bowl.

He chuckled to himself. He'd heard them arguing more than once today. Michele wanted to do more than she should with her injured hand, and River flat-out refused to let her.

A couple of days had passed since the power going off at Mercy Ring. Since that time, everything had remained quiet. He'd been staying at Michele's. Escorting her to and from work. Making sure she locked the shop door between customers.

Despite the precautions, there was a bad feeling in his gut. It damn well kept him awake at night. Had him holding her a bit tighter and longer every time he touched her.

When she looked his way, a small smile crept across her lips, then she quickly ducked her head. It amazed him that she could still get shy after everything they'd done over the last couple days. They'd barely been apart. Waking up together, showering and eating together.

She was so damn cute. At least he could touch her anytime he wanted now. His heart thudded at the thought.

He looked back to Cole, but the man was no longer talking. Jackson and Erik were in a conversation about boxing techniques, while Cole's attention was on the window. Declan followed his gaze to a teenage boy across the street. He was stepping out of a house. Before the door could close, a woman walked out behind him.

She looked early to mid-thirties, with long, wavy brown hair. She was a good head shorter than the kid. She seemed to be talking quickly while looking frustrated.

The boy turned, said something to her before climbing inside his car and pulling the door closed after him. The woman crossed her arms over her chest and watched as he drove away. Now she looked somewhere between wanting to cry, and raging mad.

Declan hadn't seen many of his neighbors yet. They all seemed to stay inside. He looked back at Cole, who still had eyes on the woman. "Have you met her, Cole?"

Finally, he dragged his gaze away, looking at Declan. "The neighbor? Nope. Seen them both a couple of times, though. Kid always has a scowl on his face."

Angry teens seemed to be a common thread in this town. Cole's gaze went back to the woman while Declan turned to Anthony.

"You doing okay, kid? You've been quiet."

Declan hadn't been home to check on him these last few days. Michele had said he was doing well at the shop, though, and Cole and Ryker had been looking after him.

Anthony nodded. "I'm fine. Just not all that chatty." He shifted in his seat like he was uncomfortable.

Interesting.

Declan leaned closer. "If there's anything else going on, anything you want to talk about, I'm here."

The kid had heard it before, but it felt worth repeating.

Another shift in his seat. "Thanks."

When the game came back on, the guys quieted. From his peripheral vision, he could still see Cole watching the woman across the road. He looked out the window to see her still standing in the yard. She seemed to be staring intently at something down the street.

~

MICHELE WATCHED as River measured out a cup of chocolate chips. The cup was already overflowing, but that didn't stop the woman from adding even more once the cup was empty.

"Uh, I think that's enough, River."

Her best friend smiled. "Can you ever have enough chocolate chips?"

"The boys will be asking for some cookie with their chocolate, so I think so."

River chuckled as she lifted the wooden spoon and went back to mixing. "Nothing wrong with that."

The sweet scent of mini apple pies filtered throughout the kitchen. They were in the oven and almost done. She hadn't been planning on baking cookies as well, but if these guys had shown her anything today, it was that they could eat. They'd demolished half a dozen pizzas and a huge bowl of pasta already.

When her gaze rose to the living room to find Declan looking right at her, a small smile curved her lips before she suddenly dropped her head. God, why did the man have to be so dang cute? These last few days, he'd been everything a woman could want. Attentive. Helpful. Kind.

Then there was everything he made her feel at night…

Her cheeks heated at the thought.

"Are you thinking about him right now?"

Her gaze flew to River. Her friend had the biggest grin on her face.

"Maybe."

"So, yes." She chuckled as she grabbed a chocolate chip from the dough. "That reminds me, I've already planned our first double date."

"Do I even want to know?"

A mischievous smile stretched River's lips. "Axe throwing."

What on earth? "You want us to go axe throwing? You, me, Declan, and Jackson?"

"Yeah. What's wrong with that?"

"Ah, how about the fact they're former Deltas and will whip our asses? Hell, axe throwing was probably part of their training. Not to mention I wouldn't be able to lift the thing with my bum hand."

River rolled her eyes. "We'll obviously wait until your hand is healed. And, yeah, that's the point. Just imagine Declan standing behind you, his hot body pressed against your back as he guides you in throwing the thing."

Okay, that didn't sound terrible...

River got this dreamy look on her face, and Michele laughed, tugging the bowl from her friend. "I think you've had too much sugar."

"Oh, I've definitely had too much sugar." She leaned over the counter, her voice lowering. "You know what sugar goes well with? Sex. The other night, Jackson and I—"

"River, I'm going to stop you there. I cannot listen to a sex story while six guys are sitting in the living room within listening distance."

Her smile widened. "Well, that's your loss. It's a good one."

"You can tell me later."

She grabbed a baking pan, and River shifted closer, spooning the cookie mixture into balls. "Is the sex with Declan amazing? Like, I know it has to be good, because how could it not be, but is it out of this world?"

Michele's cheeks reddened. She'd told River the morning after she'd slept with Declan, because she'd needed to tell *someone*. And her best friend had been just as excited as she'd known she would be.

Michele shook her head. "Nope. Not talking to you about that here, either. Not right now."

Another pout. "McDreamy over there is always around protecting you, and with this serial killer on the loose, Jackson never lets me out of his sight. When will I get to hear the sexy details?"

Her stomach churned at the mention of the serial killer. River noticed the shift in her mood and touched her arm. "Hey. You're safe with Declan. He would never let anything happen to you."

"I know, it's just…concerning. And there's been so much going on. It's like as soon as one thing ends, something else begins."

All she wanted to do was stick her head into the dirt and pretend everything with this killer and Tim wasn't happening.

River swung an arm around Michele and tugged her into her side. "I know. I feel it too. It's heavy. But we have each other and the guys. Declan and his twelve-pack are pretty good allies."

She laughed. She could always count on River to cheer her up. "Thank you." River was just leaning away, when Michele whispered, "And the sex is out-of-this-world amazing."

River squeaked. "I knew it!"

They spent the next few minutes scooping and flattening the cookies onto the baking pan, although Michele was pretty sure River did more eating than scooping and flattening. They'd just finished when the oven dinged.

Perfect timing.

River took the hot apple pies out and replaced them with the cookies, then cleaned up the kitchen while the pies cooled. Michele had just set the pies on a plate and was carrying them into the living room when the doorbell rang.

Cole was the first to stand and cross the room before tugging the door open. The guys lowered the volume on the TV. A woman stood on the porch, and her voice filtered through the room.

"Sorry to bother you. I live across the road. I just wanted to let you know that I saw some guy parked down the street. He got out of his car, and he seemed to be watching this house. He was a bit creepy."

Michele sucked in a nervous breath.

"Which way?" Cole's voice was low and hard.

She pointed to the right. "When he saw me watching, he got back into his car and drove off."

Cole stepped outside, and Jackson followed. Erik rose from his seat but didn't attempt to move toward the door.

Nerves trickled down her spine, but she shook her head. *It's probably nothing, Michele.* But regardless of the whispered voice, her stomach churned.

She moved forward again but stopped beside Erik when something on the TV caught her attention. Suddenly, everything around her faded but the screen. Because there, on a news brief, was Tim.

"Can you turn that up?" she asked Ryker quietly, her voice holding a definite tremble.

He frowned but lifted the remote and turned up the volume.

"The following is video surveillance from Miss Dean's residence in Rock Island, which recorded footage of a man accompanying her inside her home less than an hour before her murder. He was also recorded leaving alone a short time later."

Her skin chilled as the clip played—Tim walking up the porch steps with a short blonde woman by his side. It was dark, but there was no mistaking him.

Michele's breathing turned choppy. Black dots started to hedge her vision. She was vaguely aware of Anthony standing from his chair and Declan swearing, but she ignored them both. She ignored everything but the TV.

She watched in horror as Tim stepped into the woman's home, his hand on her back. The video then flicked to footage of him leaving by himself.

The reporter came back on the screen. "This man is believed to be a suspect in the recent string of murders in Washington. If anyone sees him or has any information on his whereabouts, it's important that you contact your local police immediately."

The last words had barely left the reporter's mouth when the plate of pies slipped from her trembling fingers and the black dots turned into a dark haze. The last thing she saw was Erik reaching for her before the world darkened.

CHAPTER 17

"*S*o the FBI are meeting you at the station?"

River's words pierced Michele's consciousness.

"Yeah, they asked us to come in as soon as she wakes." Declan sounded angry. It made Michele want to reach out and comfort him. "I can't believe she's been walking around by herself while this asshole has had her in his sights!"

FBI? Had her in his sights? What were they—

"How was anyone supposed to know that Tim might be the serial killer?"

River's words had Michele's last memory crashing back to her. The news. Tim. The Washington serial killer.

Oh God. It was *him*.

Her eyes flew open, and shuddering breaths whooshed in and out of her chest.

Declan was by her side in a second. "Michele! Christ, are you okay, baby?"

He sat on the edge of the bed, a hand moving to her cheek. She pushed up to a seated position and latched onto his hand, needing the warmth and comfort.

"It was him! Tim, he… He murdered all those women!"

He clenched his jaw. "It's looking that way."

Serial killer. The man she'd dated was a *serial killer*. It didn't feel real. At what point had he been planning to kill her? Because that had been his end game, right?

Oh God. This *couldn't* be real.

As if he could hear her thoughts, Declan growled and pulled her against his chest. She sank into him, wishing she could just remain there forever, cocooned in the safety of his arms.

Eventually, she pushed back, and for the first time took in the room around her. The gray sheets. The dark oak bedside tables.

She was in Declan's room. She hadn't been in it before, but she knew it was his. She glanced up to see River and Ryker standing by the door. River's eyes softened, then she ran over and threw her arms around Michele in a big bear hug. River's bear hugs were the best. She sighed into her friend's shoulder.

"I'm sorry this is happening," River whispered before pulling back and holding her shoulders. "But everything will be okay."

Michele tried for a smile, but she was sure it came out all kinds of wrong. Her gaze skittered back to Declan. "Did you say the FBI?"

"Yes. We need to tell them what you know."

"I don't know *anything*." Suddenly, a thought came to her, and it had anxiety bubbling in her belly. "I don't want to go to some safe house. That's what they do with people like me, isn't it? When a serial killer is after someone, they hide them in a safe house?"

The thought of being whisked away from her home. Her uncle with his heart issues. Declan, River, and Ryker, who were her safety... It had her skin going cold all over. And in all the books and movies, the safe houses were never actually so safe.

"Hey." Declan's hand went back to her cheek. "No one is taking you away from me. *No one.*"

He said it like a vow. Like he'd tear apart any unlucky soul who tried to get between them. The anxiety eased. She believed him. She couldn't not.

River stood, and slowly, Michele climbed off the bed, all the while trying not to think about the fact that she'd dated a serial killer. Let him into her home.

No. She needed to take the emotion out of it. Obsessing over things wouldn't change what had happened.

For now, she needed to focus on this conversation with the FBI. The sooner it was done, the sooner it would be over.

When they finally loaded into the car and drove to the station, the trip was far too short. Neither of them spoke a word. For her, it was nerves, but for him...

She peeked at him from below her lashes. At the way his muscles contracted in his arms as he undid his seat belt. At the pissed-off look on his face.

She'd barely opened her door when he was there, wrapping an arm around her waist and leading her inside. When they stepped into the station, a man walked forward and stopped in front of them. A man in a suit.

"Miss King. My name is Agent Tolson. Could you please follow me down the hall, where Special Agent Maggie Burton is waiting for you?" He looked at Declan. "Mr. James, if you could wait here."

Unease sprang to life in her belly. Her fingers tightened around Declan's, and she was moments from telling the guy she wasn't going anywhere without him when Declan spoke first.

"I go where she goes."

The man's eyes narrowed. "Mr. James—"

"I'm not going anywhere without him," she hurried to interrupt.

For a moment, Agent Tolson was silent, his face giving nothing away. Then he turned. "Follow me."

Michele blew out a loud breath. She went to slip her hand out of Declan's as they walked down the hallway, but his fingers tightened. His thumb started a slow stroke down the back of her hand. For a moment, it had the chill in her bones warming. But the second they made it into the little white room, those chills returned.

A woman in a dark suit sat at a small table, and a tall man stood behind her.

Michele stepped inside and the woman rose, stretching her hand out as the door closed behind them with a resounding click. Declan finally let go of her, and she shook the woman's hand.

"Hi, Miss King. My name is Special Agent Maggie Burton, and I'm leading this investigation."

Michele swallowed. "Hi."

The agent looked at Declan, keeping her hand outstretched for him. "Not surprised to see you here, Mr. James."

He shook her hand. "Glad to hear it."

She dipped her head toward the chairs. "Please, sit."

Michele lowered into a chair. The agent's gaze went straight to her, and all she wanted to do was squirm under the woman's scrutiny. She had a feeling Agent Burton was trying to come off as calming, but there was nothing calm about this little white room and the men in suits with visible holstered guns.

The agent pushed a picture across the table. Michele sucked in a quick breath. It was Tim.

"Do you know this man?"

Michele nodded. "Yes. That's Tim Johnson."

"Can you please tell me how you know him?"

She found a small crease in her jeans and ran her finger along it. "We met on a dating app and chatted online for a week or two. He'd said he was a winemaker. That he was looking for someone to connect with."

Declan's hand landed on top of the one on her leg, giving her a little squeeze. That was what she needed to continue.

Blowing out a long breath, Michele told the special agent about their three dates. "He was great when we chatted over texts, but on our first date, I got a bad feeling in my gut. Every-thing felt a bit rehearsed. Then on the second date, there were little red flags in the way he was behaving…subtle insults toward me, anger at any guy who talked to me. On the third date, he drank too much. When we got back to my place, he followed me in without permission and wouldn't leave. He grabbed my arms and kept pushing for a fourth date."

"I saw you made a couple of reports, too?" Agent Burton asked.

Michele had no doubt the woman had read those reports in detail. "Yes. Not straight away. He called me the day after our third date, trying to apologize and asking to go out again. I said no. It wasn't until he showed up at my apartment building that I decided to talk to the police." Declan stroked the back of her hand with his index finger. "The officer didn't seem to care. Said there wasn't much he could do unless the guy actually hurt me. There was also an incident at Mercy Ring."

"What kind of incident?"

"The power was switched off, and someone connected to the portable speaker via Bluetooth. A song about death played." She shuddered. "We reported that too, but…"

But the officer was a jerk? But the guy was lazy as hell and didn't want any more work created for himself?

The woman across the table narrowed her eyes. "I'm sorry that the officer didn't take you seriously, but I can assure you, we do." She leaned forward. "We're going to need everything you have on him. Phone number. Text message conversations. Dating profile."

Declan cleared his throat. "He deleted his profile."

Michele frowned at Declan. How did he—

"We asked some friends to search for his profile. They were able to recover deleted information, but there was nothing useful. No picture. No bank details. No address."

When had he done that? And why hadn't he told her?

The agent nodded like the information didn't surprise her.

Michele shifted her gaze back to the agent. "I can share the phone messages, but that's basically all I have."

The woman nodded again. "You're very lucky to have not gone on that fourth date, Miss King."

Her stomach cramped, and she almost didn't want to know. Still, she asked, "You think that's when he would have...killed me?"

She distinctly felt Declan flinch beside her.

The agent nodded, no change in her expression. "Yes." The word was so definitive, it was like a sucker punch to the gut. "This guy finds his victims in cafés, grocery stores—any way he can. From there, we've established that he has a clear pattern of behavior. He goes on four dates with the women, and on the fourth, they end up at the victim's house and he stabs them while playing, *Come, Sweet Death* by Bach."

Michele's heart crashed against her ribs. "That's the song that was playing at Mercy Ring."

Again, no change in the woman's features. If she was surprised, she didn't show it.

"Is there anything else that's distinctive about what he does?" Declan asked.

"He always stabs his victims exactly four times. And always at the dining table."

Nausea crawled up her throat. Since seeing his face on the news, she knew how close she'd come to death, but hearing someone say the words out loud... It was different.

"Why four?" Michele asked quietly.

"We're not sure what his obsession with four is. He grew up in foster care and experienced abuse at the hands of a couple of foster parents. Each time, he was moved to another home. He was a teenager when he was moved to his last placement. He was there for four years before he aged out."

Michele nodded. There was so much information it kind of made her feel numb.

"During his time in the last foster home, his foster mother reported that he was abusing animals. Neighbors' cats. A rabbit. He also set fire to a few things." She paused. "Then, shortly after he aged out, the foster mother was murdered."

Michele sucked in a gasp of air.

"All evidence pointed to her boyfriend. His prints were on the knife, and he was with her the entire night. But to this day, he vehemently denies it."

"How did she die?" Declan asked, his voice holding a dangerous edge.

The agent looked at him. "She was stabbed four times."

Oh, Jesus.

"Is his name even Tim?" Michele asked.

The agent nodded. "His first name is. But he's been changing his last name with each victim."

Victim. She'd said that word already, more than once, and each time it made Michele feel sick to her stomach. That was almost her. *She* was almost a victim.

"Why would he play that song while we were at Mercy Ring?"

It was Declan who answered. "He was messing with you. He's trying to scare you."

Well, it was working.

She scrubbed a hand over her face. "Why won't he just leave me alone?" She wasn't sure who she was asking. The agent? Declan? Everyone? "I didn't want a fourth date, so why is he still after me?"

The agent's voice softened. "As far as we know, you're the first woman who declined that fourth date. People like him, people who have such a specific pattern of behavior, they need things to be the same. He's probably not coping well with the fact that you got away and interrupted that pattern."

Sick. The man was sick.

"Miss King—"

"Michele. Please call me Michele." She needed to control something right now, even if it was just what this woman called her.

"Michele. We'd like you to go into a safe house."

There it was, the request Michele had known would be coming.

"No," Declan said before she could. "She's not leaving my side."

The agent exhaled loudly. "Mr. James—"

"I'm sure in that background check your team ran on me, you've seen I'm former Delta. I live with two other Deltas. She can stay with us. There's nowhere she'd be safer."

There it was again. That lethal voice, laced with danger.

For a moment, the agent didn't speak. Then she turned to Michele. "What would you like to do?"

"I'm staying with Declan and his team." No way did she want to be anywhere else.

The agent nodded. "If that's what you want, but we *will* be placing an agent outside your house every night."

The air rushed from Michele's chest. She wasn't going to be separated from Declan. She'd expected a fight. She hadn't gotten one. Good. She really didn't have the energy right now.

They remained in the room for another half hour. In that time, she handed over her phone, and the men in suits hooked it up to a computer and copied every text she'd ever received from or sent to Tim.

When they finally stepped outside, she sucked in a deep breath. The fresh air felt good.

Declan pulled her into his chest. He looked worried. "How are you doing?" he asked quietly.

"Not great. I just want this horrible day to be over."

"It will be." He tucked a strand of hair behind her ear. "Are you okay staying at my place with Cole, Ryker, and Anthony there?"

"As long as Pokey can come."

He chuckled. "I wouldn't want him anywhere else."

It was going to be a full house.

She lay her head on his chest, breathing him in. She was only just pulling away when her phone rang. An unknown number popped up onto the screen.

"Hello?"

"Hello, is this Michele King?" a woman asked.

"Speaking."

"Miss King, I'm calling from Lindeman Hospital. We have your uncle here. I'm afraid he's had a heart attack."

CHAPTER 18

*D*eclan ran a hand through his hair. God, he *hated* this. He could see Michele as she sat by her uncle's hospital bed. Saw the tears wetting her cheeks. The way she held her uncle's hand like she was afraid he'd slip away if she let go.

The worst part, the part that really tore at his fucking soul, was that he couldn't do a damn thing to help her. Not with this. He was powerless.

At the sound of fast footsteps, he looked up to see River running down the hall and Jackson hot on her heels.

River moved straight past him into the room, while Jackson stopped by his side. He touched Declan's shoulder. "How's she doing?"

"Not great." Understatement of the century. "She's been crying since the call came in. And then she saw him…"

And it was like her heart broke all over again.

Jackson blew out a long breath. "The woman's had a lot thrown her way today."

"Too much," he muttered under his breath.

"Where was Ottie when he had the heart attack?"

"In his shop. Luckily, Mrs. Albuquerque and a couple of her

friends were in there with him. They called the paramedics straight away."

Jackson shot a look into the room. "Is he conscious?"

"He was awake when we got here, but he's sleeping now. Doctors said he should be okay but will need to remain in the hospital for a while longer."

"Good. It would kill Michele to lose her uncle. He's been her entire family since her parents passed."

"I know." That very fact had been playing on his mind too goddamn much.

Jackson turned away. "How'd the meeting go with the FBI?"

"Honestly? It was messed up." That was the only way he could describe it. "The guy killed animals and set things on fire as a teenager. Goes on four dates with women, then kills them at their dining table by stabbing them four times. They even think he killed his last foster mother." If Declan ever got his hands on the asshole, he was a dead man.

"And Michele had three dates with him?"

"Yep." Too. Damn. Close.

The veins in Jackson's neck stood out. "Is she staying with you?"

"Yes. They didn't get a choice in the matter."

"You're both welcome to stay with me and River if the house gets too crowded."

"Thank you, brother."

MICHELE HELD her uncle's hand while tracing the back of his hand with her other one. He was sleeping. River had left about five minutes ago, and Declan was still in the hall giving her some time with Ottie.

While she was grateful for him trying to give her space without leaving her side, she just wished she could send him home. She didn't want him to see her like this. She didn't want *anyone* to see her like this.

Her heart was breaking. Seeing her uncle in a hospital bed... It brought back all the memories of sitting with her father while he was in the exact same position. Only, her father hadn't survived. And she'd had to watch as her last parent breathed his final breath.

It was too similar. Too heartbreaking.

A tear trickled down her cheek. "I can't lose you too, Uncle Ottie."

The doctor had said he should make a full recovery. But then what? They just wait for something else to happen? It wasn't fair. He'd done everything his medical team had told him to do. What had set off his sudden high blood pressure and subsequent heart attack? Was it stress?

Something niggled at her mind. On one of her dates, Mrs. Albuquerque had seen her with Tim. Had the woman seen him on the news and told her uncle?

"I lost my parents too young, Uncle Ottie." Her voice was low as she spoke. "That should have been it. I went through my grief and should get to live pain-free. You took me in. You saved me. And I've been so grateful to have you ever since."

She closed her eyes. "But this year..." She sucked in a shuddering breath. "It's kicking my butt. First thinking Ryker was gone. Then River being shot. And you."

Words torn from somewhere deep in her heart slipped out one by one. "I'm starting to wonder if it's worth it. Loving people. Letting people in. The world doesn't seem to mind taking the people I love away from me. Or at least dangling the fragility of their lives in my face. I don't know if I can lose anyone else."

She lowered her head onto his hand and let the tears fall again. She didn't feel strong enough for this today. Any of it. Not her uncle's heart attack. Not a serial killer having her in his sights. All she wanted to do was crawl under her sheets with Pokey and lose herself in a book. Be transported into someone else's world. A world that promised things reality couldn't.

She didn't know how long she stayed like that before someone touched her back. Then Declan was beside her, on his haunches, his face intense as he looked at her.

"Visiting time is ending, honey." His voice was as gentle as his touch. "I'm sorry."

She wasn't sure if he was apologizing about the visiting hours or her uncle. Maybe both. She looked back at Ottie. "I don't want to leave him."

Declan leaned his head into her hair and pressed a kiss to her temple. "We can come back in the morning."

She gave a slow nod, even though all she wanted to do was strap herself to the chair and refuse to leave. Slowly, she rose to her feet, but not before pressing one last kiss to her uncle's hand.

The second they reached the hall, Declan wrapped an arm around her. Usually, all she wanted to do was lean into his touch. Right now, she was too numb to feel him.

On the drive home, he kept a hand on her leg. "We'll stop at your apartment so you can pack a bag, then I'll take you to my place."

She nodded, never taking her gaze from the road. Tears were trying to press at her eyes again, but she would not let them fall. Not now. She'd cried so many tears this afternoon.

When they reached her building, they both climbed out. She didn't miss the way Declan scanned the area. The way his hand on her back felt like it was a second away from wrapping around her waist and whisking her away.

They'd almost reached the door when two men suddenly walked around the building, one from either side, approaching the front door.

Declan pulled her to a stop. Then he shot a look behind them, no doubt about to pull her in that direction. She gasped when she looked over her shoulder and saw two more men walking out from behind cars in the parking lot.

What the hell?

As the two men nearest the door crept closer, Michele frowned. Wait. The guy to the right looked familiar. He was the guy from the trailer park. The one who'd grabbed her and fought with Anthony. Her gaze flittered to his arm. It was in a sling.

She didn't recognize any of the other guys, but all four of them had weapons. Two had knives, one a baseball bat, and another a broken wine bottle.

Fear trickled down Michele's spine, causing her hands to shake.

"What the hell do you want?" Declan growled, angling his body sideways and tugging her behind him.

"You dislocated my fucking arm," the guy from the trailer park sneered. "I also had to get stitches on my head from that goddamn kid. I don't have health insurance, so I have quite the bill now. Are you gonna pay my fucking bill?"

Declan's fingers were tight around her wrist. "If you come anywhere near her, I won't just dislocate your arm, I'll break it."

"How did you even know where I live?" Michele asked before she could stop herself.

He lifted a shoulder, looking quite pleased with himself. "You said you worked at Meals Made Easy, you stupid bitch." The muscles in Declan's arms flexed. "Wasn't hard to figure out where you lived."

"Stay the hell back," Declan growled.

The guy's eyes narrowed—and before Michele realized what was happening, the man with the bottle hurled it right at her head.

In the blink of an eye, Declan had her pinned to the floor. Then the men were racing toward them.

Declan shot to his feet, and Michele watched in shock as one of the men lunged, a knife aimed right for Declan's chest. He grabbed the guy's wrist before the knife could reach its mark, twisting him around so his back was to Declan's chest.

He plunged the knife into the guy's gut.

Michele's lips separated. A buzzing sounded in her ears at the sight of the blood.

When another guy came at Declan from the other side, he shoved the bleeding man into him before grabbing the other guy's baseball bat mid-swing and whipping it out of his hands.

Michele was so busy watching Declan, she almost missed the man from the trailer park closing in on her. His knife was drawn...and there was a smile on his face.

"Shall we finish what we started?"

Michele screamed as the man dove at her.

"Michele!"

Declan's voice sounded distant as she rolled, the knife narrowly missing her. She attempted to crawl away. The guy grabbed her ankle and yanked her toward him. Then he was on her back, pressing her into the grass. Suddenly, a knife was at her throat.

The smell of alcohol brushed across her face as he leaned closer. "I figured you might not wanna pay up."

The sharp edge of the blade just touched her skin before it was torn away. Then the weight on her back disappeared. She rolled over to see Declan putting the guy in a chokehold.

When one of the men behind them rose, the one Declan had stabbed in the gut, Michele's heart stopped.

"Declan!" She screamed his name just as the guy plunged the knife into Declan's side.

Deep horror and panic flooded every part of her as red liquid seeped from his side. She pressed a hand to her mouth to stop from being sick, blinking rapidly to urge away the black dots clouding her vision.

But it was as if Declan didn't feel the wound. He didn't pause, just dropped the unconscious guy in his hold before grabbing the knife and plunging it into the guy's neck.

Another wave of nausea hit. *Oh God, Oh God, Oh God. Don't be sick.*

From her peripheral vision, she saw a car skid to a stop in the parking lot and a man run out. A man in a suit. An FBI agent.

He aimed his gun at the men who were still breathing.

"If anyone moves, I shoot."

Declan ignored the agent, moving to her side and holding her. "Are you okay?"

His eyes stopped on her neck, where she could already feel the small trickle of blood. His jaw hardened, and it looked like he wanted to turn around and murder the remaining men. Her cut was just a graze. Unlike his.

Her gaze went to his side. "You're b-bleeding."

She touched the red blood, and her insides coiled. But this time, it wasn't just because of her fear of blood. It was something else. Something that went far deeper than a phobia.

"Just a flesh wound," he said quickly.

"A flesh wound? The man stabbed you! We need to get back to the hospital!" Her entire body trembled. She tried to push him away, but her arms shook so violently she barely had any strength.

Stabbed. Declan had been *stabbed*. And her uncle had had a heart attack.

She was right. The world was reminding her yet again that the people she loved were flesh and blood. And they could be taken as quickly and easily as they could be given.

CHAPTER 19

*S*he was quiet. Had been quiet ever since the attack yesterday.

Declan watched as she grabbed a customer's meals from the fridge while Anthony worked silently at the counter beside the stove.

They'd spent the morning at the hospital. He was sure Michele would have spent the entire day there if she could have, but she'd had orders to fill. Something her uncle had reminded her of before all but pushing her out of his hospital room. There was still quite a bit Anthony couldn't do by himself, although the kid had been pretty great, opening the shop and doing everything he could until Michele arrived.

He didn't blame her for being quiet. The previous day had been a shit show of danger. Hell, she'd seen him stab men and get stabbed in return. They'd had to make a second hospital trip last night so he could get stitched up. And yeah, she'd been quiet and pale as hell then, too. She'd stared at him like he was going to bleed out in front of her or something.

"Thank you, darling," the customer said, taking her bag of meals.

"You're welcome, Connie."

The door to the shop opened, and three women stepped in, led by Mrs. Albuquerque. She walked straight up to the counter. "Oh, dear. We're so sorry about your uncle. His heart attack took us all by surprise."

The curve of Michele's mouth faltered, but she recovered quickly with a smile that was too wide to be real. "Thank you. And thank you for calling the paramedics and staying with him until they arrived."

"Of course," one of the women beside Mrs. Albuquerque said.

Connie's mouth slipped open on a gasp. "Your uncle had a heart attack?"

Michele swallowed. "Yesterday."

"Oh my gosh. I'm so sorry!" Connie reached across the counter and touched Michele's hand. "You know what? I have this amazing cookie recipe. No matter the situation, they always brighten my day. I'm going to make a double batch, one for you and one for your uncle."

"Thank you," she said with a more genuine smile for the woman. She turned back to Mrs. Albuquerque and her friends as Connie left. "I'll get your meals."

"I mentioned to Ottie that I saw that man you dated on the news. I hope that wasn't the wrong thing to do," Mrs. Albuquerque said, sounding surprisingly regretful.

Michele paused at the open fridge door, her body visibly tensing at the older woman's statement. Declan didn't miss the way her fingers tightened on the fridge door, knuckles turning white.

Shit.

Declan rose before moving behind her so that when she turned, he could slide the meals from her hands. She was shaking. He took the meals to the waiting women.

The woman to her right patted Mrs. Albuquerque's hand. "You couldn't have known what would happen."

Declan set the containers onto the counter.

The third woman shook her head. "For a moment, I thought he wouldn't make it."

Michele's head hit the underside of a shelf in the fridge. Dammit, did these women have no shred of sensitivity? She turned, and he took the second handful of meals.

"Lucky for us, he'll be okay," Declan said, trying to save Michele from responding.

"Would you like Anthony to help you carry those to your cars?" she asked. Her voice was off, but he was certain it was something only he would notice.

Mrs. Albuquerque shot an assessing look Anthony's way. Then she nodded. "Yes. That would be nice."

Declan waited until everyone was out of the shop. When Michele went over to where Anthony had been working by the stove, he moved behind her and curled his arms around her waist.

Her entire body froze, and he felt her muscles tighten and contract. He frowned. "Are you okay?"

"Yes." Her response came too quickly.

He pressed a light kiss to her neck. "I'm sorry you saw me do what I did last night. And about everything that came before that. I'm also sorry about what Mrs. Albuquerque said." He sure as hell hoped Michele wasn't blaming herself.

After a short moment, she shimmied out of his hold. Reluctantly, he let her go. She stretched up for an empty cardboard box on a top shelf, and Declan reached above her, grabbing it easily before handing it to her.

"Thank you." She set the box onto the counter before stacking meals inside. "And you don't need to apologize for what happened last night. You kept us safe."

She didn't look him in the eye. Not once.

She moved over to the fridge and opened it before grabbing

more meals to add to the box. She was going back to the fridge for another load when he snagged her wrist.

"Michele. Can you please look at me?"

She sucked in a long breath. Then, slowly, her gaze shifted up his body, pausing for a moment at his side, right where the knife had gotten him, before finally reaching his eyes.

"Talk to me. What can I do to help?" Because she was obviously pushing him away—and he needed to stop it from happening.

Her gaze darted between his eyes. Then she swallowed. "I'd like to stay with River and Jackson tonight."

Her words were like a dagger to his chest. She didn't want to stay with him. She didn't want to *be* with him.

She tried to pull away, but he didn't release her. He couldn't. Not yet. "Why?"

She blinked twice before answering. "I just... I need a night with River."

"Is that all it is?"

She opened her mouth but hesitated. And that hesitation told Declan everything he needed to know. There was more she wasn't saying.

The door opened, and both their gazes shot to Anthony. He took a step inside but paused. "Uh...sorry?"

Michele put her hands on Declan's chest and pushed. Reluctantly, he moved back, his hands dropping.

"You're fine, Anthony." She walked over to the fridge, grabbed a couple more meals, and set them in the box. "This is the last delivery for the day. It's for Mr. Sanders. He lives on—"

"Abbey Court. I remember." He lifted the box. "Thanks. I'll see you both tonight."

The door closed, and Declan's gaze went straight back to Michele. "I want to stay with you, Michele. Even if it's just in the same house to make sure you're okay."

Both physically and emotionally.

She turned away from him and grabbed an empty saucepan and spoon before rinsing them in the sink. She didn't say anything. The silence killed him. He watched her place the dishes into the dishwasher. He had no fucking idea what to say.

She switched on the washer, and when she turned around, he stepped in front of her. "Michele, what's going on?" His hand went to her cheek. He needed to touch her right now, because she was scaring the shit out of him. But the second he made contact, she pulled away and her head dropped.

"I can't, Declan. I can't…" Suddenly, she looked panicked. Her breaths came out faster. "I can't *breathe* right now. I just…" More fast breaths. "I just need some time to think and process."

His heart crashed against his ribs. "Time to think about what?"

Them? Whether she still wanted him?

She tried to step around him, but he quickly moved in front of her, blocking her way. "Michele, give me something. *Please.*"

"I can't do this," she whispered.

This? Them? Him and her? To Declan, they were a done deal. He reached for her, but she pulled back as if his touch would burn her.

"Please don't touch me."

Her words were worse than the knife to his gut last night. "Why?"

He inched closer. She inched back.

Suddenly, the door opened. Declan shot a look behind him. His eyes narrowed at the sight of Jackson and River stepping into the shop. They both stopped.

"Everything okay?" River asked.

He ignored her question and turned back to Michele. "You already texted her."

She swallowed, looking on the verge of tears. "I'm sorry. I just need some time."

Time for what?

He wanted to ask, but footsteps behind him grew closer, and he saw the glimmer of tears in Michele's eyes. So he gave a small nod. "Okay, honey. I'll give you some time."

How much time exactly, he wasn't sure.

What he *was* sure of—he wasn't giving up on her. No matter how hard she tried to push him away.

MICHELE TURNED her face into the spray of water. She'd spent the last few hours at the hospital with her uncle, with Jackson and River by her side. He'd looked tired. So exhausted, her heart hurt to see it. Every time he lifted his arm, his hand had shaken.

She swallowed, scrunching her eyes.

But what really tugged at her chest was his question. He'd asked if she was safe from Tim.

Her fault. That's how this felt. Utterly and completely her fault. Her uncle had a heart attack brought on by stress because he'd been worried about *her*. She was sure of it.

She scrubbed her hands over her face, wanting the pain in her chest to disintegrate. And the fear. God, she hated the fear. The fear of possibly losing Uncle Ottie. It tore at her.

Michele stayed in the shower until her skin was wrinkly and the room was thick with steam. When she finally turned off the tap, she got out, drying off quickly and tugging on yoga pants and an oversized T-shirt.

She'd just stepped into the spare room when she stopped short. River sat on the bed with a tray of food. The woman looked way too comfortable. "I have salami, prosciutto, crackers, olives, some pesto dip, Whoppers, and your favorite, spicy Doritos."

The first real smile of the day curved Michele's lips. "Everything we used to eat for dinner when we had our movie nights in high school." It had become quite the tradition for the two of them. She gave Pokey a pat before climbing onto the bed.

River nodded. "Yep. I could have prepared a normal adult meal, but something told me you'd prefer this."

This is why the woman was her best friend. She knew her so well. This was soul food to Michele. Exactly what she needed.

She lifted a Dorito and nibbled on it. "Thank you."

River smiled, tilting her head to the side. "Your uncle's going to be fine."

She lowered the Dorito. "I just can't look at him without..."

River leaned forward, touching her hand. "Without thinking about your father."

Of course her friend knew. "And knowing he found out Tim is likely the serial killer..." She couldn't finish the sentence. Not out loud.

Immediately, River shook her head. "Nope. Don't you do that, Chele. This isn't your fault. None of it."

"If I hadn't dated Tim—"

"Still not your fault. You didn't ask for any of this."

Michele nodded. It was one of those quick nods that didn't in any way mean she agreed.

River's hand softened on her arm. "What's going on with you and Declan?"

She'd known the question was coming. It didn't make answering it any easier. "When we were attacked last night—"

"I hate that those assholes attacked you," River seethed, shaking her head. "Sorry, go on."

"Declan got stabbed." She picked at the Dorito, breaking it into tiny bits. "And he bled. Real blood. And I just..." She stopped, not even sure how to word what she needed to say. "I lost Mom and Dad so young. Now Ottie's health isn't great. You got shot a few months ago, and Ryker had a frickin' *funeral*. Then the news-cast, the heart attack, Declan getting stabbed—all in one damn day! Life just keeps reminding me that it can take the people I love away from me whenever it wants."

She swallowed the lump in her throat. She did not want to cry.

"I don't want to love anyone else, only to lose them. I can't, River. I'm not strong enough."

River's eyes softened, then she was pulling Michele into her arms. "But you didn't lose me. Or Ryker. And you haven't lost Ottie or Declan." She pulled back, keeping a firm hold on Michele's shoulders. "And you are so much stronger than you know."

"What if I fall in love with him, only to have him die?"

River seemed to consider her words for a moment. "It's possible. None of us know how much time we have on this earth. That's why we need to live every day to the fullest. Make the decisions that scare us. Love the people who make us feel something." She cupped Michele's cheek in her hand. "I've seen the way you look at him. The way he looks at you. What you and Declan have is *real*. He's your person. And if you keep pushing him away, you won't have to wait for something to happen to him… You'll lose him right now."

She inhaled an anguished breath, letting her friend's words penetrate deep into her soul. "He's so easy to love. The longer I'm with him, the harder I'll fall. And the more it could hurt."

"Then you'll be one of those lucky people who gets to tell others about this epic love story you once lived."

Michele dropped the Dorito crumbs and tugged her friend close. This was exactly what she needed to hear. It was healing. "I don't know what I'd do without you."

"I don't know either, Chele. But lucky for you, you don't have to find out."

Michele chuckled.

When she pulled back, River smiled. "Want to watch a movie

and gorge on all this food like we used to? We could watch *Mean Girls* and throw Whoppers at Regina George whenever she comes on the screen."

As temping as that sounded… "Thank you. But I think I'm just going to go to bed early, if that's okay."

"Whatever you need, Chele. I'm gonna leave these snacks on the dresser, though, in case you get hungry."

"Good idea."

River kissed Michele's head before moving the food off the bed and leaving the room.

When the door closed, she called Pokey onto the bed and grabbed a book from her bag. But for once, she couldn't get into it. Her mind was moving a million miles a minute. And the thing that was right at the forefront…Declan's expression when she told him she needed space.

Her eyes closed. Pokey pushed his face into her side, and she opened her eyes, petting him. "Why can't life be simple, Pokes?"

She was just closing the book when her phone dinged from the bedside table. She reached over, and her heart gave a little thump when she saw who it was.

Declan: Just wanted to check that you're doing okay, honey. X

She rolled onto her side, taking a moment to figure out what to write. What do you write to a guy you'd all but pushed away just a few hours ago?

Michele: Hey…I'm okay. Just going to bed early.

Declan: Can I see you tomorrow?

Her eyes closed at his question. She hated herself for not giving Declan more in the way of explanation today. But her head had been a mess. *She'd* been a mess. She still was.

Michele: I'd like that.

Declan: Thank God.

Despite everything, she laughed at his response.

Declan: I'll see you tomorrow morning, honey. Sleep well. Xox

Her eyes grew wet again, but she wasn't sure why. Maybe because he was being so nice to her when she'd treated him so poorly. Maybe because she didn't feel deserving of this perfect man. Or maybe it was just everything.

Michele: Good night, Declan. xx

CHAPTER 20

$\mathcal{M}$ichele pulled on a pair of comfy blue jeans. The first thing on her to-do list for the day was to stop by the shop and pick up food for her uncle. Once she'd dropped it at the hospital, she needed to find Declan. What exactly she was going to say to him, she wasn't sure yet. Sorry for being a complete and utter mess? Sorry you had to save my life, get stabbed, and then have me about break up with you within a twenty-four-hour period?

Argh. She grabbed a T-shirt and pulled it over her head. Words would come to her. They had to.

She grabbed her phone and shot a quick glance at the screen. No messages from Declan this morning. Disappointment tried to skitter through her belly, but she shut it down. It was fine. She'd see him soon enough.

River's talk last night had been vital. Yes, she could be upset about her uncle. Yes, she could be scared and pissed off about Tim. But if there was anything good to have come out of the last few weeks, it was Declan. And she should be pulling all the good in her life closer, not pushing it away.

Jeepers. She wished she'd come to this epiphany earlier. But better late than never.

Blowing out a long breath, she moved to the door. She was just opening it when something from the window snagged her attention. A sound.

Glancing over her shoulder, she frowned. She stood there and waited for it to sound again but heard only silence.

You're fine, Michele. You're in a house with top-of-the-line security and a former Delta, and you have an FBI agent sitting in his car outside.

Hell, she was probably safer than ninety-nine percent of the population right now.

Shaking her head, she moved out of the bedroom. Maybe she would text Declan. Ask him to meet her somewhere. A café, perhaps?

She was pulling out her phone and stepping into the kitchen when her feet slammed to a stop. She'd expected to see River. Maybe Jackson. Not a devastatingly handsome Declan standing by the kitchen window, hands shoved into his pockets and biceps looking ridiculously thick. Then there was his hair. It had this windswept thing going on that made her want to rush over and run her fingers through it.

"What are you doing here?" she asked quietly.

When he looked at her, there was no smile on his face. If anything, he looked like he was assessing her. Studying her. "I asked River and Jackson if I could come over." The side of his mouth tilted up, and a fraction of her nerves disintegrated. "I thought they'd stay, but the second I got here, River pulled Jackson out of the house."

Of course she did. "River thinks you're my person."

His features heated, his eyes shifting from caramel brown to almost onyx black. "Your person. I like that." He took a step forward. "What do *you* think?"

"I think..." She wet her lips. "Would you like a coffee?"

She definitely needed coffee before she spoke big, important words.

She moved around the island, keeping a wide berth from the man and heading straight to the coffee machine. She was more familiar with River's kitchen than River herself.

She grabbed a pod from the jar, ignoring the slight tremble in her hand. Once the pod was in, she tried to close the lid. She tried three times before a warm chest pressed to her back and a thick arm curved around her. He adjusted the pod, then his hand slipped over hers and closed the lid.

For a moment, neither of them moved. Declan's hand remained firmly on hers, his chest as close as ever. The man surrounded her. It should be suffocating. It wasn't. It was the opposite.

When his other hand touched her hip and his mouth lowered to her neck, her eyes closed...and she realized something she should have known yesterday. Something that had been whispering inside her heart, snaking its way into her mind.

"It's too late," she whispered.

The muscles in his arm around her tensed. "What's too late, honey?"

Slowly, she turned, forcing herself to look up and meet those dangerously beautiful eyes of his. "I pushed you away because I was scared to love you. I didn't want to love another person because it made me vulnerable. It gave me yet another person to lose."

His brows tugged together, but he remained silent, waiting to hear what came next.

She ran her hands over his chest. "But I just realized, it's too late anyway. I already love you."

～

DECLAN'S HEART gave one giant thud against his ribs. His eyes shuttered and his hands tightened on her hips. After a night of uncertainty about where he and Michele stood and what their future held, her words were everything he needed to hear. They were what allowed him to breathe his first easy breath since she walked away from him yesterday.

He opened his eyes. "I love you too, Michele. I didn't know what I'd find when I moved to this town, but you're the best surprise yet. You're everything I didn't know I needed. But I do. Need you. Last night, not knowing if you still wanted to be with me…"

It was worse than any fear he'd felt on any mission as a Delta.

Pain flashed in her eyes. "I'm sorry. Everything just caught up with me and I crashed. The introvert in me was scared, and I just needed to be alone. I should have tried harder to articulate my feelings."

"You don't need to apologize. These last few weeks have been a lot, especially the last couple of days. But I swear to you, I will do everything in my power to ensure your safety."

He needed her too damn much to lose her.

He lifted a hand to her cheek. "God, I love you."

Before she could respond, he lowered his head and kissed her. This. This was exactly what he needed. What he'd been suffocating without. There'd been so much uncertainty in his chest over the last fourteen hours. He'd hated every second of it.

He swiped his lips across hers, letting the kiss soothe the jagged edges of his soul. Her hands grazed the hard ridges of his chest, grabbing onto the material of his shirt. He loved her touch. He craved it. Hell, he craved all of her.

Finally, he lifted his head. "I'll take you to the hospital to see your uncle. Do you have to work after?"

He didn't plan to leave her for a second.

She shook her head. "No, I scheduled today off. I can do some admin work at Mercy Ring, though, if you want to work. You took yesterday off for me. I don't want you missing too much."

Perfect. The woman was perfect.

He was just opening his mouth to say something when Pokey's growl sounded from the back of the house.

Michele frowned. "No one else is here. Why would Pokey be growling?"

She went to take a step, but his fingers tightened on her hip, keeping her where she was. "I'll go first. Stay behind me." His hand slipped down to hers, while he used the other to grab the gun from his concealed holster. They moved slowly down the hall.

Pokey was still growling as they stepped inside the spare bedroom. And the second his gaze rose, Declan saw why.

Stuck to the outside of the window was a single black rose and a folded piece of paper.

Motherfucker. The asshole had been in her backyard—right outside where she slept.

Michele's fingers tightened around his. "Oh my God! I heard a noise as I was leaving the room. It had to be him."

Declan saw red. But he pushed the anger down, keeping himself in check. Barely. "Stay here."

He released her hand and moved forward. He glanced out the window. No one. No one he could see, at least. He was moments from turning when he saw them. Prints in the dirt, leading to the back wall of the fence.

Goddammit!

Cursing under his breath, he walked back to her, took her hand, and led her to the front door. The second they were outside, his gaze shot to the FBI agent sitting in his car. When the guy saw the gun in Declan's hand, he was out of his car and across the street in seconds. "What happened?"

"Someone stuck a rose and a note on the outside of the

window to the room Michele slept in last night. There are prints in the dirt leading to the back fence."

The agent took off. Declan followed but at a slower pace, his hand never leaving Michele's. When they reached the backyard, the agent was already jumping the fence and disappearing.

Declan scanned the area, making sure no one was there, then he holstered his weapon and moved to the window. He tugged down the note and opened it. Inside was a messy scrawl, like it had been written in a rush.

I'll get my fourth date, Michele. One way or another, we will finish this.

Finish this.

The words had the blood pumping even faster through his veins.

Michele's breaths were loud beside him. Shit. Quickly, he folded the note and slipped it into his pocket before turning to her. "He *wants* you scared. Don't let him have that."

She glanced back at the window, and suddenly, rather than scared, she looked furious. "I hate this. I hate *him*! Why won't he just leave me the hell alone?"

Both his hands touched her face. "Because he's deranged. He needs to be locked away from people." Far away, where he couldn't touch another soul.

She nodded, but there was still the thread of anger in her eyes. When her phone rang, she tugged it from her pocket.

"Hello?"

She was silent as she listened to the other person. Then a frown tugged at her brows.

Fuck. What the hell *now*?

She hung up. "That was my super. There was a break-in at his office a couple of weeks ago. He didn't think anything was stolen, but this morning he did an audit on the keys and realized mine was the only one missing." She swallowed. "Tim was probably in my apartment the day my tire was slashed. And if Pokey hadn't been with me..."

Declan wanted to rage. He wanted to turn and ram his fist into the wall. Instead, he pulled her against his chest. "I'll say it as many times as you need me to, Chele. Nothing is going to happen to you. Not on my watch."

CHAPTER 21

*D*eclan's fist hit air as Ryker dodged the jab. Declan went again, this time throwing in an uppercut at the end. The uppercut grazed the side of Ryker's head, but his friend didn't even pause, instead countering with a right hook of his own. Declan dodged, remaining light on his toes as he circled.

He needed to be in the ring right now like he needed air to breathe. He needed the outlet for his anger. A place to direct his frustration. Tim had gotten too close yesterday morning. Leaving a note on the bedroom window where she'd fucking slept?

Ryker threw another jab, and Declan shifted his head, missing the hit and throwing a hook. It caught Ryker's cheek. The guy's head snapped back.

Declan stopped. "Dammit. Sorry."

Ryker spat blood onto the floor. "Why are you apologizing? We're in the ring. You got me fair and square."

Yeah, but they were only sparring.

Ryker tugged the gloves from his hands. "Is this anger about the note and flower Tim left yesterday?"

Even hearing the guy's name on his friend's lips was like a kick to the gut. "It's about everything. He shouldn't have gotten

172

so close. Hell, he shouldn't have had the balls to walk up to a house with a former Delta inside and an FBI agent out front."

It proved he was stupid but fearless. That was a dangerous combination.

"At least the FBI matched his handwriting and caught his face on the neighbor's cameras. It was definitely him. Everyone in the state has his picture. He won't be able to do much more than breathe without being recognized."

Didn't stop the tangled unease from poisoning his gut. "I feel better now that she's at our place."

She'd slept in his bed last night. The house had been alarmed, and Ryker and Cole had been under the same roof. It didn't get much safer than that.

Ryker nodded. The side of his face was red, and his lip was still bleeding.

Damn, he was an asshole.

The door to the gym opened and Anthony stepped in. He'd been a pretty quiet addition to their house. They'd contacted his grandmother shortly after he'd moved in, and the woman didn't give a shit about where her grandson had been. In fact, she'd told them she was glad he was gone.

Anthony stopped just outside the ring, shooting his gaze between them. "Is it okay that I'm here?"

Ryker walked up to the rope. "Drop your bag. I have one more round with this guy, then you're up."

Anthony nodded, as usual, not breaking a smile. The kid took a step toward the locker room, then stopped and turned. "Is Michele coming in?"

Declan nodded. "Yeah, she's just finishing up in the shop. You didn't work with her today?"

"Nah, she had a slow day. Said she didn't need me."

"Why do you want to see her?"

Anthony swallowed. "Just to ask about the shifts next week."

Before Declan could respond, Anthony walked away.

A punch in the shoulder had Declan turning back to his friend.

Ryker tilted his chin. "Let's go. No holding back this time."

Declan raised a brow. "You think I was holding back?"

"I know you were."

"You don't want the full force of what I'm feeling right now." No one did.

"Try me." When Declan hesitated, Ryker lifted a brow. "That's what this place is all about, remember? Now let's do this."

He lifted his fists. "Don't say I didn't warn you."

"You doing okay, Chele?"

Michele lifted a shoulder at Jackson's question. "Better than I was. Uncle Ottie should be out of the hospital soon, so that's a relief." She smiled at him. "Thank you for spending the afternoon with me."

She gave the counter one last wipe before rinsing the cloth and putting it away.

Jackson had shown up at the shop, all but kicking Declan out and telling him to get to Mercy Ring. Something quiet had passed between them. Unspoken words of agreement that he needed to be there.

"So I wasn't a terrible Declan substitute?"

She bumped his shoulder as she walked past. "You know you're awesome. And I'm so happy for you and River. You two were always going to happen. It was only a matter of time." She paused. "Is she really doing okay after being shot? She tells me she is, but sometimes…"

"She tells people she's okay when she isn't?"

Michele laughed. "Yeah, that."

Jackson held open the door for her. "I think in this scenario, having her brother back overshadows any bullet wound."

Michele smiled as she turned off the lights and stepped through the door Jackson held for her. "It's having you too, Jackson. You make her happy."

"Well, the woman may drive me crazy, but now that I have her, there's no way I'm letting her go."

Michele wanted to sigh at his words. River had loved Jackson since she was a teenager. So the fact they'd finally found their way to each other... It was everything. "I'm so happy for you both."

"Thanks." He shoved his hands into his pockets as they walked down the street. "You said Ottie should be getting out soon?"

"In a couple of days. I told him I'm going to be a thorn in his side."

Jackson chuckled. "He's lucky to have you. I'm sure the man won't be going hungry."

"Nope. I've already filled his fridge and freezer. Not sure he'll love what I've filled it *with*. There's not an unhealthy food item in sight."

"The man adores you. He'll eat whatever you make."

She smiled. Jackson was easy to talk to. She'd always liked the guy. Not in the same way as River. Heck, no one liked him like her. But he was awesome company.

When they reached Mercy Ring, Jackson held the door again and she stepped inside. There were a couple of guys hitting bags to one side of the ring, but it was the person *inside* the ring who really caught her attention. Declan. Hot and sweaty. His muscles rippling with every movement.

God, the man was lethal. Ryker too. Every punch they threw made her want to shudder with the thought of them landing. They rarely did, though; both men almost looked like they anticipated the other's move before it was made.

Jackson squeezed her shoulder. "I'm just gonna check on the kids."

Michele nodded, only glancing at Jackson briefly before

turning her attention back to Declan. Was this what the unspoken conversation was about between him and Jackson this morning? That he needed to get into the ring? Did sparring help him?

He threw another punch, and there it was, more rippling of thick, corded muscles in his upper body.

Water. She needed water.

Dragging her gaze away, she moved across the room to the kitchen. She was just about to walk inside when Anthony walked out and collided with her. He had a bottle of water in his hand.

"Shit! Sorry, Chele."

She smiled, secretly thrilled that he'd used her nickname for the first time. That meant she was growing on him, right? "That's okay. Have a good day off?"

He lifted a shoulder. "Haven't done much."

His gaze flickered to the side, then behind her, before moving back to her. And there it was again. That familiar feeling that he wasn't telling her something.

"I've been meaning to mention," she said quietly, "there are some great online courses that allow you to get your high school diploma. If that's something you want."

He frowned. "Why would I want that?"

She lifted a shoulder. "Maybe you don't. But if you do, even a little bit, I'd be happy to help you. You could even do some of your work in the shop between tasks if losing income is something you're worried about."

Anthony looked taken back by the offer. "Um...thanks. I'll think about it."

Her smile grew. She may not have known him for very long, but she wanted him to succeed. He was a good kid who'd had a tough run. Everyone needed someone in their corner to help them.

"Great." She started to step around him, but he touched her arm.

"Before you go, I just wanted to check on how you're doing. You know, because of that asshole Tim being after you and everything." Anthony's eyes darkened when he said the guy's name. It kind of reminded her of when Declan said the man's name.

Her voice lowered. "I'm doing okay. Probably as good as I can be when a serial killer has me in his sights."

Anthony nodded. "So nothing else has happened?"

Michele frowned, not sure how to take the hard edge to Anthony's voice. "Um, there *was* something. A black rose and a note were stuck to the bedroom window at River's house the morning after I stayed there. The FBI followed the footprints he left in the dirt but couldn't find him."

Anthony's eyes narrowed. "Why couldn't Declan track him? Wouldn't he have learned that stuff in the military?"

"He stayed with me. Tim was already gone anyway."

Anthony's jaw clenched.

She stepped closer. "Are you okay?"

"So what's the plan? Are the FBI using you as bait to set up a sting?"

Her brows rose. "No. The guys are going to make sure they stick with me, and an FBI agent will remain outside the house so I'm safe."

Anthony's features darkened again. Suddenly, he grabbed her arm. "That's it? This man is *killing* women. He needs to be caught and have a fucking knife stabbed into his chest! He needs to pay for what he's done!" Anthony's fingers tightened on her arm.

"Anthony, let go. You're hurting me."

It was like he didn't hear her. "*You* can end this. You need to tell me you're doing more! Tell me you're going to do something to find him."

"Anthony!" She pressed her hands to his chest…and felt something inside his jacket. Wait. Was that…? "Do you have a gun?"

"Hey!"

She shot a look over her shoulder at Declan's hard tone. He and Ryker had stopped sparring, and both of them were watching the exchange between her and Anthony. So was Jackson. They all looked ready to race over and shove Anthony away from her.

Anthony's hand dropped and he took a step back. The look on his face... It was as if he couldn't believe what he'd just done.

Her arm would be bruised, but she ignored the dull throb, trying for a reassuring smile toward the guys. "It's okay."

At the sound of Anthony's footsteps, she swung her head back toward him as he disappeared into the kitchen.

"Anthony, wait!"

He didn't. He unlatched the back door and went outside.

She moved fast to catch up to him. "You're sixteen years old. Where did you get a gun?"

He didn't so much as pause, instead continuing into the parking lot.

"Anthony, tell me what's going on. Let me help you!"

When Anthony suddenly stopped, she collided with his back. She stepped to his side to find him frowning at something. She followed his gaze—and a puff of air slipped from her lips.

Was that...

Suddenly, Anthony was sprinting.

"No! Anthony, stop!"

Shit!

It was Tim, crouched behind a car on the road behind the parking lot. And Anthony was going after him with a gun! She started to give chase but didn't get three steps before Declan wrapped an arm around her waist, while Jackson and Ryker raced past her, running after Anthony.

"What the hell's going on?" Declan asked, his voice laced with anger. "Where's he going?"

She waved in the direction he'd run off. "Tim was behind a car! Anthony took off after him."

Declan's eyes turned to steel, and the arm around her tightened. "Tim's here?"

She nodded. "Yes, and Anthony has a *gun*. I felt it under his coat."

His gaze flew to where his friends had gone, then back to her. His hand slid down her arm, stopping at the spot where Anthony had grabbed her. "Is this from him?"

She looked down. Crap. She was wearing a short-sleeve T-shirt, and there were very visible red fingerprints from where Anthony had grabbed her. "It's nothing."

His gaze lifted to hers again, his eyes dark and deadly. His voice quieted. "It's Anthony's *handprint*."

She swallowed, her gaze almost involuntarily skirting in the direction everyone had run. When she looked back to Declan, he looked ready to kill.

"He wasn't himself," she said quietly, feeling an inexplicable need to protect the boy. "He was asking about Tim and what I'm doing to help bring him down. When I said nothing, he got upset."

Upset being a massive understatement.

"He bruised you. I'm going to kill him!"

"No!" She touched his arm. "Declan, he's a kid. He has a gun. He ran away from home, and he's clearly hiding something. He needs our help."

"He *hurt* you," Declan said through gritted teeth.

"He didn't mean to." She was certain. "Please, Declan!"

His jaw worked. "Fine—but he tells us what's going on, and he tells us today. And if he touches you again, I'm really *am* gonna kill him, kid or not."

CHAPTER 22

"*E*xplain." Declan was barely holding himself in check. All he could see were the red marks on Michele's arms. They were at his house, and she'd pulled on a sweater, but he remembered exactly what they looked like. "And this time, you're going to tell us the full story, not just the parts you feel like sharing. Starting with—where the hell does a sixteen-year-old get a gun?"

He caught every little emotion that washed over the kid's face. Guilt. Regret. But also that same seething anger he'd had on his face since the day he arrived in town.

Declan stood in front of the couch Anthony sat on, while Cole leaned against a wall with Ryker beside him. Michele was perched on a different couch.

"I found it in my grandmother's sock drawer, and I took it," Anthony finally admitted.

"Why would you need a gun?" Ryker asked.

Anthony's gaze shot to Ryker, and fire danced in his eyes. "So I can shoot the bastard who stabbed my sister!"

Michele gasped. "Stabbed? You said your sister was beaten to death."

Anthony's chest moved up and down rapidly, like he was barely holding himself together. "I lied. I knew you'd figure out the real reason I was here if I told you the truth and then you'd send me back to live with my grandmother."

"And what's the real reason?" Michele asked quietly.

"To find and murder the Washington serial killer."

The room fell into a heavy silence.

Anthony's jaw ticked as he glanced out the window. "My sister, Alana, went on four dates with the guy. I even met him at the door one time. On their fourth date, I was out with friends. It wasn't until I got home that I found her…"

Jesus. The kid had found his dead sister.

"Alana Garcia," Michele breathed. "I remember seeing her picture on the news." Pain laced her words. "I'm so sorry," she whispered, moving to stand near Anthony.

For a second, the kid's eyes misted. Then his jaw turned to granite, and he blinked. "I came here because the last few murders were in towns surrounding this one, and I don't know, I just had this gut feeling that here was where I needed to be. I didn't have a plan, other than to bring a gun. I just… I had to *do* something! I couldn't just stay at home and accept that this asshole was still out there after he'd killed my sister!"

Below the guilt and the anger, Declan saw his desperation. To avenge his sister's death? To ease some misguided sense of guilt?

"That day I didn't show up for my shift, I was leaving Mercy Ring when I saw Declan reading the paper. There was an article on him and it said—"

"He was driving a light blue Honda," Declan finished.

The kid nodded.

"And what was your plan today?" Cole asked. "Shoot him and get yourself sent to prison?"

Anthony's eyes darkened. "It would have been worth it. He needs to die for what he did."

"He does," Declan agreed. "But you need to be smart. And what you did today wasn't smart."

Suddenly, Anthony was on his feet. "I don't *want* to be smart! All I want is to see that fucker rotting in the ground! He took my sister from me, the one good person I had in my life, and I want to kill him for that! I want to kill him like he killed *her*!"

The kid was shaking with rage and grief.

Declan stepped forward. "Believe me when I say, the man's going to die. But a sixteen-year-old chasing him down the street with a stolen gun is not the way to achieve that."

Anthony's voice shook. "Then what are we supposed to do? Just wait and watch as he kills a dozen more women? More sisters and daughters? Maybe even mothers? Michele could draw him out, but she won't!"

Michele flinched where she stood.

Declan took a small step forward, and his voice lowered. "You're grieving, so I understand that your head's a mess right now. But Michele's given you a job and helped you in ways others wouldn't have. Expecting her to put her life on the line is no way to repay her."

Anthony opened his mouth to speak, but Declan continued before he could.

"Michele has no responsibility to risk her life to end this. Anything Tim does is firmly on *him*." He paused, letting that soak in for a second. "The only thing we're *supposed* to do is let the police and the FBI do their jobs and catch this guy. Which they will."

For a moment, the kid remained silent, his chest once again rising and falling in quick succession. Then he turned, moving toward the stairs.

Declan snagged his wrist. "I don't want to see you pulling the shit you pulled today ever again. He's not worth a life sentence. Got it?"

Another grinding of his teeth. "Got it."

The second Anthony disappeared, Declan scrubbed a hand through his hair.

Cole pushed off the wall. "Well, that makes me want to kill this asshole even more."

"No shit," Declan muttered. His gaze skirted over to Michele. She was still watching the back of Anthony as he moved up the stairs, her bottom lip between her teeth.

Was his jab about her not doing anything upsetting to her?

He moved over to her, urging her to sit, before crouching to his haunches and putting his hands on her knees. "He's grieving, Chele. Don't listen to his accusation."

Slowly, she drew her gaze to his. Her eyes held sheer pain. "But he's right. This guy clearly wants me. I could use that to end this. The longer it takes to find him, the more women will die."

"Michele. The man knows you're working with the FBI. Even if we wanted to"—which Declan sure as hell didn't—"a setup won't work because he'd be smart enough to recognize one."

That lower lip slipped between her teeth again, and a crease formed in her brow. "But couldn't we do *something*? Maybe we could ease up on the guards. Like lose the FBI agent. Make it look like I'm less protected so he makes an attempt."

His chest clenched at the thought. "What you're suggesting wouldn't just make it *look* like you're less protected. It would *make* you less protected. You'd be at a greater risk. I'm not willing to risk you, Michele."

"But Declan—"

"No." It was that simple.

In much the same way as Anthony's had, her jaw clenched.

"He's right, Chele," Ryker said quietly from where he stood. "The FBI will find him. And in the meantime, his photo is out there being blasted on every news report, social media platform and newspaper. It won't be long before he's caught."

Her gaze slid back to the top of the stairs one more time

before returning to Declan and Ryker. She nodded…but he knew it didn't mean she agreed.

~

"WHERE ARE YOU TAKING THAT?"

Michele stopped at Declan's words. Oh, and at his giant frame standing in front of her, blocking her way out of the kitchen as she held a plate of cookies. "To Anthony."

"I don't know if the kid wants company right now, Chele."

"I'll just leave them in his room, then." But she was hoping he'd at least hear what she had to say.

Declan sighed.

She pressed a hand to his chest. "I know what you're thinking. That he's going to say something to make me feel guilty again."

"That's exactly what I'm thinking. And I haven't forgotten those bruises on your arm."

He swiped her upper arm, and her skin tingled.

"He's a kid," she said quietly. "He lost the only person in the world he cared about. I know what that's like. I want him to know I'm here for him if he needs someone to talk to."

There was a beat of silence before he spoke again. "Fine. But don't be gone long." He lowered his head and pressed a kiss to her lips. "Or I'm coming to find you."

That didn't sound so terrible. She hummed against his mouth. "Deal."

When she walked past him, his hand tapped her butt, and she chuckled as she moved up the stairs. It felt good to laugh.

The smile slipped when she reached Anthony's closed bedroom door. She took a moment to suck in a large breath before knocking.

"Yeah?"

She wet her lips. "It's me. Chele. I made some cookies for you. I thought we could have a chat."

A moment of pause. "Could we do it later?"

She'd been expecting that. She wasn't giving up that easily, though. She took a small step closer. "Please, Anthony. I'll be quick. I promise."

Another beat of heavy silence. Then he spoke again. "Fine."

Victory. Slowly, she slid the door open and stepped into the almost empty room. There was only a suitcase on a chair and the bed that Anthony was lying on, his phone in his hand. He looked about as far from wanting to talk to her as possible.

Well, too bad. She had words to say.

Quickly, she closed the door and moved to the bed, perching on the edge and setting the plate beside him. "These are my emergency cookies. A special recipe I save for dire situations."

One of Anthony's brows lifted. "Is this a dire situation?"

"I think so." She darted her gaze between his eyes. "My dad baked these for me the week my mom died."

Something flickered in Anthony's eyes, but he remained silent.

"Then, at my request, my uncle helped me bake them when my dad had a heart attack and then again when he died a few days later. Now, whenever my world crashes down around me, I either want a book or a wooden spoon in my hand." She traced the edge of the plate with her finger. "I think it's the escape. Or maybe it's that I finally feel like I have control over something."

She paused, considering her next words. "I couldn't talk about what my parents' deaths did to me for a long time. Whenever someone tried to get me to talk, I'd just…shut down."

Still, Anthony remained quiet. But his gaze… It held hers like she was a lifeline. Like he was taking in every little thing she said.

"My uncle Ottie was amazing. It was like he knew what I needed. He'd sit with me in silence. Occasionally, he'd fill the silence with talk about everything and nothing. But not once did he force words from me that I wasn't ready to speak."

Her uncle had saved her in so many ways. Wetness filled her eyes at the memory, but not enough for tears to fall.

"Something he did that really helped," she continued, "was making sure I knew that when the time came when I *did* want to talk about it, he would be there. An ear to listen. A shoulder to cry on. And that was everything to me. It was safety."

Just like in the living room, Anthony's breaths turned rapid, like he was trying to hold himself together.

"So, Anthony, I want you to know that I'm here. To sit in silence. To listen. Or to be a shoulder for you to cry on. I'm whatever you need. Because I know the pain of losing your whole world. You feel alone and angry and like nothing is safe anymore. Everyone deserves someone to be there for them in their time of pain."

She gave Anthony a moment to speak or respond or nod. When he did none of those things, she gave a slow nod and rose to her feet.

She'd just reached the door when his voice stopped her.

"She was eight years older than me, and she was more of a mother than our real one ever was." Michele turned, seeing the turmoil in Anthony's eyes. It was like a storm brewed there. "She was the person who made sure I had food to eat every day. She cleaned my clothes so I didn't go to school dirty. She made me feel loved. She protected me." There was a heavy pause. "But I didn't protect her."

When his eyes filled with tears, she crossed the room and pulled him into her arms.

"It wasn't your job to protect her," she whispered. "Your job was to be her little brother."

Anthony's arms went around her, and she felt tears wet her shoulder. Tears she had a feeling were long overdue. She held him tightly, wanting to hold his world together, even though she knew she couldn't.

Anthony's tears brought fresh wetness to her own eyes. She

held it in, but only just. She wanted to cry for his pain, his loss and the injustice.

When she finally pulled back, she kept her hands on his shoulders.

"I just wish I could have been what she needed when she needed it," he whispered. "Like she was for me."

She held his cheek. "It took me a long time to realize that we can't always protect the people in our lives. We can only love them. And I have a feeling she knew you loved her." She pushed a lock of hair from his forehead. "She would want you to be happy. To live your life."

He dragged in a long breath and nodded. "I don't know how to do that without her."

"It'll get easier. Life will never be what it was before you lost her. But one day, you'll have moments when her memory won't cause you so much pain."

He looked down at his lap, nodding.

"Anytime you need anything, you come to me. And when I go back to my place, you're welcome to stay if you get sick of these guys." He chuckled softly. "And if you want to get a different job or go back to school, I'll support you in any way I can."

They may not have known each other for long or still even know each other well, but this kid needed a person. And she wanted to be that person.

He lifted his head. "Thank you."

CHAPTER 23

*M*ichele glanced up from her book to see Cole walk past the couch and head into the kitchen. It was midafternoon and she'd been reading for at least an hour. Ever since Declan had popped into the back room for a workout. Apparently, you still needed your own workout room with a bag, even when you owned and ran a boxing club.

The funny part was, he'd asked if she wanted to join him. Hmm, sweat her face off in a gym and possibly pass out, or get comfy on the couch with a book boyfriend? She'd wanted to tell him it was a tough decision, but she wasn't that good at lying.

Pokey rose from where he sat at her feet and plodded into the kitchen. Cole bent down and gave him a pat. Michele smiled at the way Pokey nuzzled into his hand. Pokey loved affection, and it appeared, where dogs were concerned at least, Cole liked to give it.

He opened the fridge and stuck his head in for a moment before tugging it back out.

Michele snapped her book shut and headed into the kitchen. "Want to help me make some sticky buns?"

Cole frowned as he faced her. "Sticky buns?"

"Mm-hmm. I don't mean to toot my own horn, but whenever I make these for my customers, they die. Literally, drop to the floor in awe."

Cole raised a brow.

"Okay, maybe not actually die, but everyone raves about them."

She rolled up her sleeves. Cole was still looking at her like she was promising rainbows when there wasn't even rain. He leaned his hip against the counter. "I doubt we have the ingredients."

A smile tilted her lips as she opened the pantry door and grabbed what she needed before placing everything on the island. "Actually, Dec and I went to the store this morning, and I grabbed all the ingredients."

"Why would you do that?"

Next, she opened the fridge. "Because I wanted to make something nice for you guys to say thank you for letting me stay. And because I love to be in the kitchen." She tossed a smile over her shoulder. "Cooking's my love language."

She was just turning with the milk and butter when Cole was there, taking the ingredients from her hands. "Love language?"

"Yeah, there are five. Words of affirmation, gift giving, giving quality time, acts of service and..." It took her a moment to remember the last one. "Physical touch. Which is yours?"

He shook his head. "I don't have one."

"Everyone has one."

"Sorry to disappoint you, but not me."

She sighed. He was like a big, grumpy bear. "Come on, I'll show you how to make these. Maybe you can share *my* love language."

"Doubtful."

"But not out of the question?"

She got a half smile. That was a win in her mind.

Out of all four of the guys, she found Cole the most reserved. He seemed to have a tough exterior and gave very little of himself away. But then, she'd known Ryker and Jackson for a long time, and she was dating Declan, so it shouldn't really surprise her that she knew Cole the least.

She kind of expected him to say no to the whole making-sticky-buns thing. So it surprised the heck out of her when he nodded.

"Great. Okay. Can you warm up half a cup of water? We need to dissolve some yeast into it."

As they worked, she gave Cole instructions, all of which he followed to a T. He didn't give her many words, but he was a good listener. More than once, she saw his gaze flick out the window to the house across the street, almost like he was looking for someone.

When he suddenly stopped kneading the dough and went still, she followed his gaze to see a woman in front of the house. She was on the phone and had a pained expression on her face.

Cole never took his eyes off her. Not while she talked. Not while she walked around her lawn, running a hand through her hair. Not even when she looked up at the sky like God was spiting her or something. He didn't continue with the dough until the woman was back inside her house.

Michele cleared her throat. "Have you spoken to her? Apart from that day she came over, of course."

"Why would I do that?"

Michele could have laughed. *Ah, maybe because you're staring at the woman like she's all you see.* Instead of saying that, she lifted a shoulder. "Might be nice to get to know your neighbors. It seems like a great street."

"I don't need to know my neighbors."

Fair enough. "Does she live there by herself?"

He shook his head. "A teenage boy also lives there. Her brother maybe?"

She measured out some butter. "Well, I think you should go

introduce yourself. Maybe you could take her some of these sticky buns."

He laughed. The sound was deep and rumbly. "I don't do that."

Michele frowned. "Do what? Be a friendly neighbor?"

"Introduce myself to neighbors with baked goods."

Oh, yeah, that would be way too polite. She almost laughed. "Okay, that's probably enough kneading. Can you roll out the dough and spread this butter on top?"

He started dividing it while she poured some sugar and cinnamon into a small bowl.

"Why don't you believe in happily ever afters?" The question was out before she could stop herself.

His brow lifted, and he almost looked amused. "You remember the happily ever after comment, huh?"

"Of course." The guy had said it a few months ago in River's kitchen, and Michele had wondered about it ever since.

He angled his body to face her, ignoring the dough altogether. "When I said I didn't believe in happily ever after, it was in regard to River trying to set me up with someone."

Michele frowned. "So, it wasn't happiness in general you were talking about, but—"

"The idea that love is what gets you there. I've seen love result in tragedy more than happiness."

Her stomach did a little roll. "What tragedy have you seen as a result of love?"

He shook his head and went back to the dough. "It doesn't matter."

Michele's lips turned down. In just that one comment, her heart hurt for the man. She knew he hooked up with women occasionally, from stories she'd overheard from the guys. But to close yourself off from love and anything long term? *That* was the tragedy.

"Who taught you that?" she asked quietly.

"Everyone." His response was instant, without a single shred of hesitation. "Now, let's get back to baking these buns."

DECLAN STEPPED out of the shower. The smell of sugar and cinnamon hit him right in the face. Michele was baking. Why did the thought of her baking something sweet have his dick twitching?

He tugged on some briefs and sweatpants and went into the hall. On the way, he passed Anthony's room and was about to knock when the door pulled open, Anthony on the other side. He was wearing jeans and a black T-shirt.

Anthony frowned. "Hey."

"You going out?" He'd become so used to seeing the kid on the bed with his phone the last few days, seeing him up and about was a surprise.

"Yeah. I've been messaging some people from the local school. Thought I might catch up with them tonight."

Whatever he'd been expecting the kid to say, it wasn't that. "The local school?"

He lifted a shoulder. "Chele was saying if I wanted to get my high school diploma, she'd help me. It's something I'm thinking about. But even if I wasn't, getting to know other kids my age wouldn't hurt."

God, his woman was amazing. "That sounds great."

He dipped his head before moving out of the room. They walked down the stairs together, and the kid said a quick goodbye before he disappeared out the front door.

When Declan turned his head, a laugh burst from his chest. Was that Cole, slicing dough? He moved into the kitchen, squinting his eyes like they were playing tricks on him. Whatever they were making smelled even better up close.

He moved behind Michele and slipped his arms around her

waist. She was mixing up some sort of syrup that smelled sweet as hell. Or maybe that was her. "Whatever this is, it smells amazing."

She melted back a little bit into his hold. "Cole and I are making sticky buns."

"So my eyes *aren't* playing tricks on me." Declan lifted a brow at his friend. He'd never seen the guy bake a thing in his life, and they'd known each other a long damn time. "You just need an apron, and we can start calling you Julia Child."

Michele elbowed him lightly in the stomach. "Don't poke fun at him. He's been super helpful."

One side of Cole's mouth lifted. "The asshole's just jealous because you taught me to bake and not him."

Yeah, he was. Anyone who got to spend one-on-one time with his woman made him jealous. "You're lucky you're making baked treats for me."

"Who says they're for you?" Cole asked.

His fingers grazed Michele's belly. "Something tells me I'll get some."

Michele grabbed his hand, stilling his movements. "Only if you play your cards right."

He nuzzled her neck. "Don't I always?"

Cole shook his head, moving to the sink and washing his hands. "All right, I'm out. I might go to Mercy Ring for a bit. I think Ryker's already there."

Declan chuckled. "A kiss too much for you to handle?"

"Nope. But you are."

Declan laughed again.

Cole's gaze shot to the dough, then to Declan. "There'd better be some left when I get back."

"Sorry, no promises."

He got another whack in the gut from Michele. The second his friend was gone, he nuzzled her neck again. "You're very violent today."

She hummed. "You need to stop."

Nope. Not enough conviction in her words. He nuzzled her again.

"I need to get this syrup and dough into the pan so they can bake."

"I'm too impatient." Even the promise of sticky buns didn't feel worth it.

His hands crept beneath her shirt while his mouth trailed down her shoulder. But when footsteps sounded on the stairs, she pulled out of his hold.

Cole opened the front door before pausing to look at Declan and Michele. "Be back in a couple hours. Feel free to get this PDA stuff out of your system while I'm gone."

"No promises." Absolutely none. Was "getting it out of his system" even possible?

When the door closed, Michele tried to move away, but Declan wrapped a hand around her wrist and tugged her back into him. "Finally, we have the house to ourselves."

He pushed some hair behind her shoulder and started kissing the warm skin of her neck yet again.

"Declan..." She breathed his name this time, her voice sounding more like a plea than the protest he was sure she was aiming for.

He pushed the shoulder of her T-shirt and the strap of her bra down, leaving a trail of kisses along her bare skin.

A ringing phone trilled through the silence.

"Ignore it," he whispered.

She slid out of his hold, and he almost groaned.

"It could be Uncle Ottie," she said as she lifted the phone and glanced at the screen.

He lifted a brow. "Is it?"

She turned away, lifting the phone to her ear. "Hi, Connie."

So, no. He moved over to the window, closing the blind so the agent on the street couldn't see inside the house.

"No, sorry, I'm not in today. But I can have meals ready for you in a couple days."

He walked up behind Michele and lifted her onto the kitchen counter before slipping between her thighs.

"Yes, that's not a problem." Her voice was a little breathless this time.

Declan leaned forward and pressed a kiss to her cheek, then her neck. His mouth trailed down, over her clothing, and when he reached her breast, he found her hard nipple, closing his lips around it, sucking her through her bra and shirt.

A gasp slipped from her lips. "Connie, I—"

His tongue flicked back and forth, while his fingers crept between her thighs and grazed her through her yoga pants.

Another gasp. "Yes. That's all fine. I'll talk to you later."

He sucked the nipple again, rubbing her harder through her pants.

She hung up the phone as Declan switched to her other breast, not trying to remove any of her clothes yet.

"Declan…" Another breathy murmur of his name. Fuck, he liked it.

He rubbed his thumb in a small circle, and she latched onto his shoulders.

He almost chuckled. "Yeah, honey?"

"I can't think when you're touching me."

His mouth trailed up her neck again, kissing behind her ear. "That's the point." He found her tight nipple with his hand, rolling it between his thumb and forefinger.

Her breaths became shallow and quick. "You don't want me thinking?"

"I want you completely and utterly *consumed* by me and everything I do to you."

"I'm already there."

His lips stretched into a smile against her skin. He lifted his head. Her eyes were glazed. "You have syrup on your cheek."

She frowned, scrubbing both her cheeks and looking at her hands. "No, I don't."

He grabbed the bowl and set it beside her. Then he dipped a finger in and trailed a line of syrup from her cheek all the way down to her shoulder.

Her lips separated. And when she lifted a hand, he grabbed it gently. Then his head dipped, and his lips closed around the syrup on her skin.

CHAPTER 24

*M*ichele's heart fluttered as Declan's mouth closed over her cheek, his tongue lapping at the syrup on her skin. Slowly, agonizingly so, his mouth followed the line of syrup down her shoulder, sucking up every little drop. Her body had already been in overdrive from his mouth on her nipples. From his grazes between her thighs.

When his hands went to the hem of her top, her skin tingled at the contact with her bare skin. Then the shirt was tugged over her head.

A ghost of a smile stretched his lips. He reached behind her, his thick arms pressing to her sides and fingers tickling her back before unlatching her bra. Cool air hit her breasts.

His eyes darkened. Then he dipped a finger and thumb into the bowl of syrup before switching and dipping his other hand. When she realized his plan, her belly flopped. His fingers found her nipples, rubbing the melted butter and sugar onto her tips. Her lips had barely parted when his mouth caught hers, his tongue plunging inside.

He tasted sweet, the syrup tingling across her tongue.

His fingers never slowed from their torturous circles and grazing on her peaks.

A low moan slipped from her chest and lava pooled between her thighs. She wanted to squirm under the onslaught, but at the same time, she needed to stay perfectly still. To surrender herself to everything this man had to offer.

Slowly, that mouth of his trailed down her cheek again, then her chest, before closing around her nipple. He sucked, and her back arched, an explosion of raw desire rippling inside her. It had the dull throb pounding to life.

His tongue licked and flicked her tight bud, sucking her nipple clean of the syrup. Then he was shifting over to her other breast, and the torture started all over again.

Her mind fogged. She barely noticed when his hands went to the waistband of her yoga pants.

"Lift up for me, honey." His breath brushed against her already sensitive peak, and she had to roll his words around in her head a few times to make sense of them. Then she did as he asked, pushing up as he pulled her yoga pants and panties away from her body and dropped them to the floor with the rest of her clothes.

At the back of her mind, she was vaguely aware that she should probably be concerned about being completely naked in a shared house. About an FBI agent sitting outside.

"What if…" Man, it was hard to speak right now. Thinking felt too hard. Oh God, his tongue was still moving against her, rolling over her nipple. She forced the words out. "What if someone walks in?"

"Cole and Ryker will be out for hours." More breaths brushing against her. "And Anthony's meeting some people."

Declan's fingers dipped back into the bowl. She barely had time to process what he was doing when wet fingers touched her core and rolled the warm syrup over her clit.

She cried out as every coherent thought left her head. Her

hips lifted from the counter and she wasn't sure if she was trying to get closer or away. It didn't matter. She didn't get anywhere, not with Declan's hand on her hip, keeping her rooted to the spot.

After a final swipe of her nipple, his mouth trailed down her ribs and stomach. Her lower abdomen warmed. Then he crouched down, and his mouth closed over her center and sucked. Her world grayed, and a loud, guttural cry left her lips.

He swirled his tongue around her clit, flicking her bud. Even the way his arms wrapped around her thighs, his thumbs grazing skin so close to her core, added to the torment.

Her head rolled from side to side as her breaths turned choppy.

Finally, those lips left her clit, but as his mouth trailed back up her stomach, his fingers touched her entrance. His mouth had just reached hers, his tongue slipping inside, when two fingers pressed into her.

A whimper tried to escape her mouth, but he swallowed it. Every thrust of his fingers was a ripple of wildfire throughout her body, and the thumb swirling against her clit made each thrust more intense.

She reached for the buckle of his jeans with desperate fingers, needing to touch him like he touched her. Needing to feel him in her palm. And the second she did, the second her fingers closed around his thickness, a hum slipped from her throat. It rivaled the growl from Declan.

She moved her hand from his base to his tip, reveling in the way his muscles strained. She explored him thoroughly, his length thickening in her hand and the veins in his neck cording.

It wasn't enough. She wanted more. With two hands to his chest, she pushed him back a step. Then she hopped off the island and lowered in front of him.

"Michele…" There was warning in his voice.

She ignored it and closed her lips around his tip.

Another growl, this time almost pained. She heard the creaking of the countertop as his fingers tightened around the edge. She swirled her tongue, tasting him. Sucking.

Knowing she could do this to him, bring such a powerful man to a standstill, made her greedy for more.

She pumped her hand at his base as she moved her mouth up and down his thickness. She'd barely begun when strong hands latched onto her arms, tugging her back onto the counter in one powerful move.

He pushed between her thighs. "I need you now." There was a quiet danger to his voice and an almost wild look in his eyes.

He inched in and then stopped. "I'm not wearing anything."

He started to pull out, but she grabbed his arm. "I'm clean, and this is a safe time of the month for me."

"I'm clean too. But are you sure?"

She wanted to feel the man bare inside her. She kissed him. "I'm sure."

A low moan slipped from his lips, then he slid inside her.

Oh God. The feel of him... It made her forget everything that came before this moment.

He slid his hands down her legs and lifted them around his waist.

Then he was thrusting. Long, deep thrusts that filled her so completely she could barely breathe. He leaned over her body, his mouth once again latching onto her neck, sucking. She groaned as her breasts bounced against his chest, the grazing of her nipples an added sensation that pushed her closer to the edge.

Her breaths grew heavier with each thrust, her skin heating and tingling.

Suddenly, he pushed her back onto the island, moving aside the sticky buns.

He leaned over her body and began thrusting again, now hitting her at a new angle. His front pressed against her as they kissed. At the same time, his hands found hers, fingers interlacing as he held her hands to the surface beside her head.

It was a symphony of sensations. His hard, deep thrusts, her nipples brushing his chest, Declan caging her against the counter.

His tongue began to thrust faster inside her mouth, claiming her. She held onto his hands like they were a lifeline. Like she'd drift away if she let go.

His mouth moved to her cheek, then her ear, nibbling on a sensitive spot she didn't even know existed.

Oh God, she felt him *everywhere*. Her breaths quickened, her heart pounding.

His mouth unlatched and his forehead touched hers, his thrusts unrelenting. "Fuck, you're everything."

Those gravelly words vibrated down her limbs, and that was it. Her body began to spasm. She threw her head back and arched into him.

Declan latched onto her nipple and kept thrusting, prolonging the orgasm. Then his forehead returned to hers, and he tensed and shuddered, his thickness pulsating inside her.

Minutes of heavy breathing passed. Of stillness. Moments where they both sucked in uneven gasps. Then, slowly, he slid out of her before lifting her up against his body. "God, I love you."

She wrapped her arms around his neck. "I love you too."

DECLAN GRAZED a finger down Michele's shoulder. The second they left the kitchen, he'd carried her to the shower, where he'd made her come apart a second time. After that, she'd insisted on remaking the syrup and finishing the sticky buns to get them into the oven. Then he'd carried her to the bedroom.

They still needed to have dinner and clean up the kitchen, but right now, he didn't want to be anywhere else.

Long minutes of quiet had passed. She'd started drawing

circles on his chest, grazing his bullet wound, leaving a trail of flames in her wake. And hell if it wasn't making his dick twitch again.

"You're quiet," he said softly.

Her hand paused. "Just thinking about some stuff Cole said."

He almost laughed. "Uh, baby, I don't know that I like you thinking about another guy while we're naked in bed together."

Best friend or not, the guy had no damn place here.

She glanced up. "No, not like that. He just…"

When she paused, Declan's brows drew together. "What?"

"He said some stuff about love ending in tragedy. It was sad."

Yep, that sounded like the cynical bastard. His friend had told him bits and pieces about his upbringing. About the relationship his mother and father had before his dad died. And about his sister.

He ran his finger up her shoulder this time. "I think it has to do with some family stuff. He lost his dad, and his sister's gone through some stuff."

Michele pulled in a sharp breath. "His dad died?"

"Yeah. They were particularly close. It affected him." Another stroke. "Don't let anything he says get to you."

The guy would never say it to discourage anyone else. In fact, he was surprised Cole had said anything to Michele at all.

"I won't. I just feel sorry for him. He's closing himself off from the possibility of love. It's sad."

He could see how someone like Michele, a woman who filled her head with love stories, would find Cole's stance tragic.

He rolled her to her back. "Maybe one day"—he pressed a kiss to her neck—"he'll find a woman who will change everything." She hummed as he eased more of his weight onto her, her nipples hardening against his chest. "Like you did for me."

A long breath released from her chest. "I changed everything?"

"Yep. I've always been open to love"—another press of his lips—"but finding it… That's been another matter completely."

He sucked her neck, and she'd just started purring when a knock sounded on the door downstairs.

Declan frowned. It wouldn't be Cole, Ryker or Anthony, because they all had keys.

He pushed up and tugged on some jeans and a T-shirt. Before he left the room, he leaned over the bed and pressed a kiss to her lips. "I'll be back in a sec."

He moved down the stairs, and when he looked through the peephole, he frowned again. There was no one there. Quickly, he moved across the room and grabbed a gun his team had stashed inside the TV unit. Then he returned, opening the door slowly.

That's when he saw it. Not a person, but another fucking note—this time stuck to the door with a knife.

His eyes narrowed as he snatched the thing off the wood and opened it.

I never liked law enforcement anyway. They were never any good at keeping me safe. How many more have to die before we go on that fourth date?

His gaze shot straight to the car on the street.

His insides iced at the sight of the agent slumped over the steering wheel.

Gun still drawn, he moved outside and around the car to the driver's side. He was just reaching inside the open window to feel the guy's neck when he saw it—the slash to the throat.

He grabbed the guy's wrist instead. No pulse. There was blood running from a wound in his chest. He'd also been stabbed.

Quickly, he jogged back across the road and had just reentered the house when footsteps sounded from the stairs. He whipped the door closed.

Michele stopped in front of him. The second she scanned his face, a flicker of unease washed through her gaze. "What is it?"

"Nothing." Fuck, he'd said that too quickly.

"It's not nothing. You look like you want to kill someone." Her gaze slid down to the note and the gun.

She swallowed. "He left another note?"

He remained silent.

"What does it say?"

"Michele—"

"What does it say, Declan?"

She grabbed it from his hand, and the blood drained from her face. Her gaze lifted to the door. "The agent. Is he—"

"Yes." He sighed heavily. "He's dead."

CHAPTER 25

"*H*ow did he get close enough to your agent to slit his throat and stab him three times?" Declan growled.

He was beyond pissed, just like Cole and Ryker beside him. This shouldn't have happened. And Michele shouldn't be standing in his living room with the FBI, clawing at her arms, thinking the agent's death was her fault. Because he was sure that was exactly what she was thinking.

Agent Burton blew out a breath from where she sat on the couch. "That's information we don't have right now, Declan. Agent O'Donohue had his window open, and it doesn't appear he reached for a weapon, so we can only assume Tim snuck up on him."

Cole stepped forward. "Or he has a partner."

"The footage we have from a previous victim, Ms. Dean, only shows one man entering and leaving the frame. Tim. And every woman who's been killed has dated him—and only him—before being murdered. There's no indication of a partner."

Declan worked his jaw as he shot a look over his shoulder at Michele. She'd been standing silently, hugging her waist or scratching her arms, since reading that note. She was pale and shaky and clearly terrified. He hated it.

"Do you have any more information on why he waits until the fourth date to kill?" Ryker asked.

A man standing behind Agent Burton answered the question. "We believe four dates is something he does for an emotional reason. What that reason is, we're not sure."

"The asshole's sick in the head," Declan muttered. "There's your reason."

"Yes, he is," the man responded, looking directly at Declan. "It's highly likely unreported abuse occurred from either his last foster mother or one of her many boyfriends, and it had some kind of a negative effect on his already fragile psyche."

"Why do you suspect there was abuse?" Michele asked quietly.

The guy's attention shifted to her. "Most serial killers either suffer from mental illness or experienced childhood trauma. The note he left about law enforcement would support the latter. Maybe he *did* report his foster mother or her boyfriends, but nothing was done." His attention flicked around the room. "It's possible he holds resentment toward his last foster mother, or previous foster parents, for neglect or abuse he experienced at their hands, and when he dates women, he's projecting that anger and taking it out on them."

Jesus Christ.

"You're a profiler," Cole said.

"I am."

Declan shot another look over at Michele. She wasn't looking at any of them now. Her gaze was out the window.

Clenching his jaw, he moved over to her, touching her hands. She flinched, as if she'd been in her own world and hadn't heard him approach. Christ, her fingers were ice cold.

He lowered his head, trying to meet her gaze. "Hey. You doing okay?"

She nodded. He grazed her cheek as the door to his house

opened and another agent walked in. The guy had been directed to go around to the neighbors and see if anyone had street footage.

"Got anything?" Agent Burton asked.

"I do." He stopped, clicking something on his tablet. "The woman across the street has a security camera on her front yard, which covers the street. The camera caught footage of Agent O'Donohue's car."

He rubbed Michele's arms. The agent placed the iPad on the table and pressed play. Declan released Michele and inched forward, along with everyone else in the room.

On the small iPad, they saw the agent sitting in his car, watching the street. His window was open and his elbow on the door. Then his gaze shifted slightly, and he straightened, as if watching something farther down the street.

When a person wearing loose black pants and a cap walked into view, Declan straightened. The guy had his back to the camera, making it impossible to see a face.

It looked like some words were exchanged, then suddenly, the guy outside pulled a knife and slit the agent's throat. The footage actually caught the motion of the guy's arm. The agent reached for his throat while the attacker stabbed him in the chest and gut three times.

Jesus Christ.

It was messed up. But it fit the MO. Technically, the victim was still stabbed four times with a knife.

Michele's soft gasp sounded behind him, and he cursed under his breath. He hadn't realized she'd joined them to watch.

He turned, tugging her away from the screen. "You shouldn't have watched that."

She tugged herself out of his arms, turning to Agent Burton. "Did he have a family?"

The agent hesitated. Declan's gut clenched.

"He did. Two teenage boys and a wife."

The last bit of color left Michele's face.

The others started talking about the agent and how this person, if it had been Tim, had managed to get so close without the agent drawing his weapon. Declan barely heard a word they said. His entire focus remained on Michele.

She wasn't listening either. Her gaze flicked out the window to the spot where the agent was killed, like she was picturing the entire thing in her head. When her chest started to move up and down with panicked breaths, he took a step toward her—but she was already turning and racing toward the back door.

MICHELE COULDN'T BREATHE. The knife slicing the agent's throat, the stabs to his chest before his head fell forward, it was all on repeat in her mind. The man was a husband. A father.

Nausea stirred in her belly, and the room around her started to shrink. Her gaze shot across the road to the spot where the man was shot. And it was like she was seeing it all over again.

Dead. A husband and father was dead—and she was doing nothing but hiding out in this house with Declan while he'd been protecting her from the street.

A buzzing sounded between her ears, blocking out whatever the agents were talking about. Her fault. *This was her fault!*

She tried to suck in a breath, but her chest was too tight. It felt like there was a band around her, squeezing, stopping any air from getting to her lungs and causing black dots in her vision. And why was the room getting smaller?

The whole house was closing in on her while she was suffocating!

Outside. She needed to be outside!

Blindly, Michele turned and ran to the back door before all but falling out. She didn't stop until she felt the grass beneath her feet. But it wasn't enough to quell the panic. Oh my God! Why couldn't she breathe?

She closed her eyes, pressing her hands to her face. The second her eyes shuttered, it wasn't darkness she saw... It was kids mourning the loss of their father. A wife who would never see her husband again.

"Michele."

The tremble in her hands worsened, but at the same time, those hands felt numb. She was pretty sure she was having a panic attack, but as much as she wanted to stop it, she couldn't.

"Michele, stop."

The words confused her. She *was* stopped, wasn't she?

A hand suddenly grabbed her arm. That's when she realized she was walking toward the front of the house. When exactly had she started moving again? Or maybe she'd never stopped.

"Michele, talk to me."

She looked up at Declan, but he blurred before her eyes. She wasn't sure if it was from tears or her vision refusing to center. Maybe both. "It's my fault."

"Don't say that."

"It is!" She tried to yank herself away from him, but the hold on her arm tightened. "Anthony said this would happen! He said more people would die if I didn't help drag this guy out. And it *happened*! Another man has lost his life. And the worst part is, I knew it was a possibility—and I didn't do a damn thing!"

A weird vibration started in her body, like she was trying to escape her own skin. Like her soul was trying to get away from her.

A hand latched onto her other arm, and she was pulled forward against a warm chest. "Michele, listen to me. What this asshole does is *not* your fault. It's not even close."

"But I could have done something!" She was yelling now, but she couldn't stop. The combination of guilt and devastation from the last week was pressing on her chest, choking her. Her uncle.

Declan. Agent O'Donahue… "People are getting hurt, *dying*, and I'm doing nothing when I'm probably the only person with a chance of stopping it!"

Selfish. She was so selfish.

"Michele—"

"I need to do something." She gave a big push on his chest, but again, his hands were like iron manacles, refusing to let her go. "I know the pain of losing people I love! I don't want anyone else to lose a husband or a father or a daughter or a sister!"

"Chele—"

"I need—" A sob cut off her words. She tried again. "I need to *end this*. Please, let me help end this. I have to do something!"

Another deep sob. Her knees caved. Declan caught her before she hit the ground, lifting her body against him, one hand on her back, the other behind her neck. He touched his temple to hers, his warmth and strength chasing away some of the demons.

"You *are* doing something. You're staying safe."

She took deep gulps of air, trying to settle her nerves. "I don't want another agent's death on my hands."

"Michele—"

"I don't, Declan!" Her heart pounded harder at the thought of any more agents dying because of her.

He stroked the back of her head, sighing. There was a long beat of silence. "We'll consider some ideas…and after that, we can discuss our options."

The band around her chest finally loosened. The light-headedness began to fade. Nothing would bring the agent back, but if they devised a plan that worked, a way for her to help, it might just save the next victim.

"But we're only considering a plan if we can absolutely guarantee your safety," he added quickly, his voice lethal. "And if you're comfortable with whatever plan we come up with."

Her eyes shuttered, her hand running through the hair at the back of his head. "Thank you."

CHAPTER 26

"When are you meeting the FBI to talk options?"

Michele rubbed a cloth over the counter with one hand while holding the phone to her ear with the other. River was on the other end. "When I finish my shift. They're meeting us at Declan's house."

The meeting had to wait a few days, and for Michele, it couldn't come soon enough. She needed to be *doing* something. She needed to use the fact that this guy wanted her to get him locked away so he couldn't hurt anyone else.

River was quiet for a moment. Michele could almost hear her overthinking. "What is it, River?"

"Just be careful. The guy knows you've been working with the FBI. Like Declan said, I doubt he'd fall into any trap easily."

Michele paused mid-swipe. "Declan will make sure it's foolproof."

River sighed. "I know. I'm just worried about you."

"I appreciate it. It's better to do something rather than nothing, though. The profiler said this guy wouldn't give up on me. That there's something inside him that needs to finish what he starts. I'm counting on that being true. And I'm counting on

Declan and the agents coming up with a plan that both catches him and protects me."

Another sigh from River. "I hope whatever this plan is, it involves you carrying a gun."

"You know I don't know how to use those things. But they *did* give me a tracking device yesterday, in case…well, you know why." In case Tim somehow got his hands on her. She touched a hand to the tiny device Declan had stuck to the belt buckle on her jeans.

She cast a glance outside. She couldn't see Declan, but she knew he had eyes on her. Something he'd reluctantly agreed to try until they could meet with the FBI, and only because he knew Tim couldn't get into her shop without being buzzed in. When she drove away, he'd be behind her, and if she shouted for help before then, he'd be by her side within minutes.

"Okay, honey. But I'm here if you need anything."

"I know." River was always there when she needed someone. It was what made their relationship so important to Michele.

Seeing Anthony at the door, she pressed the button in the kitchen and he stepped into the shop. "I gotta go. Anthony just got back."

"Okay. Catch up soon. Love you."

"Love you too."

She hung up, attention turning toward Anthony. "Hey. Everything go okay?"

He nodded. "Yep. People were especially happy to see the brownies in their orders."

Michele smiled. They'd been a little surprise for her customers this week. People always raved about her brownies.

Anthony frowned. "Mrs. Albuquerque wasn't home, though, which was strange."

Michele paused. That *was* strange. The older woman was very particular about her orders and liked to go through the box while ticking items off her list, making sure everything was accounted for. "Are you sure? Maybe she didn't hear the knock."

"I knocked a few times and rang the doorbell twice. No one answered, and her car wasn't in the driveway. I left the order by her front door."

"Hm. Maybe I'll give her a quick call."

She lifted the phone and dialed the older woman's number, but after half a dozen rings, it went to voice mail. She left a quick message, letting Mrs. Albuquerque know her food was at the door before hanging up. That was about all she could do.

She smiled at Anthony. "Ready to go?"

Anthony switched off the lights. "Ready."

It had been his suggestion that they drive to work together. He knew Declan was trailing her, and he'd suggested he take Declan's place in the car so she'd have company. But she had a feeling it was more than that. He wanted to be there if Tim showed up. She just hoped that if the guy *did* make an appearance around Anthony, the kid didn't do anything stupid.

She grabbed her stuff before heading outside and locking the door after them. Just like the last few days, the second she stepped outside, she scanned the street. Anthony did the same. She briefly wondered exactly where Declan was. A few days ago, a man in a sweater had brushed past her on the sidewalk, and Declan had jumped out from seemingly nowhere and grabbed the poor guy, scaring him.

She unlocked her car doors before sliding behind the wheel. Every few seconds, she glanced into the rearview mirror, looking for a tail.

Stop, Michele. Get out of your head. You're fine.

Dragging in a long breath, she shot her gaze to Anthony. "You doing okay today?"

"Yeah, I'm okay." He was running his finger over the base of the window in almost a nervous gesture. "I actually wanted to say something to you."

Michele frowned. "What is it?"

"The other day, when you went outside and Declan followed, when the FBI were at the house... I was sitting in my room with the window open."

Why was he...

It hit her. Oh shit. His bedroom was right above where she and Declan had stood. "You heard my panic attack." It wasn't a question. She could hardly remember what she'd said or done, but it couldn't have been pretty.

"I did."

When he shuffled in his seat like he was uncomfortable, she shot another look across to him. "What is it, Anthony?"

"I'm sorry. I shouldn't have said it was your fault if someone else dies. None of this is your fault. I was just angry and—"

She grabbed his hand, stopping whatever he was about to say. "It's okay. I was having a panic attack, and if you hadn't said it, I'm sure my mind would have gotten there on its own. Honestly, I know none of this is my fault—I really do—but you weren't entirely wrong when you said that if I could do something to stop this, I should."

He looked her way. "Still...I'm sorry."

"It's okay." She squeezed his hand before putting her own back on the wheel, her attention returning to the road.

"I think I'm going to go back to school," he said quietly.

Her brows lifted. "You are?"

"Yeah. The guys were saying I can stay with them for as long as I want. Said they'd contact my grandmother again to make sure I can stay, then help me enroll in the local high school."

She beamed at him. "That's amazing, Anthony! I mean, I'm sorry that I'll have to replace you at the shop. You've been an amazing help. But if finishing school is important to you, then you should do it."

"Thank you."

She'd just turned a corner onto a backstreet when she saw it—

a car crashed into a pole. She slammed her foot on the brake. The entire hood of the car was crumpled, and thick smoke was coming from underneath. Then she noticed a woman hunched over the wheel.

Wait... Was that—

"Mrs. Albuquerque's car," Anthony said, leaning forward in his seat.

"Oh my gosh!" Frantically, she turned off her car and reached for her seat belt. Anthony did the same. She'd just opened her door when Declan suddenly appeared beside her.

"Stay in the car and lock the doors." He had a gun in hand, and his voice was hard. "I'll check on her."

"Hurry! That's a lot of smoke coming from the hood." Too much.

Michele tugged her door closed and watched in horror as flames suddenly leapt from the hood.

Anthony cursed under his breath. "Should I—"

"No. Stay here." She reached for the lock.

A split second from pressing it, the back door behind Anthony opened. Michele turned her head...

Her stomach cramped, blood draining from her face.

Tim. And he held a gun to Anthony's head.

Panic flared through her chest. "What are you—"

"Drive the car or I shoot him."

Michele's gaze shifted to Anthony, and she saw his jaw clench. Then it flew to Declan. His head was in the car, and he was pulling Mrs. Albuquerque out of the vehicle.

Anthony's voice drew her attention back to him. "Let him shoot me, Chele."

Michele gasped. "No!"

Tim growled. "I'm not fucking around, Michele. He means nothing to me, and if I have to, I'll kill him. Then I'll shoot lover boy over there."

Declan was pulling Mrs. Albuquerque from the car.

Tim clicked off the safety—and Michele's heart stuttered. With shaking hands, she started the engine.

Immediately, Declan looked her way. A mixture of shock and rage flashed over his face. He dragged Mrs. Albuquerque to the sidewalk and gently eased her down before running toward them.

Michele drove slowly, trying to give him a chance to catch up.

When a gunshot rang out, she screamed and Anthony shouted, grabbing his thigh.

"Press your foot to the fucking gas or I put another hole in the kid," Tim seethed. "Next will be his head."

She pressed her foot down as hard as she could. When she glanced at Anthony's leg, a quiet sob slipped from her lips. Blood. There was so much blood!

Familiar buzzing started between her ears, and nausea rose in her stomach. She breathed deeply. She had to keep it together. For Anthony's sake.

When she looked at him again and saw the pain marring his features, her fear turned to fury. She grabbed hold of that anger with both hands, letting it snuff out everything else.

"I don't know where I'm going," she said, voice low.

"Take the next left."

She did as he asked, and it took everything in her to keep from crashing the car on purpose. "Are you okay, Anthony?"

"Don't talk. Both of you throw your phones out the window."

She ground her teeth, tugging her phone from her pocket before lowering the window and tossing it out. Anthony took the blood-soaked hand from his thigh and used it to toss his own phone.

"You didn't have to shoot him," she growled at Tim.

"And you didn't have to drive ten miles an hour. We'll share responsibility for this one."

She breathed through her rage, shooting another glance

Anthony's way. When he met her stare, he was breathing deeply, his mouth in a thin line.

"I'm okay," he said through gritted teeth.

Was he, though? Even with the pressure on the wound, he was still bleeding a lot.

Tim shoved the muzzle of the gun against Anthony's head. "Faster, Michele."

She tightened her hands on the wheel, and she sped up again, driving as fast as she could without losing control. "He needs a hospital. Let me stop the car so he can get help."

Tim laughed. "And lose my leverage? I don't think so. Take the next right."

The tires squealed as she turned.

"You thought I was stupid, didn't you?" Tim said, once they were driving on a straight road again, surrounded by wooded trees. There were no shops and no people to see she was driving too fast. "That I would just walk up to your store and take you while lover boy was hiding in his car."

She shot a look in the rearview mirror. *Come on, Declan, where are you?*

"A lot of people in my life have thought I was stupid. I like proving them wrong."

Prove people wrong by what? Killing them? "Do you really hate women so much that you need to go from town to town murdering them?"

"You think I'm doing all this for hate?" He laughed, but it was a maniacal sound that made her stomach turn. "Everything I've done has been for *love*, not hate."

What the hell was he talking about?

"That's always been my problem, really." He almost sounded like he was talking to himself now. "I love too hard."

Delusional. The man was completely delusional. "Tim. Take the gun away from Anthony's head and let me stop the car. You want me. You have me."

His voice hardened. "No. We're doing this fourth date my way."

"Is that why you killed my sister?" Anthony growled There was a darkness to his voice she'd never heard before, and it had her skin chilling. "Because she went on that fourth date with you? Because you *loved* her too hard?"

"Who's your sister?"

"Alana. You stabbed her to death. I met you at the fucking door when you picked her up."

"Ah, that's why I remember you. And, yes, Alana…" Tim said her name like he still thought fondly of the woman.

In her peripheral vision, she saw the veins in Anthony's forearm cord as he clenched his fist.

Don't do anything stupid, Anthony.

"I liked her," Tim finally said. "She was nice. Dressed a bit slutty, but—"

Suddenly, Anthony ducked his head and spun around. The gun went off, splintering the windshield as Anthony launched into the back. As he flew over the seat, he kicked Michele's arm and the wheel twisted.

She cried out as she lost control, their speed sending the car spinning. Even if she could've controlled the vehicle, she could barely see through the smashed windshield.

Madly, she rotated the wheel, trying to adjust. The tires squealed seconds before the passenger side of the car smashed into a tree.

Michele flew out of her seat, hitting the passenger-side window hard, and she heard the guys in the back do the same.

For a moment, everything was still. Pain skittered down her right shoulder and from the right side of her head. She reached up, touching wetness at the spot where her head had hit the glass.

A new wave of nausea bubbled in her belly from the sight of the blood on her fingers, but she breathed through it. When she glanced into the backseat, it was to see both Tim and Anthony still, huddled against the passenger side of the car in a tangled heap.

Oh God, Anthony! He already had a bullet wound to the leg, and now he was unconscious. He needed an ambulance, and he needed one *now*.

A whimper of pain slipped from her lips as she sat up. Everything hurt. Her chest. Her arms. Blood slipped down her head into her eyes, but she wiped it away. She couldn't think about her injuries or the blood right now. Anthony needed her.

Slowly, she reached into the back and touched his shoulder.

There was movement, but it wasn't from Anthony.

She snatched her hand back. Tim tried to sit up, groaning. "I'm going to fucking murder you, bitch!"

Oh Jesus!

Ignoring the aches in her body, she climbed over the middle console to the driver's side. When the door didn't open, she pushed harder. She leaned her shoulder into the door as she yanked on the handle.

Finally, the thing flew open.

She was crawling out when a hand latched onto her ankle and tugged her back. Frantically, she kicked her foot, looking over her shoulder.

Blood dripped down Tim's face, his expression enraged. With a hand still on her ankle, he was climbing into the front when her foot collided with his face—hard. He cried out, letting go, and she fell out of the car and down to the ground.

When she rose to her feet, her legs immediately threatened to buckle. She didn't let them. With a quick glance around, she spotted something that looked like a big dilapidated warehouse in the distance, set back from the road. That was it. That was all there was in the immediate area.

She didn't want to leave Anthony, but Tim didn't seem to be after the boy at the moment. He wanted her. The best thing she could do for Anthony was draw Tim away—hopefully while Declan made his way here with help.

She took off as quickly as she could toward the warehouse, knowing Tim would follow. Knowing she needed to move faster than she'd ever moved in her life if she wanted to survive.

CHAPTER 27

The second Declan heard Michele's car start, his gaze shot up and his limbs iced. Michele, eyes wide, and Anthony looking like stone. But it wasn't Michele's fear or Anthony's anger that had him going cold.

It was Tim in the backseat. The gun at Anthony's head. And the sight of them driving away.

Fuck!

He lay Mrs. Albuquerque on the sidewalk, then he was running. He'd just slipped behind the wheel of his car when someone else pulled up. An FBI agent.

"Call an ambulance for her," he shouted.

The guy climbed out. "Where's Michele?"

"Tim's in her damn car, and they just drove away!"

He pressed his foot to the gas and lifted his phone.

"Special Agent Maggie Burton speaking."

"I need the location of Michele's tracker. Tim has her and Anthony."

The woman cursed. She spoke to someone else, then there was the sound of typing over the line. "How long ago was she taken?"

"Just now. He slid into the back of her car and put a gun to Anthony's head."

More typing. "Getting her location."

It was taking too damn long. He took a hard left, the last direction he'd seen Michele take, not giving a shit about the speed limit as he careened around the corner.

It felt like a lifetime passed before Agent Burton finally came back. "Okay, got her."

"Tell me."

"She's driving on Brick Mill Road, and she's driving fast."

Then he needed to drive faster. He took another sharp turn, driving toward the highway. "I'm heading there now."

"I'll send agents."

The second he was off the phone, he called his team. He needed their backup. He just had to hope like hell they weren't too late.

MICHELE SHOT A GLANCE BEHIND HER, almost stumbling over her own feet when she saw how close Tim was. He lifted his hand, and she saw the gun.

Oh God.

The second she reached the metal door of the warehouse, she grabbed the handle, pushing it down and falling through when it opened easily. She slammed the door closed behind her. Her fingers shook as she flicked the lock.

Her entire body flinched when bullets peppered the door.

She stepped back, sucking in deep breaths, eyeing the door as if waiting for Tim to break through and shoot her. She stayed like that for two long seconds, then she pulled herself out of her daze, turning and running again. She ignored the ache in her muscles and the pounding in her head. All she could concentrate on was keeping Tim away from Anthony.

The warehouse was huge, and there were tall aisles stacked with boxes wrapped in plastic. At the end of each aisle stood pallets with yet more boxes.

"Hello?" Her shaky voice echoed throughout the cavernous space. "Is anyone here?"

Please, God, let someone be here. There had to be. The door wouldn't have been unlocked if someone wasn't here, right? And that someone would have a phone for her to call a paramedic. Maybe even a gun...

Just as the word ticked over in her mind, a gunshot went off in the direction she'd run from. Glass shattered, and it startled her so badly, she stumbled and her knees hit the concrete floor.

Blood dripped down her forehead again. A droplet hit the floor beneath her. Using her sleeve, she madly scrubbed at the small speck, knowing she couldn't leave tracks. For once, the blood didn't affect her. She was in fight-or-flight mode, and she was choosing flight.

More glass shattered behind her, now accompanied by a new sound, like something hitting shards of glass from a frame. Pushing to her feet, she forced her legs to hold her as she ran to the end of an aisle, only stopping when she heard footsteps inside the warehouse.

She hid behind a stack of boxes, working hard to silence her breaths.

"Where are you?" he shouted in almost a singsong voice. He sounded like he was still near the door. His footsteps grew louder though, so she knew he was drawing closer.

She swallowed and scrunched her eyes closed. *Breathe, Michele. Just breathe.*

"Come on, darling. You're just delaying the inevitable. This always ends the same way."

No. The pattern of women dying at his hands stopped today.

"Death won't be so bad," Tim continued. "Think of every bad thing that's happened in your life. Every demon inside you that you've battled day after day. All of it will just cease to exist."

Yeah, because *she* would cease to exist. Psychopath.

He laughed. "Kind of hypocritical of me, really. To tell you not to fear death when I myself fear it."

She scanned the boxes and crates around her, looking for somewhere to hide.

"There was once a time when I craved death. I had nothing. I *was* nothing. Then, I found something to live for."

Was he talking about murder? Had killing people become his reason for living? If so, that was the sickest thing she'd ever heard.

"I'll let you in on a little secret, Michele. I don't do this because I want to. I do it because I have to. Because it's the only way for me to—"

A door opened somewhere, cutting off whatever Tim was about to say.

Her eyes widened. Who was that? Declan? *Please, God, let it be Declan.*

"Who the hell broke my window?" The voice wasn't one she recognized. A man with a southern accent. "We're frickin' closed. No one should even be here!"

Shit. Did he work here? He'd be walking straight into Tim—and Tim wouldn't hesitate to shoot.

Knowing she couldn't stand by and listen to an innocent man being shot, she stepped into the aisle.

"Who the hell are you—"

The gunshot was loud, bouncing off the walls of the warehouse. Then came the thud of the man's body.

Michele shoved her hands over her mouth to stop the cry. Or at least she tried to. Noise still escaped her hands. Then she heard the rapid footsteps.

Tim was running.

Terror snaked through her limbs as she ran in the opposite

direction, toward the back of the warehouse. Her head pounded from the crash, and every limb felt heavy, but she forced herself to push forward. To not stop.

His footsteps drew closer, and the sound had fear spiraling in her gut.

When an office came into view ahead, she pushed her body to move faster. She'd almost reached the room when another gunshot sounded. A scream tore from her chest as a bullet sailed over her head, hitting the wall.

She fell into the office, then slammed the door closed after her. She could have cried when she saw the lock. She flicked it quickly before falling backward onto the floor, then crawling on all fours to the back of the room.

Breaths sawed in and out of her, and when the knob rattled, her heart leapt into her throat.

Desperately, she scanned the office. It was small, with a rectangular table in the middle, piles of paper on top, and filing cabinets against the walls. When she saw a utility knife sitting on a box, she grabbed it before looking back to the door. He was going to get in. It was only a matter of time. Probably seconds. She needed to be ready.

Sucking in a deep breath, she moved to the wall beside the door and lifted the retractable blade. Then she steadied her breaths and waited.

Another gunshot went off, but she didn't flinch this time. She steeled her spine.

The second he stepped into the room, she lunged, plunging the small blade into his neck.

When she yanked the knife out, she stumbled back, watching as the gun slipped from Tim's fingers and he grabbed at the wound. He turned slowly to look at her, and even though blood began trickling from his mouth, it was his eyes that had a new wave of terror rushing through her.

Anger. Hate. And the promise of pain.

He lunged.

She tried to stab him a second time, but he seized her wrist, and they both crashed to the floor. As he hovered on top of her, he pressed her wrist to the concrete floor. His other hand went to her throat, and he immediately tightened his fingers.

She grabbed at his arm with her free hand, digging her nails into his flesh.

"You should have just gone on the final date," he choked out through gritted teeth.

Blood from his neck and mouth dripped onto her face as darkness began to hedge her vision. The knife slipped from her numb fingers as her world began to fade.

CHAPTER 28

The second Declan spotted Michele's red car, he pressed his foot harder to the accelerator.

"I see her car," he said to Burton over the speaker.

"Her tracker has veered toward a structure."

He shot his gaze to the large building sitting off the road.

"We're not far," Burton said quickly.

"I'm going in."

The second his car stopped, he sent a pin of his location to his team, then slid the phone into his back pocket. He grabbed his gun and ran to the vehicle.

His chest seized. The entire right side of the car was smashed into a tree. She was hurt. She had to be.

He shut down his emotions. He needed a clear head right now so he could handle whatever came next.

He stopped beside it—and his muscles tightened. Anthony lay in the back.

When he rolled over, groaning, their gazes caught.

"Go," Anthony wheezed. "I'm okay."

"Stay here. I'll get the paramedics." The words had barely left his mouth before he took off toward the warehouse. As he ran, he took the phone from his pocket and dialed Burton again. "Anthony needs an ambulance!"

The sound of an engine was loud across the phone. "Calling one now."

He muted the phone and slid it back into his pocket.

Footprints and specks of blood left a trail through the dirt leading to the warehouse. His insides coiled. Tim's blood...or hers?

When he reached the open door, he barely gave a glance to the shattered glass. He stepped in quickly but silently, immediately spotting a middle-aged man on the floor. He paused, bending down and touching his pulse. No heartbeat. The man was dead.

His jaw clenched as he rose. Tim needed to die, and he needed to die *now*.

Declan moved toward the back of the warehouse, gun aimed in front of him. He scanned every aisle as he went.

A loud thud sounded—bodies hitting the floor.

Fuck.

He took off, sprinting toward the back of the large space. He reached an office...

Tim lay on top of Michele, his hands tight around her throat.

He aimed and shot—catching Tim in the shoulder.

The guy jerked and dropped, partially on top of Michele. Declan ran over and yanked his heavy body away. He kept his gun aimed at Tim while Michele rolled to the side, gasping for air.

His chest seized at the sight of her—and the deep red marks on her throat. "Are you okay?"

She nodded, her breaths still too ragged to speak. He tracked every inch of her body with his gaze. There was blood, but no bullet or knife wounds he could visibly see.

His attention returned to Tim. He pulled the asshole up by his shirt and shoved him against the wall. He was pale, bleeding from the neck, shoulder and mouth. He wouldn't be alive for long. "Are you working alone?"

The guy spat blood into his face and growled, "Fuck. You."

His eyes started to close. Declan pulled him forward before slamming him back against a wall. "Don't you fucking die on me yet! Are you working alone?"

Tim opened his mouth, but his next breath rattled as blood gurgled in his throat. His eyes closed, and his chest stopped moving.

Dead. The asshole was dead.

Declan dropped him to the floor. When he turned, he saw Michele sitting up.

"Anthony—"

"Is awake. And paramedics are on the way."

A relieved sigh whooshed from her chest.

Loud footsteps sounded from somewhere else in the warehouse. From the street, he could hear the distant sound of an ambulance.

He lowered beside Michele and touched her cheek. "You sure you're okay?"

Michele looked up at him, nodding, and all he could see was relief reflected in her blue eyes. "He's finally dead."

MICHELE STOOD in the shower so long the water started to cool. She was back in her apartment. Back with Pokey. It was probably close to midnight. She hadn't eaten dinner because she hadn't been hungry...but then, she had a feeling she wouldn't have an appetite for a while. They'd spent a long time at the hospital with Anthony, until finally Cole had told them to leave, and he'd stay.

Dead. Tim was dead. Was it finally over? Was she actually safe?

She tilted her head back, letting the cool water rain over her face.

If it *was* over, why did she still have this dread pitting her stomach...like something wasn't right? Maybe it was PTSD. From being kidnapped. From Anthony being shot right beside her. From all the blood. God, there'd been terrifying amounts of blood. Her stomach rebelled at the very thought.

A knock sounded at the door. Then Declan's voice. "Honey, you doing okay?"

Exhaling a loud breath, she turned the cool water off. She'd just gotten out and grabbed a towel when his smooth voice sounded again.

"Can I come in?"

"Of course." Was there ever a time she *didn't* want Declan around her? Close was never close enough.

The door opened, and there he was, all six and a half feet of him. He wore sweatpants and his chest was bare. Her big protector.

He stepped up to her. One hand slid around her waist, the other gently caressing her neck, over the bruises caused by Tim's fingers. A low sigh reverberated from his chest. "I'm so sorry I didn't protect you from being taken today."

He'd been saying sorry all night.

"Please don't say sorry anymore. Nothing about what happened today was your fault. If you hadn't pulled Mrs. Albuquerque from that car..."

A shudder rocked her spine. The woman was okay. That's what counted. She'd been at the hospital too, but only for a concussion.

In the end, Michele hadn't had to lure Tim out, after all. Apparently, Tim had finally gotten tired of waiting. He'd found a street on their familiar drive to Declan's and walked straight out in front of her car, and she'd veered to miss him and driven into the pole.

"It should never have happened," Declan said quietly. "Any of it. He should never have gotten close enough to touch you."

She pressed both her hands and head to his chest, taking a moment to just breathe him in. To appreciate that she was here. That Declan was here. That they were both safe and she'd never have to worry about Tim coming after her again.

"I should have locked the door faster."

Stupid. She'd been so distracted, so worried for Mrs. Albuquerque, that she hadn't been thinking.

Declan stepped back, took her hand in his, and led her to the bedroom. Instead of grabbing one of her shirts, she reached for one of his. The second it was on, his scent surrounded her.

Declan sat on the bed and pulled her onto his lap. His hand went to her cheek, worry glazing his eyes. "You're still so pale. What can I do?"

She hated that he looked so worried. She was sure he must've lost his mind when she drove away from him today. He didn't need more anxiety on his plate.

She ran her fingers along the hard ridge of his jaw. "I'm okay. I just… My tummy feels sick. Like this isn't over."

There it was again. Those flames in his eyes. That hard jaw and those flexing muscles, like he was ready to go to war for her. "Why do you say that?"

"There are just so many things that still don't add up. Like why, if it was Tim who killed the FBI agent, the guy would have let him get close enough to slit his throat? And why, when you asked if he was working alone, he didn't just say yes? Wouldn't he have wanted to take all the glory? Isn't that what most killers want?"

Declan's brows tugged together. "I agree. Those things don't add up."

"He said something in the car too." Her gaze went to his chest, and she frowned. "He said he was killing people for love, not hate, and that just doesn't make sense to me."

When she looked back up, it was to see Declan's eyes soften. "I wouldn't try to understand the mind of a killer, honey. It doesn't work like yours or mine."

His hands went to her back, and he pulled her close. Immediately, she shifted to wrap her legs around his waist, her arms circling his neck.

"We'll continue to communicate with the FBI. And until we know you're definitely safe, I'll stick by your side. Even after that, I'll stay with you every second until you feel safe."

What had she done to deserve this man? "I love you so much."

A slow smile spread across his face. "Can't possibly be as much as I love you."

She wasn't sure she agreed. But before she could argue the point, he was kissing her. And in the kiss, she felt her first tendril of safety all day.

CHAPTER 29

"Yes, Uncle Ottie, I'm sure I'm okay. It's *you* we should be worried about."

Michele moved over to the stove and mixed the pasta sauce. It felt so good to be cooking in her apartment again. Almost a week had passed since Tim's death, since Michele had moved back home, and she was still grateful. Maybe it was the introvert in her who liked quiet and her own stuff around her.

When a warm chest pressed to her back and thick arms curled around her waist, she smiled. Declan nuzzled her neck.

She bit her bottom lip to stop from groaning.

Ottie sighed. "That's not true, Michele. My heart's fine. That's why they let me go home. In fact, it feels like a lifetime ago that I was in the hospital."

A lifetime ago? Uh, no. Try a couple of weeks ago.

One of Declan's hands trailed up her rib cage and closed around her breast. Her breath caught. She tried to swat him away, but he didn't move an inch.

She cleared her throat. "Well, I'm okay. Tim's dead and everything's been quiet. In fact, I'm finally starting to feel like things are going back to normal." A new normal. A normal where

Declan stayed at her place every night and kissed and touched her every second he could. It was bliss. "Please don't worry about me, because then I'll only worry more about *you*."

Declan's thumb grazed her nipple. She dropped the wooden spoon and grabbed his wrist. Her attempt to stop him did nothing.

"I'll always worry about you," Ottie said quietly.

And that's why she loved him. One of the million reasons. "Don't forget that Dec and I are coming over tomorrow night. I'm going to bring some prawns and chicken and make cold rolls."

Declan's mouth trailed down her shoulder, and it took everything in her not to hum. She pushed at his head, trying to move away, but the damn man was relentless.

"I'm already looking forward to it," her uncle said. "I love you, darling. Say hi to Declan for me."

Considering how close Declan was, he probably already heard her uncle. "I love you too, Uncle Ottie."

The second she hung up, she set the phone onto the counter and spun around. "Excuse me. I was trying to talk to my uncle."

A deep, gravelly sound vibrated from his chest. "And you did." The late-afternoon sun hit his face in the most perfect way, warming his features. When he tugged her closer, she felt his hardness.

"But your hands on me are distracting."

He wet his lips, and her gaze zeroed in on his tongue. Then one of those torturous hands touched the hem of her dress and slid up her thigh. "But it was worth it, right?"

His breath brushed against her neck again as that hand reached her core, his finger sliding over her slit.

"Declan..." She choked on his name.

"Yes, honey?" Another graze.

"I need to finish this meal first." Even though all she wanted to do was drown in the guy. "After. You can have me after."

"That's not enough."

She groaned at another swipe, her core throbbing. "All night! I'm yours all night."

Another growl. "Promise?"

His finger continued to move against her. Holy Christ. "Promise," she breathed.

When he finally let her go, she almost whimpered, but this time for a completely different reason.

No. Finish this meal, then you can have him.

Sighing, she turned back to the stove. Over the last week, the man had gone out of his way to distract her from every memory of what had happened. In fact, everyone had. River had barely left her side. Ryker and the other guys had been hanging out constantly, cracking jokes left, right and center. They'd all come to her house to avoid media attention. It had been crazy. The media coverage had been massive, and Michele was hounded on more than one occasion.

There had been a couple rare moments of quiet pause, when her mind flicked back to Tim. When the snake of unease slithered in her belly.

Anthony was also still in the hospital and pretty much the only reason she left her apartment. Each time she stepped into his room, she felt the unease return. It was to the point where her stomach dipped at the thought of going there. The second she saw Anthony, everything came back. Tim. The things he'd said to her. Anthony being shot. The unanswered questions.

"Stop."

Her head swung up at Declan's voice. He sat on the couch petting Pokey, eyes on her.

"What?" She tried to sound innocent, but by the look on Declan's face, she knew she hadn't pulled it off.

"You're thinking about it all again."

When her mind got too quiet, it was hard not to. "You're right."

Declan rose and moved back to her. He pressed a kiss to her head, embracing her in a long hug before walking toward the bathroom.

Michele was just pouring the sauce over some pasta when her phone rang. "Hey, Connie! Your meals will be finished soon, then we're going to drive them over to your place."

Michele had spent the week working from home, wanting to be around the comfort of her apartment and Pokey. With Declan's help and River delivering the meals, she'd managed to get all the orders out to her clients. Just. Connie was the only customer this week who didn't live in Lindeman. She was about half an hour's drive away, and with River busy this afternoon, she and Declan offered to make the drive outside her normal route.

"Hi, Chele. Actually, I made a last-minute trip to Lindeman. I'm just passing Ashton Street. I can be at the shop in a couple minutes."

Crap. The woman would be waiting at the shop for a while. "I'm so sorry, they're not quite ready yet." She nibbled her bottom lip. "You know what, Ashton is only a street away from my apartment. Come here instead. You can have a coffee while I finish these. I would feel terrible about you waiting outside in the cold."

"Are you sure?"

"Yes. I'll text you the address now."

"Great! See you soon."

She hung up and quickly texted the woman her address. Five minutes later, Declan stepped back into the room. She shot a look at him over her shoulder. "Connie's saved us a trip. She's in town, so she's going to pop over and pick these up."

Declan frowned. "You gave her your address?"

She paused, surprised by his tone. "Yes. I mean, I used to work out of Uncle Ottie's house before opening the shop, since he has a bigger kitchen. People picked their meals up all the time."

He gave her a look like that didn't make him any happier, but when a buzzer sounded, he pressed the button to allow her client into the building.

She was just taking out containers when Declan opened the door and Connie stepped inside.

Michele smiled from across the room. "Hey! I've finished the pasta. The chicken Kievs are just about done. They need to cool a bit, then I'll container everything. Sorry it's not ready to go." She definitely missed Anthony's help. How she had ever survived without the kid, she had no idea.

Connie smiled. "Oh, don't be silly. You just went through—" She stopped halfway to the kitchen, eyes falling on Pokey.

Michele paused at the scared look on the woman's face. "Are you okay?"

"Yeah, I just… I have a bit of a fear of big dogs."

Michele's brows rose. "Oh, I'm sorry. Declan can put him in the bedroom."

Declan walked to the bedroom and opened the door. "Come here, boy."

Connie's gaze never left Pokey. Once he was out of the room, she visibly relaxed again. "Sorry. I was attacked as a kid, and now I just don't like to be around them."

"You don't need to apologize. Pokey's almost as big as me, so he'd scare most people." Though he was a giant teddy bear, just the way she liked him.

She went back to the oven and opened the door. The Kievs were perfectly browned and crispy. Smiling, she used the oven mitts to scoop out the tray of chicken.

Connie groaned. "Oh my gosh. They smell unbelievable."

Michele beamed. Even though she'd been doing this for a while, she'd never tire of people complimenting her cooking. "I don't think I've made these for you before. You'll love them. They're a hit with almost all my customers."

She set the tray on the stove just as Declan sat at the table and took out his phone.

"Oh, I know I'll love them." Connie sat down on a stool on the other side of the kitchen island. "Tell me, how have you been?"

Michele's smile turned tight. Everyone had been great the last week, but she didn't want to talk about Tim with a client. It was bad enough her name was all over the news, prompting questions from well-meaning locals. "I'm managing. It's helped that I have so many wonderful people around me."

"That's good. I've been so worried about you. Having a support system does make the world of difference in tough times." She reached into her bag and pulled out a container. "Which reminds me, I finally brought you those cookies I promised. Enough for you, Declan, and your uncle."

"The special recipe." Michele had actually been looking forward to those. It wasn't often someone baked for her. Usually, it was the other way around.

Connie opened the lid, offering one to Michele. "Here, try one. I just baked them, so they're probably still warm. I'm dying to know what you think."

Michele's stomach growled at the divine smell. She grabbed one and took a bite. They were perfect. Just the right amount of fluffy and crunchy. "They're amazing. What's the secret ingredient?"

Connie laughed. "Sugar. *Lots* of sugar."

Michele chuckled as well. Of course.

Connie stood and offered the container to Declan, who shook his head.

"You have to, Dec," Michele said as she swallowed her mouthful. "They're delicious!"

He gave her a small smile. "Okay. Thanks." He took one. After a bite, he nodded. "It's good."

No. Not good. Un-freaking-believable. She needed to get this woman's recipe.

"Here, have another. You can never have too much sugar

before dinner." Connie set a second in front of him before returning to the island.

"You have to share this recipe," Michele said as she took another bite.

Connie replaced the lid and set the container onto the counter. "Uh, no way. You have a *ton* of amazing secret recipes. Let me keep this one, then I can make them for you whenever I want as my way of thanking you for all your beautiful cooking."

"You thank me by supporting my business." Michele was grateful to all her customers.

When Declan's phone rang, he stood and walked out of the room. She didn't miss the fact that he'd grabbed the second cookie. She chuckled, and received a wink from him before he disappeared into the hall.

Connie sighed. "You two are adorable."

Michele smiled, grabbing the lids for the chicken containers. "I'm very grateful to have him."

"Just as I'm sure he's grateful to have you."

She was turning back toward the containers of chicken when she saw a small frown tug Connie's brow together. "You doing all right, Connie?"

"I've actually had a bit of a tough week," the woman said quietly.

Michele returned to the island. "Is everything okay?"

"Someone close to me passed away."

Michele's lips separated. "Oh my gosh. I'm so sorry."

Connie lifted a shoulder. "Thank you. We weren't blood related, but he was closer to me than anyone else."

"Connie..." She lifted her hand to touch the woman...and frowned. Her arm felt heavy. Why did her arm feel so heavy? Slowly, she lifted her hand in front of her face.

Her fingers suddenly blurred before her eyes, her hand looking further away than it should.

What the hell?

"I'll get through it," Connie continued. "Just like I've gotten through everything else life has thrown my way."

Connie's voice sounded like it was coming through a tunnel—far away and small.

Michele tried to tell the woman she didn't feel good, but before the words left her mouth, her knees gave way. She hit the ground with a thud, and her world darkened.

∾

"HEY, ANTHONY. EVERYTHING OKAY?"

He popped the last bite of cookie into his mouth. God, they really were good. What the hell did the woman use?

"The agents were talking outside my room. I think they thought I was asleep, but I heard everything."

Declan stilled. Anthony sounded anxious. "What did you hear?"

"They were talking about a possible second person. Someone working with Tim. But they weren't talking about it like the person was some kind of small player. They think his partner actually made all the kills."

Declan stopped, his skin chilling. "Why?"

"Because Tim used a gun in the warehouse, not a knife. He shot me and tried to choke Michele. The profiler doesn't think the killer would change his MO." There was a rustling noise, like Anthony was getting out of bed. "And because that agent outside the house let his killer just walk up to him, with the car window open. Something he wouldn't have done for Tim."

They'd always questioned the agent's kill. But the first part about the kills at the warehouse? Why the hell hadn't the FBI shared this information?

Connie's voice filtered down the hall. "Someone close to me passed away…"

Anthony voice drew him back to the call. "The agents were

talking about some foster sister in the last house Tim was placed in. He spent a lot of time with her, and they were similar ages. They've been trying to locate her but can't. Said she might have changed her name."

"Why would they want to locate her?"

"After studying the video of the agent being shot, the profiler thinks it was a woman who killed him."

Connie's voice pricked his ears again. "We weren't blood related, but he was closer to me than anyone else."

His heart thudded against his ribs. "I've got to go."

He took a step toward the door—and suddenly, his world tilted. He grabbed the wall to remain upright. His brows tugged together when the hallway swam around him.

Fuck!

"I'll get through it. Just like I've gotten through everything else life has thrown my way."

Michele. He had to get to Michele!

He took another step, but his legs were barely holding him. A thud sounded from the other room, and everything in him iced. He was too late.

Connie was the killer. And she had them.

His knees caved and his vision turned black.

CHAPTER 30

*M*ichele sucked in a ragged breath. Then another. Was she asleep? Why did her body feel so heavy?

She tried to shift but stopped at the sound of creaking wood. Was she sitting in a chair? Not a sofa or something equally comfortable. No. This felt more like a dining table chair.

Nausea swelled in her belly, but she used deep breaths to keep it from crawling up her throat. Slowly, she peeled her eyes open.

Candles. They were the first things she saw. They centered the small four-person dining table and offered almost the only light in the room. The golden flames flickered, the light reflecting off the wineglasses. There was food, too. Food she'd just cooked, sitting on the plates in front of her.

Her gaze lifted—and terror sealed her throat shut.

Declan.

He was hunched over in the dining chair opposite hers, his head hanging at an odd angle, chin to his chest.

"Declan?" Her voice scratched her dry throat. She tugged at her hands, but they barely moved. Something was wrapped around her wrists, holding them captive behind the chair. Duct tape?

Oh God!

Next, she tried her feet. They were bound too, but unlike her hands, which were only tied together, her ankles were bound to the chair legs.

"Declan, wake up. Please, God, wake up!"

Her heart pounded in her chest. Was he breathing? Was he alive? Her gaze zeroed in on his chest. At the small rise, the air whooshed from her lungs. He was alive. Unconscious, but alive.

"Do you know how long it took me to get him in that chair?"

Michele's head flew up at the words. There was a slight ache in her head, but she ignored it, her entire focus on the other woman. Connie. She leaned a hip against Michele's kitchen island, a long, sharp blade in her hand.

Michele swallowed, trying to ease the sudden fear and uncertainty in her chest at the sight of the knife. Not fear for her. Fear for Declan. He was unconscious and vulnerable while she was duct taped to a chair and unable to protect him. "Connie? What are you doing?"

A slow smile crept over the woman's lips, but it was unlike any smile she'd previously given Michele. This one made her skin crawl and her stomach do a sick little roll. "You already know the answer to that, don't you, Michele?"

She shook her head, but again, the movement caused small flecks of pain, this time accompanied by nausea.

Her gaze lowered to the container beside Connie. The cookies. Connie had laced the cookies. That's how she'd gotten both Declan and Michele down.

"No." Her voice was so damn croaky. "It was Tim. The FBI told us it was Tim! He was abused in foster care. He... He killed animals and set fire to things. He was unhinged. Unstable." Even as she said the words and willed them to be true, flickers of doubt began to ravage her mind.

"No, dear. The fires. The animals. It was me. All of it. He willingly took the blame, though." She pushed off the counter, and the knife glinted in the candlelight. "I met Tim when I was sent to a foster home at twelve years old."

Connie smiled, like she was recalling a fond memory. "I gave the idiot a bit of attention, and he loved me. Probably because I was the only person to ever show him affection. He experienced a lot of neglect in his life. Abuse too. The man would have done *anything* for me."

Connie had taken advantage of a neglected and abused kid while she'd only been a child herself?

"Did they tell you about my birth mother?" Connie asked. "Oh, of course not. Because no one suspects me. The police have cared very little about me throughout my entire life."

Did she even want to know? "What… What happened to your mother?"

Connie's eyes flashed with anger. "The woman was a *whore*. She used to bring men to our house. She'd pass out and then… Well, you probably know."

Michele's mouth dropped open. "Oh my God."

Abused. Connie was saying she'd been abused too.

"I thought my mother overdosing was the best thing that had ever happened to me." She started stroking the knife like it was a pet. "But then I got put into that foster house with Tim, and you know what happened? The same. Fucking. Thing. The abuse started all over again."

Connie lifted a shoulder. "At first, I blamed the men. But that was naïve of me. The older I got, the more I realized men are pathetically weak. I shouldn't have expected better from them. It's the *women* who are at fault. Both those women—my mother and my foster mother—were supposed to love me. Protect me and keep me safe. But they didn't."

Connie never raised her voice, but the quiet rage that laced her words was impossible to miss.

Michele quietly struggled against the tape on her hands. She tugged her right wrist, then her left. The left was looser.

Loose enough to get free?

"Connie, I'm so sorry. I really am. But you need therapy."

And to be locked up, far away from people and knives.

Connie laughed, and it made Michele's stomach dip. "Oh, don't worry, darling. I've tried therapy. Although, to be fair, I didn't tell her everything. I was smarter than that." She tapped her head. "I didn't tell her that I was nine when I had my first aggressive fantasy. I still remember it so well. My mother had some classical music playing throughout the house, like she always did. She'd passed out somewhere. The couch maybe. I walked into the kitchen, lifted a knife, and I imagined plunging it into my mother's chest."

At the mention of classical music, Michele finally heard what she'd missed until that moment. A soft song in the background. The same one that had played at Mercy Ring. *Come, Sweet Death* by Bach.

Her skin crawled.

"I *did* tell the therapist about the abuse by my mother's boyfriends," Connie continued. "I told her about some of the darkness that ravages my mind. And do you know what she said to me? That she was *sorry*. That the trauma may have caused borderline personality disorder. Then she wrote me a script for medication."

Connie blew out a long sigh. "I didn't want medication. I wanted vengeance. So I stopped therapy and tried something else."

Michele swallowed, tugging at her left hand again. Hope flared in her chest when her hand slipped out of the tape a scant inch.

"I killed my foster mother."

Michele paused in her struggle. Hearing the woman say those words with absolutely no remorse... Disturbing didn't even begin to describe it.

"It was a Saturday night. Her and some guy had already

passed out. I had just turned sixteen, Tim was eighteen and had aged out. And guess what? She had more foster kids. And I knew if I didn't do something she'd continue to whore around and allow her boyfriends to do to them what they'd done to me. So I stabbed her. Four times. She was so wasted she didn't even wake up. I put the guy's prints on the knife and made it look like he did it. Then I left with Tim, and guess who came looking for me? No one. Because no one fucking cared about a foster kid. No one but Tim."

How had this woman seen a therapist and *not* been locked up? And how did the police not look for a missing foster child?

Connie's eyes glowed. "And you know what happened after that?"

Another tug.

"That voice in my head, the one that torments me with dark thoughts, makes me want to rip off my own skin... It quieted. And I knew. That was the only way I could live with myself."

By killing women?

Sick. So sick.

"And what?" Michele asked. "Tim just collected these women for you?"

Another smile. "Like I said, men are pathetic. Driven by the most basic instincts. I told Tim what I needed. Showed him some love and affection. Told him we'd be a team and that this was the only way I could survive and make the voices in my head quiet. He hopped on over to the grocery store and picked up our first victim."

At the sight of Declan's eyebrows scrunching, Michele's breath stopped. Was he waking? Would he be able to get out of his bonds?

"At the end, he started getting sloppy," Connie continued. "I watched your dates from a distance. I could see he was losing your interest." She shook her head. "The night of your third date, I told him if he didn't do better, I'd have to replace him. It was the biggest fight we'd ever had. He was scared to death of losing me. And what did the idiot do? He got so worked up he drank too much and you ended things."

Even if he hadn't drunk too much, Michele would have ended things anyway.

"Why four dates?" she asked, needing to keep Connie talking.

She shrugged. "I've always had this weird fascination with the number. Maybe because I was four when I started preschool and realized I was different than other kids in class. Or maybe because I stabbed my foster mother four times, and it just felt...*right*."

Out-of-her-mind crazy. "Don't you ever feel remorse? These people you're killing—they aren't your mother or foster mother. They're random women, and most likely good people."

Connie shook her head. "Not random. They're women who agree to go out with men they don't even know. Sluts. *Whores*. Look at you—you didn't know Tim for shit, yet you agreed to go out with the guy."

"Dating. It's called *dating*. And it's normal. It doesn't mean I'm anything like your mother or foster mother."

"My foster mother seemed normal too. Until she brought predators into the home where I was supposed to be safe." Connie stepped closer to the table, the light from the candle glinting off the knife again. "Did you know that sixty to eighty percent of criminals have past physical or sexual trauma? Kind of poetic, isn't it? That the best way to channel my inner demons is to rid the world of people like *you*."

Michele tugged her hand again. Half out. She was nearly out of the tape.

There was no arguing with Connie. She was going to believe what she wanted to believe. Michele just needed to keep her talking until she got her hand free. "That footage from the woman's front porch only showed Tim entering and leaving the house. Why?"

"I was already in there. Snuck through a back window. People usually leave at least one window unlocked. And if they didn't, Tim would unlatch it for me."

Another tug. So close. "Aren't you sad that he died?"

"Why would I be? It just means I have to change up how I do things. But there are always plenty more pathetic men out there to rope in and groom." She frowned. "Makes me sound a bit cold, doesn't it? But I don't tend to fall in love or become attached to people. Guess that's the borderline personality disorder the therapist was talking about."

Okay, Declan's head definitely just shifted.

"And the FBI agent? Why kill him?"

Connie lifted a shoulder. "I wanted to send you a little message. So I padded my clothes and off I went."

Finally, Declan's eyes opened. Immediately, his brows tugged together. The second his gaze met hers, his eyes darkened to the color of the sky when it was devoid of stars. All rage and torment and...something else. Something dangerous. Lethal.

His expression was granite as he looked up at Connie, his chest moving up and down as his breaths came faster.

Connie hadn't seen him yet. Michele had to keep the woman's attention on her. "What about the flat tire? Was that you, too?"

"You're good at this." She laughed. "I was going to kill you that night. Tim and I were up here waiting for you. We'd stolen your key from the super. We were all ready to go. Then that damn mutt of yours growled." Her gaze shot to the bedroom door. "That's okay. We got here in the end."

She caught the slight tensing of Declan's muscles. He was testing his bounds like she'd been testing hers.

Connie stepped closer.

Panic filled Michele's chest. "You don't want to do this, Connie. Declan has three former Delta best friends. If you kill him, they'll hunt you down and murder you."

The woman's smile was the creepiest thing she'd ever seen.

Connie leaned her face close to Michele's. "Let them try." Then she straightened. "Time for my favorite part. Only, tonight, I get double."

When Connie turned to Declan, fear spiked through Michele's limbs. "No!"

Connie ignored her. She took a step toward him and lifted the knife.

His eyes flew open again, startling Connie enough for her to stumble back. Michele gave one final hard tug of her arm. Her left hand released. She shot forward and grabbed one of the candles before thrusting it into Connie's side.

The woman screamed, dropping the knife as her top caught on fire. The second the blade clattered to the floor, Michele lunged forward, almost toppling the chair. She grabbed the knife to cut the tape binding her feet.

"Are you okay?" Declan shouted.

"I'm okay!" She didn't look up. There wasn't time. "I'll cut you free next."

She was vaguely aware of Connie running into the kitchen. Of the sound of the tap running and Connie's pained cries. Michele ignored it all, working to free her ankles.

She'd just gotten both loose and stood from the chair when Declan shouted.

"Watch out!"

That's when Connie landed on Michele's back and sent them both crashing to the floor.

"I'm gonna fucking kill you, bitch!" Connie growled.

The woman spun her around, and the second Michele was on her back, Connie threw a punch that connected with her left cheek.

Declan struggled in his bonds. "Get the hell off her!"

For a moment, Michele was dazed. When she saw that fist rise again, she shifted her head just before it landed. Connie cried out as her hand connected with the floor.

Michele didn't pause. She reached up, grabbed Connie's hair and tugged it to the side as hard as she could. The woman screamed.

Declan's chair screeched across the floorboards as Michele released Connie and grappled for the knife. The woman was back on her before she could grab it. Michele bucked and rolled, trying to get her off. They hit the dining table, jolting everything on top—including the candles.

Suddenly, the room lit up as flames raced across the tablecloth.

CHAPTER 31

$\mathcal{T}$he second Connie's fist collided with Michele's face, Declan saw red. The woman had drugged them. Bound them. Now she was hurting his woman.

The bitch needed to die.

He tugged at the bonds around his wrists and ankles again. His feet were bound to the chair, but his hands were only fastened to each other. That was Connie's mistake.

He tried to stand, but dark dots danced across his vision. He blinked them away. He needed to push through. Get the hell off this chair and protect Michele.

With a deep breath, he stood again, this time willing his body to remain upright. He clenched his fists, his muscles contracting, which in turn made his forearms bigger. Then he pushed his hands away from his back as far as they'd go before driving them forward in a hard, violent thrust. The tape tore.

The second his hands were free, he shot a quick look at Michele. She was reaching for the knife as Connie grabbed her. They rolled, hit the table, and flames immediately ignited the tablecloth.

Declan growled as he bent and frantically tore at the tape on his ankles. Every second that passed had the fogginess in his head fading a bit more.

He'd just torn off the last of the tape when Connie grabbed the knife. Her arm swung high as Declan lunged and tackled the woman to the floor.

The second she was on her back, she tried to headbutt him. He dodged the hit and pulled her hands above her head, lifting them off the floor and slamming them back down hard enough for the knife to fly from her fingers.

When the fire alarm sounded, he heard doors opening in the hall.

Connie tried to knee him, but he immobilized her legs easily with his own, still holding her hands over her head. He flipped her onto to her stomach and tugged her to her feet.

"Get the hell off me!" she screamed.

"Not a fucking chance."

He glanced up to see Michele throwing water on the fire. It wasn't enough. The flames had spread and were now racing across the floorboards and catching on the curtains.

When Michele glanced their way, her eyes widened. "Declan—"

Connie kicked her leg up, bringing it back down on the edge of the burning table. It tipped toward them.

Declan released her and lurched to the side, barely missing the flames. Connie, on the other hand, didn't move in time. The table fell on her. She screamed, dropping to the floor and rolling.

Michele raced to his side. "Are you okay?" She scanned his body frantically, looking for any injuries.

"I'm okay." His gaze flew to her bruised cheek, anger tearing at his gut as he took in her already bruising flesh.

At Connie's horrific shrieks, both their heads whipped up. The flames on her body were out, but she was badly burned. She lay on her back, almost still now, her shuddering breaths barely lifting her chest.

Michele started to cough as smoke filled the apartment.

He needed to get them out, *now*. "Let's go."

The smoke was thick, darkening the room rapidly. There was an alarm sounding from the hallway, accompanied by pounding footsteps. People were getting out.

"Pokey!" she choked out between coughs.

He put an arm over her shoulders and crawled them over to the bedroom. The second the door opened, Pokey ran out. He made a whimpering sound as he dug his head into Michele's chest.

Okay, now it was really time to go. Declan was just turning them back around when Michele screamed.

He spun in time to see Connie no longer where they'd left her. She was on her feet, face contorted in a maniacal grimace, knife clenched in her charred hand as she stumbled toward them.

Michele attempted to lunge in front of him. He pushed her out the way just in time to avoid a swipe of the knife.

Then with quick, practiced moves, he grabbed Connie's wrist, spun the knife, and plunged it into the woman's chest.

She dropped back onto the floor.

The thud had only just sounded when he heard the racking coughs from Michele. Dammit. She was inhaling too much smoke.

He scooped her into his arms, then he was moving. Pokey followed closely behind as they sprinted from the apartment.

Doors to the surrounding apartments were open. People were rushing down the halls.

Michele's breaths were ragged. "I'm...fine," she gasped out.

Another cough racked her body, and when he looked down, he saw her eyes scrunched, like the simple act of breathing was painful.

"Slow breaths, Chele."

When they finally reached the ground floor, firefighters were hurrying toward the stairs. He stepped in front of one of the guys, stopping him. "Level two, apartment ten."

The guy nodded before continuing.

The second Declan saw the ambulance, the air rushed from his chest. He raced forward and climbed inside. Then he lay her down on a stretcher. The two startled paramedics immediately leaned over her as Declan barked, "Smoke inhalation. She needs oxygen."

An oxygen mask was placed over her face. As they looked over her body, she pulled her mask down. "I'm sorry."

He frowned. "For what, honey?"

He should be the one apologizing. He'd let her down tonight. Again. He'd told her, *promised* her, she was safe. Then he'd let the woman drug them. Bind them. Almost kill Michele.

"I told you to eat the cookie."

If the situation wasn't what it was, he would have laughed.

Gently, he took the mask from her hand and set it back on her face. Then he pressed a kiss to her forehead before whispering, "It's over. And I promise on my life that no one will ever hurt you again."

It was an oath to both her and him.

CHAPTER 32

Sweet pastry. Unsalted butter. Flour. Sugar. And the boys even had—would you believe it—eight apples. This had to be Anthony's doing. He'd bought all the ingredients for her apple pie recipe. She'd have to thank him later.

Smiling, Michele pulled the ingredients out and placed them onto the counter.

God, she'd missed this over the last week. Declan had barely allowed her to leave the house, let alone stand for a period of time and bake a pie. She was about to lose her damn mind. It was just a bit of smoke inhalation. She hadn't gone this long without baking since… Well, she couldn't even remember.

Humming to herself, she got started on weighing the butter, then cutting the apples. When she needed a baking dish, she sighed, glancing up at the top shelf. Why they kept all the baking pans in the top cupboard only they could reach, she had no idea. Maybe they assumed no one would ever use them.

Shaking her head, she reached up for the pan. Before she could touch it, someone was behind her, grabbing the pan easily and lowering it to the counter.

"Shouldn't you be resting, Chele?"

She turned to smile at Cole. Whenever Declan wasn't hovering, this guy or Ryker were. Not to mention Jackson and River whenever they were around. "Nope. I'm all rested up."

He crossed his arms over his mammoth chest. "You shouldn't be baking."

Pfft. "I've been off my feet for a week. Declan won't let me help him pack his stuff, and I've finished my latest book."

So what the heck else was she supposed to do? Twiddle her thumbs? The book was the tenth she'd read in the last week. Yes. She'd read more than a book a day. And no, she did not have a problem. Oh, except for the enforced bed rest. That was annoying as hell, and she definitely considered it a problem.

Cole grabbed a piece of apple. "You can't just relax until the man's ready to leave?"

"Could you?"

A ghost of a smile touched his lips. "Fair enough. How's the apartment going?"

She sighed, coating the pan in butter before grabbing the pastry. "It will probably be a few months before the damage is fixed and it's habitable again."

The fire had destroyed a huge chunk of her living room. She wasn't even going to think about all her destroyed books. That was a heartache that would take a while to heal.

She and Declan had been living here with Cole, Ryker and Anthony, but that was just too much testosterone. Lucky for her, she had a best friend who didn't mind her and Declan moving in for a while. Having another woman around would be heavenly.

"You doing okay?" Cole asked quietly.

She smiled again. Cole liked to act all tough, but she'd started to suspect he was really a big softy at heart. He'd been ridiculously overprotective and terribly gentle this last week. It was sweet.

"I am. I still can't believe Connie was part of it." Not just part of it. The brains. The damn *knife wielder.* She shuddered at the thought. "I'm just glad it's actually over this time."

There'd been no more pit-in-her-stomach moments, like something else was coming. No more fear when looking at her phone.

"She was good at hiding her true nature," Cole said. "I'm glad you and Dec are okay."

She nodded. "Me too."

He grabbed some more apple slices just as Anthony stepped into the kitchen. He took in the pastry and the apples before shooting his gaze back up to her. "You sure you want to move out? No one else around here can bake for shit."

She chuckled, grabbing a saucepan and popping in the butter. "I'm sure Cole will bake you a pie if you ask nicely."

Both guys scoffed. Cole pushed off the counter. "That won't be happening, kid. You're on your own."

"Not on your own." She shot a look over her shoulder. "You're still going to be working for me around your school hours. I'll make sure you have food to take home in case Cole and Ryker are neglecting you."

The guys had made contact with Anthony's grandmother again. Of course she hadn't cared at all that he wanted to stay. And she certainly hadn't cared whether he went back to school or not.

Michele added water and sugar to the saucepan. When she turned, she saw both Cole and Anthony were now eating the apple slices. God. She snatched the board up. "Will you both stop? These are for the pie. There are perfectly good apples in the fridge."

"No one's cut them up for me, though," Anthony said, humor in his voice.

She wanted to act mad, but she just couldn't. Not when he was making jokes—and even cracking smiles every so often.

As she headed back to the stove, her gaze caught on the

window. Or more accurately, the woman *outside* the window. "The lady across the street just got home, Cole."

There was a small pause before he answered. "And?"

"You can take her a slice of pie."

When Anthony scoffed again, she turned and said, "Or *you* can. There's a boy who lives there, and he looks about your age. He's probably at your school."

Anthony rolled his eyes. "Thanks, but I can make my own friends."

Jeez, what was it with these boys and being so antisocial?

She was just arranging the apples in the pastry when she heard footsteps on the stairs. A second later, she saw him. Declan strode toward her, his thick biceps stretching the material of his dark blue top, a hint of a dimple on his cheek. Then those muscled arms were wrapping around her waist, tugging her against him.

"Mm, thought I smelled something good."

She chuckled. "The pie isn't in the oven yet."

"I wasn't talking about the pie."

There was a choking noise from someone behind them, probably Anthony. Then Cole spoke up.

"That's our cue to leave."

She turned in Declan's arms as the guys left the room, yet again reminded of how unbelievably lucky she was to have this beautiful man in her life.

THE SECOND THE guys left the room, Declan swooped in, pressing a kiss to her neck, and yet again, he felt it. The peace. The love. She was his sanctuary. Fuck, he was a lucky son of a bitch.

Since the attack last week, he hadn't been able to get enough of her. He sure as hell hadn't been able to leave her side. Every time he thought about that day in her apartment, he saw the image of her struggling with Connie again. It could have been so much worse.

He pressed another kiss to her neck. "I'm all packed."

A soft hum slipped from her chest. "Okay. I'm just going to get this pie on and set the timer, then we can go."

He swiped his hand over her cheek lightly. The bruising from where Connie had hit her was faded, but he could still see it. And he hated it. "How's the breathing?"

Her gaze flickered between his. "Amazing. Back to normal."

Hm. She'd been saying that for a while. "I hate what happened. I was right there. I should have been able to protect you."

She shook her head. "It's not your fault. I shouldn't have encouraged you to eat that cookie."

"I'm sure she had a plan B if I hadn't taken it."

She stiffened at his words. Yeah, plan B probably would have been worse.

He slipped a hand beneath her shirt, grazing the skin. "Neither of us suspected Connie. Why would we have? The FBI didn't tell us everything they knew."

Agent Burton had given some bullshit excuse about not being able to disclose all information since him and his team weren't part of the investigation. He'd been mad as hell.

"She's gone now," Michele said quietly. "I'll be fine with us never thinking about her again."

Damn straight. He stroked the bare skin on her back. "You sure you're okay?"

"I'm great."

Hm. He wasn't sure she'd tell him if she wasn't, but he'd accept her words. For now.

His head lowered and he kissed her lightly. "I can't wait for us to get back into our own space."

He felt her smile. "Me too."

"Maybe," he said quietly, pressing a kiss to her cheek between his words, "we can start looking for our own place. Somewhere with a yard for Pokey. A reading room with a big bookcase for you."

At her silence, he lifted his head to see a frown on her face.

She swallowed. "You want to buy a place with me?"

"Yes." It wasn't even a question in his mind. Why did she sound surprised? "You don't want to?" He tried to keep his voice even, but he felt anxious as hell at her uncertainty.

"Of course I do. I just… Buying a place together is a big long-term commitment."

"Do you *not* see this as long term?"

Her hands pressed to his chest. "I do. But we're still so new, and there's been danger, which has caused forced proximity. You might change your mind—"

He laughed. "Honey, with you, there's no changing my mind. Since the day I first laid eyes on you, I knew you were it. Not for now. Not for a while. Forever."

She sucked in a quick breath. "Really?"

"*Yes*. I love you, Michele. And my love for you is not temporary or dependent on circumstance. It's forever. You and me— we're forever."

Her smile grew watery. "My love for you is forever, too."

Thank God for that. "Good. Then make me the happiest man around and buy a house with me. Let's create our forever home together."

She laughed, and it was music to his soul. "Yes. A thousand times, yes!" She paused. "But when you said bookcase, you meant *cases*, plural, right? My forever home has less of a reading room and more of a library."

"Mm." He lowered his head, his mouth hovering over hers. "You're putting ideas into my head about pushing you up against those bookcases and making love to you."

She smiled. "Yes, please."

God, the woman killed him. With a growl, he dropped his head and kissed her.

CHAPTER 33

*A*t the sound of the oven timer going off, Cole pulled off his gloves and moved out of the gym. Well, less of a gym and more of a room with a heavy bag and a few weights strewn around. It was all he needed, though. And if he wanted to go a real round, all he had to do was head down to Mercy Ring. Something he did regularly even outside of business hours.

Sweat ran down his bare chest as he headed toward the kitchen. He'd spent a year healing from a broken back. That last mission had almost destroyed him, and it was something he didn't like to think about. They'd all come too close to death.

While he'd healed from the broken back, he'd lost strength. Endurance. Things he'd only just gained back in recent months.

Working out was food for his soul. He didn't just prioritize it. He centered his whole life around it. And it felt damn good to move easily again.

The smell of apple pie filled the space as he stepped into the kitchen. If it tasted anything like it smelled, the other guys would be lucky to get a piece. Anthony had a point earlier when he'd said Michele couldn't move out. Cole couldn't bake for shit, and Ryker wasn't any better.

Using the hand mitts, he grabbed the pie out of the oven. Fuck, it looked as good as it smelled.

For a second, his gaze shifted out the window, to the house across the street. He'd been finding his gaze drawn there more and more, and he had no fucking idea why.

Sure, the woman was pretty, with her caramel-blonde hair, and those tight jeans that hugged her perfect ass. But why was he constantly thinking about those aqua-green eyes? He had no idea.

Shaking his head, he turned away, lowering the pie to the stovetop.

He needed to get out. Go to a bar. Have a drink with a woman. He'd spent too long cooped up inside, and too much time watching his friends couple up.

He loved women, but dating was something he didn't do. And he always made sure any woman he hooked up with knew the score.

It wasn't like he thought the guys were making a mistake, falling so quickly. But there were only a few ways a relationship could ever end. And not many people found a fucking *Notebook* ending.

The front door opened seconds before Ryker and Erik stepped into the kitchen. Erik visited sometimes after sparring at Mercy Ring. The guy was quiet and easy to be around, so Cole didn't mind.

"What the hell smells so damn good?" Ryker called.

Cole nodded over his shoulder. "Chele made an apple pie before she left."

Erik stepped forward, inspecting the pie. "And you guys just let her go? Someone baked me an apple pie, I would have kept her here, willing or not."

Ryker smirked. "You would've had to fight Declan."

"I'd take that challenge."

Cole wouldn't. The guy was consumed with the woman. He'd fight to the death.

He was about to leave the kitchen when Ryker stopped him. "What are you doing tonight?"

"Thought I might go to Lenny's Bar and Grill. Have a beer." Get the damn woman across the street out of his head.

Unbidden, his gaze flicked to the window again.

He immediately regretted it when Ryker followed his gaze, then raised a brow as he looked back at him. "Is that right?"

"Yep." He needed to get the hell out of the room before Ryker asked him any questions. Because Cole had no answers.

"Maybe we'll join you," Ryker called out.

"Sure. The more the fucking merrier," he called over his shoulder.

He moved toward the stairs, but one more time—because there was something very wrong with him—he shot a glance outside toward the street.

This time, he stopped in his tracks. Because not only was his neighbor outside her house, she wasn't alone. The kid who lived with her was out there too. He was tall but young. Maybe sixteen. And he always had an angry sneer on his face. Reminded Cole a lot of Anthony when he'd first met him.

Cole watched as the woman stepped between the kid and the car. Not a good idea. Not with the way the kid was currently looking at her.

The second he shoved her, Cole took off.

He stormed out of the house and across the street. He may not believe in relationships and all that shit, but he *did* believe that guys needed to treat women with some fucking respect.

The woman recovered quickly and grabbed the car door as the kid tried to open it. She was barricading it with her body. The kid looked seconds away from shoving her again. His hand grabbed her shoulder just as Cole shouted.

"Hey!"

Both the kid and the woman looked up. Cole stepped into their driveway.

The kid frowned. "Who the hell are you?"

The woman stared at him, her gaze flicking from him to the kid.

"I'm a neighbor who doesn't like seeing women get shoved around."

He grabbed the kid's hand and tore it off her. He wasn't sure if they were siblings or cousins or friends, but the boy needed to keep his hands to his goddamn self.

"Mind your own business!"

And the other thing Cole hated—kids being disrespectful. He stepped up to the boy. "You want to push someone, push *me*."

The woman gasped, touching his elbow. "Hey. It's okay."

He didn't take his eyes off the teenager. "No. It isn't. It's okay to be angry, but you take out that anger in a safe space. Not on *her*."

The kid's eyes narrowed. "You don't know me. Don't tell me how to deal with my fucking emotions."

For a moment, Cole was quiet, his eyes narrowed as he assessed the kid. At the silence, the boy swallowed, seeming more unsure by the second.

"You feel angry, you direct it somewhere else, like a bag. You can punch that as much as you want."

The kid's jaw clenched. "I don't need a bag. I just need to get into my car."

Cole's voice lowered. "Don't push her again."

Another beat of silence. Then a small nod.

Good.

When the kid reached for the door handle, the woman stepped forward, touching his shoulder. "Zac—"

"I'll be back later." The kid remained still for a moment, waiting for her hand to drop. When it did, he slid into his car and drove away.

Cole stepped toward the woman. "You okay?"

She looked at him, crossing her arms over her chest defensively. "I had that handled."

That wasn't exactly a thank-you. "Didn't look that way to me."

She shook her head, moving around him. "What you did… It's just going to make things worse."

He disagreed. "He shouldn't have shoved you."

"He's angry."

"Doesn't make it okay."

She stopped and turned before stepping close to him. Too close. Hell, she made the pie in his kitchen smell like trash. There was some sweet citrus-mixed-with-vanilla scent coming off her. "Don't do that again."

"If he pushes you again, I will." That was non-negotiable.

Her mouth fell open, and damn, all he wanted to do was keep his gaze on those lips. "Who do you think you are?"

"A neighbor who doesn't like seeing a woman get abused by an angry teenager."

She sighed, and those aqua eyes sparked with frustration. "Look, I know it's not okay. I'm dealing with it."

"Like I said, there are safe places for him to purge those emotions."

She blew out a breath, some of the frustration leaving her features, only to be replaced with something he couldn't read. Desperation, maybe? "Thanks for the suggestion."

She moved away from him and stepped up to her porch before opening her door. She was about to walk inside, but at the last minute, she turned again. "Thank you." Her gaze flicked to her house, then back to him. "For coming over here and helping me."

"I'm Cole, by the way."

She watched him for a moment before answering. "Aria."

He rolled her name around in his head. He liked it. It suited her. "Is he your brother?"

A small smile tugged at her lips. "No. He's my son."

Son? Cole frowned. "But he's…"

"Sixteen. The same age I was when I had him." Then she disappeared into the house.

Fuck. Why did that little bombshell intrigue the hell out of him and make him want to learn more?

Order COLE today!

ALSO BY NYSSA KATHRYN

Cole

JOIN my newsletter and be the first to find out about sales and new releases!

~https://www.nyssakathryn.com/vip-newsletter~

ABOUT THE AUTHOR

Nyssa Kathryn is a romantic suspense author. She lives in South Australia with her daughter and hubby and takes every chance she can to be plotting and writing. Always an avid reader of romance novels, she considers alpha males and happily-ever-afters to be her jam.

Don't forget to follow Nyssa and never miss another release.

Facebook | Instagram | Amazon | Goodreads